WELL-LIT SHADOWS

REBEKAH ANDRESS

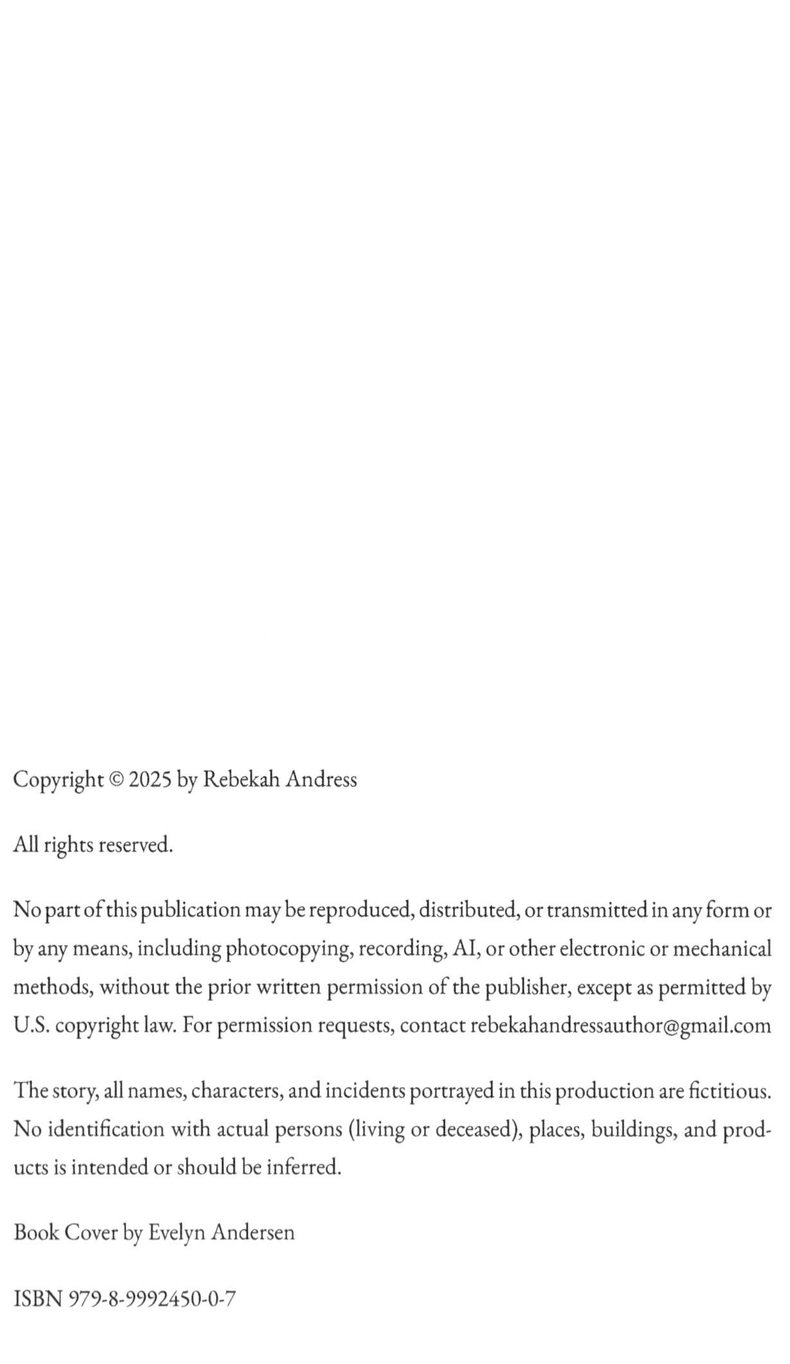

ISBN 979-8-9992450-0-7

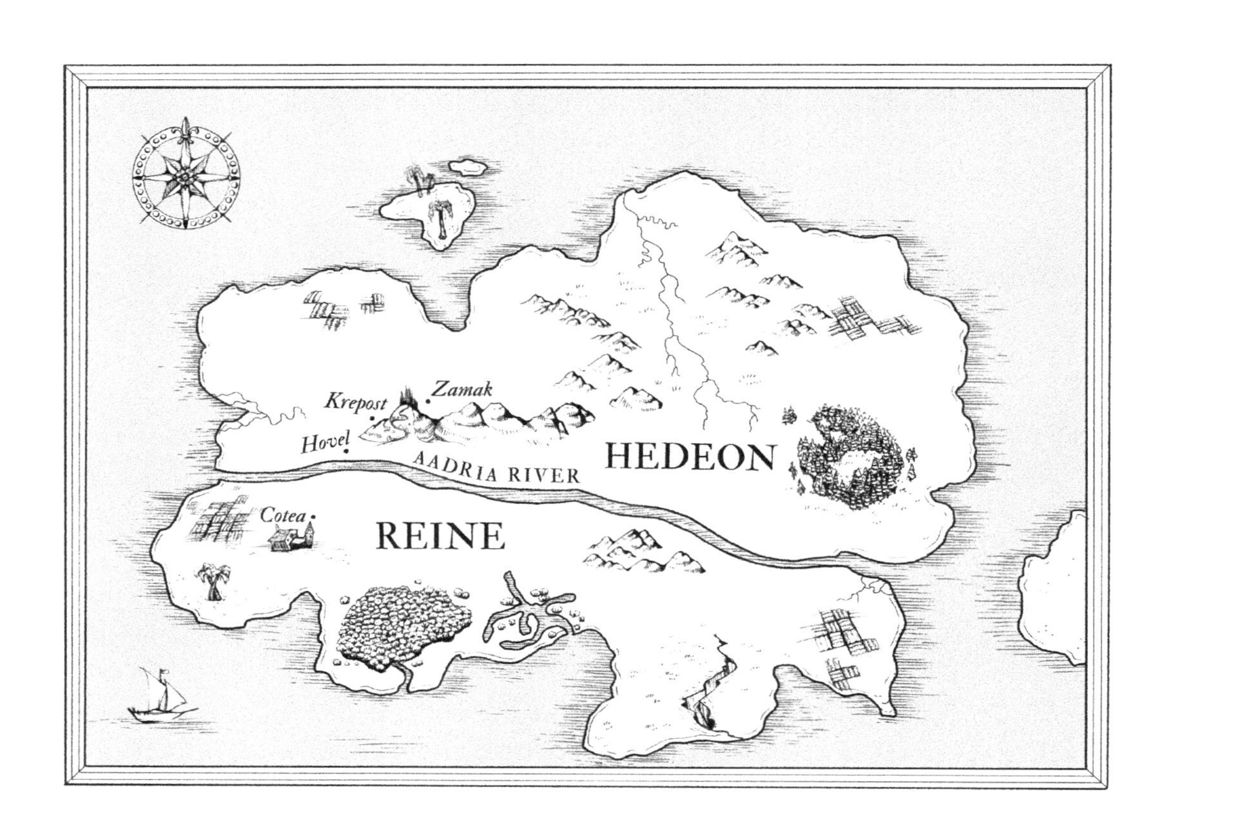

HEDEON
REINE
AADRIA RIVER
Krepost
Zamak
Hovel
Cotea

To Mags, Hans, Quel and Ruman.

Without y'all this book wouldn't exsist. You were the first ones besides myself to love these characters. Thank you for loving me in a way that made me believe I could tell this story. Every artist needs people like y'all, my found family.

1

I HAVE LOOKED LIKE my enemies most of my life—dressing to their trends, eating their food, living in their streets. But this is the first time I have ever felt like a traitor. I have two months until the show premieres for the Spring Revel. Two months to write a story, prepare the legendary Arman actors, create the sets, and have everything ready for opening night.

"Are you sure you mean for me to do this?" This isn't where I die. At least not today. I knew that if this were a summons to the Zamak for torture or execution, all parties would look more excited. Their indifference is a good sign for the longevity of my life, but I never could have imagined this.

"The war on Reine has been raging for far too long." Queen Milena ignores my question.

She looks me up and down, deciding if I will fit whatever part she is conjuring up. I concentrate on my feet, old boots sewn a few times over from wear. They have no way of knowing I am from Reine, but still the stares of everyone in the room weigh my shoulders down, compressing my spine.

"Our people are getting tired. I want you to write something that will bring hope to Hedeon. A play that will reinforce our values and reinstate nationalism in an exhausted kingdom. Write hope, Damira Letsov."

My name from her mouth is a curse.

The queen floats up the steps and sinks into the throne with a golden bat lurking atop it. The princess, who sits at her left, must favor the runaway king in looks—skin paler than her mother's, about as interested in me as she would be a fly annoying her. A throne remains vacant to their right—waiting for the missing prince following in his father's footsteps. Though, unlike the long-gone king, the prince is planned to return in time for the Spring Revel.

"That will be all. You will start tomorrow." She dismisses me with a single nod.

Lev, the man who brought me here from my neighborhood—the Hovel—takes me by the arm and leads me back through towering doors and down the hallway. He is older—old enough to be my father. Sun-worn and wrinkled, a bald head peeking out from beneath the top hat he wears.

Our steps echo through the quiet hallways as I follow Lev through an opening to the right. Portraits hang from wallpapered walls, all done with a still hand and immense talent. We descend a set of stairs to ground level, and out a back door of the Zamak. A stone path cleared of snow leads us to the forest line.

"How did the queen find my stories?" The silence shatters between us, Lev's eyes snapping over his shoulder to me.

"She found a maid reading them." His words are sharp. Precise. A quick papercut on a pointer finger.

Aunt Selah says it comes from my mother. She seemed to always have ink-stained hands. It never occurred to me if I was good or bad at it, it was a compulsion. I wrote and wrote and wrote, and then eventually, Uncle Sumood suggested I start sharing my stories. So I did. I hadn't even known my stories left the Hovel, but for them to carry all the way up the Krepost—

I can't think about that right now, I will surely spiral, so I focus on my feet and on the path we walk. If it wasn't so elegant, I would call the small house we arrive at, a cabin. It can't be more than a bedroom and kitchen. White columns make the bright blue house appear striped, like colors borrowed from a candy shop. Above the door, the word *Dramaturg* is painted on a wooden plaque. *Playwright*.

Lev leads me into the small sitting room but stays close to the doorway, hands folded behind his back.

"What supplies will you be needing to complete your job?" I'm not sure of his title, but when the Crown isn't around, he slips on their authority as if it were his own.

"Notebooks and ink pens should be all."

"A guard should be assigned to you tomorrow to show you around. Until then, feel free to wander about the Krepost, but be assured, there are eyes everywhere. Comply, and we will keep safe you and your family, but if you try to flee, none of you will like the consequences." He turns to walk the path back to the castle.

The Zamak is towering in the distance, across the snow-covered field. It is covered in deep shades of oranges and yellows and blues, all darkened and worn because of its age. I would have expected the castle that the Crown lives in to be sharper, like knives threatening even the eyes of those who dare look upon it, but its peaks are rounded, its turrets more delicate than foreboding. It is an interesting castle, one that calls to be painted, however, it would take a lot of mixing paints for me to get the colors correct.

"Lev," I stop him, a thought of excitement bringing forth the words. "Are there painting supplies available?"

"Do you require those to write?"

"Yes." More a want than a need, but making something with my hands has always helped my mind find what words to write.

That is, if I decide I want to write at all. I don't know how to betray Reine like this, writing a story against them. I could refuse to do this job entirely, tell the queen what I really think of her and be sentenced to a lifetime in jail—or the mines, or death. The Faits know I have earned a quiet end, so maybe being beheaded for not writing a story of hope would be poetic in some way.

If only my conscience was as willing as my tired soul.

"I'll see to it." He leaves just as quietly as he collected me.

I lower myself to the floor, the rug underneath me thick, clean, red-patterned leaves and vines in hues of red. I run my hand through it slowly as I can't help but stare out the open door. I am stuck. Alone without even the advice from my aunt and uncle about what I should do. I've been prepared for many things in my life, but being alone was never one of them. Being asked by the Queen of Hedeon to write a play was not one of them.

The bad luck keeps me company for a while, but before long I pull myself up, needing to be anywhere but sitting still in this house. If I steep in these thoughts any longer, surely I will drown. I take Lev's suggestion of going out to explore the Krepost. Luckily, the path is pretty straightforward from my new house and takes me down the side of the mountain.

I wrap my lavish coat tighter around me, bracing from the chill in the air. Before I spoke with the queen, I was bathed and changed into an outfit suitable for presentation. The dress is a bit too short, and the shoes they had weren't my size, so I kept my worn boots. I suppose they guessed I would have had the courtesy to take up less space than I do.

It's a short descent through the gates and down the road to the bustling life below. The Zamak sits atop the Krepost like the prowling monster it is—the perfect height for the castle to watch us all. I am too stubborn to admit that it's all rather impressive. Where the Hovel had to build up because they didn't want to infringe on the poverty of the next towns over, the Krepost built up so that no one misses out on the connections of Court. The hues of vibrant homes stick out against the grey skies, promoting just how much happier they are than the rest of the kingdom.

I have seldom been out of the Hovel in the eight years I've lived in Hedeon. I know nothing about life on the Krepost, only that the one road that switchbacks the length of the mountain is only ever witnessed by those who have high status. I suppose I now have as much status to be here as anyone else, but it still seems like a role I will never be worthy to fill.

Streaks of orange cut through the sky as the sun starts to set, the clouds finally dispersing for the show. Markets trip over themselves for people's attention, windows displaying ostentatious tastes of what's inside. Courtiers weave through the shops, arm in arm, while others sit outside in tavern patios, surrounded by furnaces that keep the snowy cold away. It's hard to peel my eyes away from the sight of the ignorant denizens living a life devoted only to themselves.

In the Hovel, no one has dealt in coin for years, not in all my memory at least. We trade things back and forth, usually passing them around in order of need. It gives people something to do, gathering in the mornings, manning their wagons of borrowed things.

I'm more of a borrowed thing now than I was mere hours ago.

If I write the play the queen demands, then it will result in more war, more hope for a future found at the tip of a sword. My people will continue to be slaughtered. If I don't write the play, then I will be slaughtered. Either choice results in more senseless death.

Unless—

Unless I write the play and write of hope, but a different hope than the kind the queen spoke of. Hope that will inspire conversation, hope that maybe the Hedeon citizens can be more than pigs raised for slaughter, hope that this war no longer has to be their legacy. It will, most likely, still result in my death, but at least it won't be senseless.

I always thought that when it came down to choosing between Reine and my own life, the decision would be easy. But staring death in the face, it's hard to accept him as a friend. It's hard not to be persuaded by the other side. The Arman Company is not only recognized around Hedeon, but they have toured all over the world. The shows they turn out set the tone for the way of all theatre productions. They're trailblazers and visionaries, top in their fields, hand-picked by the Crown. I had never daydreamed of working with them, for even such fantasies seemed out of my reach. Is the only way to work with them through submitting to the queen's will?

The choice between the two swings back and forth in my head like a pendulum. A clock ticking down the moments I have until I must decide. Write for Hedeon or write for my own people. Write for Hedeon or write for my own people. Back and forth in an annoying chant.

I round a corner, crashing into something. Someone. A man's chest. I stagger back, looking up at him. He is just as disheveled as I am. His hand goes to his chest where I hit him. My breath runs out of my lungs from the collision. We turned into each other, both hugging the wall as we came around.

"All that is good and the Divine!" He stumbles back but regains his footing easily, offering a laugh from a crooked grin full of pearly teeth.

"I am so sorry. I should pay better attention to where I am headed." I take a step back, giving him space to collect himself.

He pauses, waiting to see if I am going to add anything more. I'm unsure what more he could want. He gives a small chuckle after a moment and then answers.

"Yes, well, we can't all be dancers of the ballet." He runs a hand through his already tousled dark curls.

"Oh, are you a part of the Arman?" What luck that would be.

"A figure of speech, darling. Do I look like a performer to you?"

I have never seen a true performer in my life, so I wouldn't know how to answer even if he was genuinely asking, but he scrunched his nose as he asked the question which was served more like a complaint.

"Do you have something against it?" I am already defensive of the people I haven't met. They could be like the rest of Hedeon, like this man, but the arts already connect me to the Arman Company, and for that, I know there must be some redemption in them.

He pauses to take me in again. I shift uncomfortably under the authority by which his eyes roam over me. "I'd much prefer a sword to a stage. Besides, the Krepost has more entertaining activities to waste my time than watching shows."

"You sound like an expert in such matters. You've lived here a while, then?"

"We are all servants of the Crown, whether we live here or not. Might as well extract the benefits of Court if we can." I'm not sure if it is the way his hair refuses to lie down or the mischief in his uneven grin, but the mix of the two with his green eyes has struck my curiosity more than I would like to admit. Probably more than is safe.

"Well, once again I am sorry, and I promise to pay more attention to my surroundings. I hope I didn't do any permanent damage." I start back down the road, toward a flower stand far in the distance and away from my potentially deathly curiosity.

"You're not from Court." He doesn't let me go so easily, matching my stride down the cobblestone.

"What gave me away?"

"Most girls in Court pride themselves in letting their dresses wear them; you, on the other hand, wear your dress." A compliment or criticism—I am not sure which. He doesn't look at me when he speaks. The natural lean to his back makes him come across as perpetually uninterested.

"I am not sure I can bask in all that Court has to offer, knowing how those luxuries were obtained."

"Careful, those words border on treason," he warns, but with an ease which betrays the fact that it wouldn't concern him, even if it was outright treasonous.

"It's a fine line, and you don't grow up where I did without learning how to walk that high wire."

"You don't approve of the war?" He baits me, testing my resolve.

"I don't approve of the way the Crown spends coin when there are thousands of people starving, and quite actually freezing to death in Hedeon streets."

"Sounds like you should be the one on the throne." His grin surpasses the crookedness with ease, pulling into a full smile.

"I hardly think that would be wise, but I would care for these people. It is a curiosity, though, that it is not common knowledge why the war started in the first place. Seems it would cause more speculation than it does." My words are neutral, only revealing my true feelings in tone.

"Back when the lands were peaceful, and death was a distant cousin, King Glavnok of Hedeon fell in love with Queen Estée of Reine." He holds his arms out like a storyteller, mocking in his bluster. "Their love was like an eternal spring for the kingdoms, prosperity in every corner. The Aadria River that divides the kingdoms today was only an unimportant channel during that time. And yet, Estée still wasn't content. She became betrothed to another, and it was in that obliterating heartbreak that Glavnok started the war."

I stare at him.

"How would you know that?" Some stories are so old, so sacred, that few people have the privilege of repeating them. This is one. And he treats it like a joke.

"Just whispers." He winks.

The stranger halts at a split in the alley.

"This is where I leave you—I didn't actually get your name." The breath his words float on, clouds the air between us, a chill creeping up my cheeks from being out so long.

He takes a step closer. I don't bother pulling back. Hedeons pride themselves on prudishness. Even if he has an air of uncaring, there are some things you don't escape growing up here.

"Damira."

His eyebrow rises, Another grin.

"Very nice to meet you, Damira." My name comes out in a purr. All these years, and I still am not used to the way the language cuts your tongue on the way out. I hate the way my name sounds on everyone's tongue. Until now.

"I will be seeing you around." He moves so close so suddenly, my breath catches. His eyes trace my face, my lips. Maybe he has forgone the beating of Hedeon virtue.

"Goodnight, darling."

He turns quickly, his shoes making a hushed rhythm against the stone as he walks back up the street. It's only when he has fully disappeared that I realize I hadn't gotten his name in return.

2

I HAVEN'T KNOWN SILENCE since I was in Reine. My memories of home are sparse. My uncle says the trauma of my early years blocks any memories I might have, but I can still see the open spaces of home. The swaying of grass in the breeze and flowers blooming because no one was there to stomp on them. I'm sure Reine doesn't see many flowers these days. I was ten when I left home. Eight years later, and I still wear the anger like an overcoat. I can't find a closet big enough to hang it in.

Not many people roam the library this morning, the only sound my footsteps and those of the guard who leads me. Books are hard to come by in the Hovel. They are traded as precious commodities. Sometimes I think that's why my stories are so popular, because people are desperate for possibilities of a life outside their own, and we've read all the proper books kept in circulation. Sometimes a story can become so familiar you can pretend you lived it yourself. So, I wrote new stories for them, new lives, new adventures.

I can't keep my mind from wondering what everyone will be told of me. The Network keeps close eyes on their spies. I know our contacts have most likely already learned of my predicament, undoubtedly passing the information to Aunt Selah and Uncle Sumood. Faces run through my mind, the ones Hedeon has failed, the ones I grew up beside. If I could write those faces, I would. If I could express the horrors I have seen in the Hovel, I wouldn't hesitate. But how am I to give words to something so nameless, something so inhuman?

Turns out, I have some time to figure it out, as the legendary Arman Company won't be back from touring with their latest show until later this week. In other words, I have a week for inspiration to hit, to have something to give them when they return. To decide if I am going to write for Hedeon or Reine. Time has never been a friend, and I don't suppose it will show me kindness in this new quest.

The guard turns out of the main floor and continues us down a few staircases to a lower level of the library. He wears the standard grey uniform with a black stripe down the side. The only thing consistent in all of my nightmares.

Scripts from hundreds of years of the Arman Theatre are carefully filed away in this windowless room. I have to light each torch manually, no help offered from the guard who lingers at the door.

The room has been kept clean of dust, but it's clear that many of the tomes have not been touched in some time.

All the scripts are bound in leather, each a color of a jewel, but more valuable than any gemstone could ever be worth. I wish I could bottle the smell of ancient paper and turn it into a candle. The titles are embossed in gold on their spines. *The Dragon's Son. Knives and a Thief. Queen Elida.*

For years, I have been tracking down newspapers with small mentions of such plays, but I never even imagined the privilege of seeing them in full. And now they are all at my fingertips.

The sight brings tears to my eyes and confirmation of the decision I was always going to make.

No matter how I tried to lie to myself, it was never a choice, not really. I will write for my people. Anything less, and I would not have been able to live with myself, despite the survival I may have secured. That realization has been hiding beneath the adrenalin, the dread, the fear. But it has been there nonetheless, and now it bears its ugly head—the truth that somewhere in me is a story that will help Hedeon to realize how this war has wrapped its hands around all of our throats and demanded more than any of us have to give.

I sit down at a desk among tapered candles. The manuscripts have annotations in the margins, stage directions, directors' notes, all I could need in ways of help. I knew the plays of Hedeon focused on the fantastical and always ended happily, but reading the words, understanding the story in a way I hadn't been able to before, ushers in a new level of intimidation to wash over me. I am horribly unexperienced, not at all distinguished like those who have worked at the Arman Theatre before. Why did the queen think this was a good idea?

Book after book, I scan, learning the tales and the cadences of Hedeon until my eyes hurt. The hours pass by, evaporating with the smoke of the flames that light my reading. Because of the lack of windows, I can't tell what time it is, but I am sure by the distraction of my stomach that I have missed lunch. The guard who tracked me here left some time ago, I suppose either getting hungry himself or deciding that I am less of a threat than Lev made me out to be.

I lean back in the chair with a sigh, hands resting on the crown of my head. The feat ahead of me is a gaping hole in the ground that I have to cross, and I have never been good at jumping.

"Is this what we are paying you for? Reclining in our archives?"

I turn around quickly, so quickly the chair and I collapse in a heap on the floor.

"We've barely met, and I am already sweeping you off your feet, darling. I find myself devilishly charming too, but I will say it usually takes a few more conversations before I am having to scoop women from a puddle on the ground." The man from last night floats across the archive room, not bothering to help me up. I straighten the chair and pull myself back into it, knowing the tweak in my bad ankle is going to give me a sleepless night.

"Who are you?" I surpass his conceited comments. He thrives in the shadow, his sharp features cutting through the darkness.

He grins.

His suit is clearly expensive, too well dressed to be a servant, too comfortable in his skin to be anything less than someone of importance.

"Calix Hendricks." The grin only grows.

The prince.

Prince Calix has always left lore in his wake. He's said to have been away for the past two years, fighting on the front lines as a lead general. Others say he has been behind rebel lines acting as a spy in what's left of Reine's Court. I've also heard that he has been living aboard a ship, going to the kingdoms across the sea, asking for help with the war. One thing remains in all the speculative stories about him—he is the face of nationalism, as relentless as his grandmother.

"How dare you!" I stand, pressing closer to him, finger pointed in accusation.

"Careful how you speak to your prince, Mira." He puts a hand in his pocket, leaning back, slouching more than a prince should.

"You knew who I was last night, didn't you?" I ask, the question already answered. His silence and smug smile are proof enough.

"You knew, and you didn't announce yourself. You let me believe you were as miserable here as I was." I look up into his pine-colored eyes. They find joy in my discomfort.

"I didn't lie," he laughs.

I walk off, past him and into the stairwell, not wading into whatever game he is playing.

"I'm not done with you, darling." Calix follows after me.

"But I am done with you. And stop calling me darling," I grumble, which causes his laugh to grow.

We come out of the stairs into the large chamber of the library. The main hub of the library has tall shelves of books around the perimeter and desks in the middle, clumped together. Only a few people linger between the shelves, all eyes diverted as Calix and I walk by. Had I missed the looks thrown his way last night, or had I not been the only one to not notice who he truly was?

"I would love nothing more than to leave you alone."

Though his clothes tell of his regality, he is the picture of rebellion. His shirt untucked and wrinkled, dark hair disheveled. The only missing piece from his ensemble is a goblet of wine in his ring-clad hand.

"What does that mean?"

"My mother has been rambling on about the arts and how they will be the thing to save our kingdom. All our efforts and coin should be going to the warfront and our soldiers, not some silly little play she hired you to write."

I was glad when the guard left, but if he is being replaced by the prince, then I would like the reminder of my nightmares back.

"Please, don't soften your feelings on my behalf."

"You can ignore me all you want, but I am afraid in all my bickering with Mother, she assigned me to keep track of you."

"A war hero like you should have no problem getting out of it." I throw one of the many rumors at him. He shrugs, taking the accusation like a compliment.

"Queen ranks higher than any of my wishes. I am just as miserable as you are about it." He is silk and iron. His words don't match the bite at which he delivers them. Hard to peg down, like the scales of a fish that turn colors depending on what angle you look at it. He studies me, and I him. I don't bother hiding the irritation on my face, and as much as his demeanor is arrogant and indifferent, there is true frustration in his tone.

"Where is the theatre?" I finally ask. No one has bothered to show it to me yet, and it seems the prince is the guard that Lev promised would show me around.

"Right this way, darling." He draws out the endearment I asked him to quit, followed by a flash of his too-white teeth. He walks past me and right out of the library.

I wrap my scarf back around my neck, bracing against the wind. The library is just one bend down the road from the Zamak, tucked into the trees, and one bend further, we come upon the Arman Theatre. It isn't as offensive as the library and Zamak are. The colors of the Arman are softer, neutral, except the emerald dome hiding on the top. Stairs stretch out in rows leading to the columns, doors that shine in gold, taunting wealth to anyone who looks upon it.

Calix doesn't stop to admire its splendor, just graces the steps with no permission—he is the one who gives approval, not the one who waits for it to be granted. I follow after him, not knowing what I did to be allowed to walk up these steps. These infamous steps.

The door groans under Calix's hand, leading us into a grand foyer. I don't have time to take in the magnitude of gold and mirrors, for Calix rushes us to the next set of doors that lead to the stage.

A sanctuary. A haven. Rows and rows of velvet-covered seating, gold filigree draped around balconies, and heavy red curtains concealing the stage. A chandelier as large as my bedroom hangs from the domed ceiling. Thousands of jewels in crimson and azure and jade decorate the charcoal-colored iron of the fixture. Even from a far distance, I can make out the vines and flowers of the piping. It is startlingly hideous, extravagance taken too far. A golden bat with outstretched wings watches over the seats, installed right above the apex of the stage.

I sit in a velvet chair at the back, ignoring the looming presence of the prince.

The stage is haunted with ghosts of past shows. The Arman has seen the most renowned companies, the most renowned ballets, the most renowned playwrights. Even when the kingdom is in flames, when the war is at its height, the Arman stays open. This might be the one thing I can admire about Hedeon. People need this hope.

My words will be spoken here. Actors will be on the grand stage, playing out the things that will fill this notebook in my hands. I don't have even a seed of an idea yet, but I can almost see the blooming that will take place on the stage in two months. I will put my words, my thoughts, my story on this stage. This is how I will make penitence to Reine. I try to convince myself the cost won't matter, but it seems I need to make a friend of the fear that now accompanies my every breath.

"Are we done gawking yet?" Calix remains at the back of the theatre, leaning against the doorway.

"Feel free to leave, Prince." I motion with my hand, still watching the empty stage. Calix shuffles behind me.

"If you need any help, please don't hesitate to ask literally anyone else." And with those dull words, the door closes with a thud.

I sit a while longer, making promises to myself I pray to The Faits I can keep.

3

U PON CALIX'S REQUEST THAT I ask anyone other than him, I find the room Lev set up for me with all of my painting supplies in a back corner of the Zamak. Uncle Sumood used to tell me of the many greenhouses we had in Reine. Sheds full of flowers and plants that would thrive even in the most extreme conditions outside. That is the closest thing I can compare to this room. A greenroom.

One wall has rounded corners, windowpanes cutting through the glass wall vertically. Warmth pervades the place, despite the snow just outside the windows. Amidst green plants, an easel and dozens of canvases litter the room. Paints of all shades match the colors of flowers in pots, various-sized paint brushes lie out on tables—all more luxurious than anything I had been able to scrape up in the past. It is not ideal conditions by any means, but I will take what I can get. There are plenty of rooms in the Zamak, so I am sure Lev put me in here just to make my life that much harder.

I get to work, preparing a canvas by spreading a small amount of water on the back to make it taut. I have painted for as long as I have written. It doesn't always work, but at the very least, painting helps silence my thoughts so the stories can come to center stage. The size of my new commission is too daunting, but painting a canvas I can do.

I start drawing out in charcoal lines what the canvas will eventually become. The sun starts to go down in the distance, and the direct light causes the room to grow warmer. I persist, though, wiping sweat as I start arranging paint on a pallet. I barely get the first layer of one portrait done when Lev comes in to gather me. I am not any closer to a story of the magnitude I need it to be. He watches as I untie my smock, and though it should have protected the paints from getting on my skirts, browns and blues streak my lap, dried and staining the fabric.

"That will have to do," Lev sighs, eyeing the unfortunate accident.

"Where are we going?" I follow behind his long strides as he hurries us down the hall.

"It's time for dinner." His words are as sharp as the first time we met.

My paint-stained hands and dress give me no help to make a good impression on whoever I am dining with. At the speed Lev walks, I don't suppose I will have time to go and change. I tie my hair back, tucking the pieces that fall out behind my ears. I keep it fairly short, everyone does in the Hovel, for hygienic reasons.

I try to rub the dried paint from my hands, leaving a faint trail of color in my wake.

"You could have given me time to prepare for dinner."

Lev doesn't dignify me with a response. I stare at him in the silence. I have to glance up, but not as much as I do with Calix. He isn't dressed in any kind of uniform, a plain suit with a missing top hat today. Perhaps I could form a character after him, though I'd have to learn what exactly his job is.

I hadn't thought the castle could get less friendly, but with the silhouettes of darkness, every corner is concealed, every alcove holding a possibility of a monster on the prowl. Though we are inching toward spring, it still is winter, and the afternoons darken early, so unfortunately, many of these frights will continue in my future. We are in a quiet part of the Zamak, hardly anyone passes us, though when they do, maids, servants and guards alike scurry to the sides of the hallway to make room for Lev and me.

We wind down some spiraling hallways and up one flight of stairs. I don't bother mapping the Zamak in my mind, I have no chance of remembering it. One would think logic should accompany such a large layout, but I can't find any reasoning for the way the hallways spread.

Lev turns us into a dead-end hallway, void of any windows, so candlelight illuminates our path. The hallway is dedicated solely to the doors that wait at the end, flanked by guards in grey uniforms with a black stripe down the sides. The man to the left of us holds my stare. His blue eyes dig into mine as we approach. Lev pulls the door open, the guard's eyes snap back into place to the distant wall, and my own eyes go forward. I follow Lev in, trying my best to silence the feeling in my core that says I should run quickly in the other direction.

The queen sits at the head of the table. Calix and his sister, who I first saw in the throne room, sit in the middle of the table, talking with each other. The youngest prince and princess, not more than eight, run around giggling as a maid follows, leading them to the large table in front of me.

The heart of the monsters' den.

Lev nudges me to a chair, one down from Calix. His younger brother sits between us. The young princess and her sister sit across from us. I keep my head down, focused on the table cluttered with plates and cutlery.

"Damira." The eldest princess demands my attention. The resemblance she and Calix share is startling. I had known they were twins, but seeing them side by side, I am not sure how I missed it yesterday. Calix is notably taller, but their dark hair, pale skin and even their sharp cheekbones are replicas of one another. Calix doesn't bother to acknowledge my presence.

"Moi Nachalnik." *My superior.* Hedeon's language always chooses the most degrading words, but I still give her the respect she expects.

"You probably already know this, but I am Cantrella. Everyone in the Krepost calls me Raven, though. A childhood nickname that unfortunately stuck, and now I can't outrun it, so might as well lean into it." She gives a flip to her black hair, drawing attention to where the nickname must have come from. With it, she smiles, the previously intimidating face defrosted by the casualness of her words.

"Nice to meet you, Moi Nachalnik." I only need to talk enough to get me through this dinner. Ten minutes at a time. I just have to get through the next ten minutes, and ten minutes is nothing. I can do ten minutes. Being here, around these people, puts ice in my veins, freezing even my best of intentions. But ten minutes is a shorter eternity than some.

"Oh, now you deign to speak with respect." Calix laughs a dry laugh from down the table, across the head of his brother.

My eyes grow wide, the consequences of his words, in this room specifically, are sure to come down on me. Cantrella, Raven, rolls her eyes and leans forward across the table to catch mine and Calix's gaze.

"Don't be silly, Cal. You can speak however you want, Damira. You are a guest here, there is no need for designations or formalities. Cal just likes to be an ass. Right, Mother?" Raven rolls her eyes at her brother and turns her gaze to the queen. She's been so still, I've managed to ignore her presence. A deadly ability for a queen.

"I will not speak to Cal being an ass, however, Damira, please speak as freely as you'd like. My invitation to eat with us doesn't come with strings attached, no sense in putting on a show." I don't comment on the queen's words. I am here to put on a show, my whole life is a show. No matter how freely she thinks I am allowed to speak, I have no doubt I would get my head taken off if I were to truly speak my mind.

The doors behind us open loudly, saving me from the duty of a reply. I take a deep breath as the attention turns from me to the door.

"Oh, Mother, finally you stoop so low as to join us." The queen stands, no one else does though. I freeze in my seat. Faits, send help.

The queen mother.

The Crown has done many despicable things, and most of them began with this woman.

The war has been burning for generations, a small ember until the queen mother turned it into a flaming wildfire. The tale of Cassis still circulates. An inconsequential Reine town that was going to make their soldiers' march a day longer. And so, she burned it to the ground in the span of only a few screams. No warning for children to run, no ceasefire request. She was bored, and fire was entertaining, she was remembered as saying. All over Reine, she left similar stories, about similar towns, in her wake.

"I hear we have a guest." The crone hobbles to her seat at the end of the table, right beside me. Her voice shakes as much as her hands, worn from a lifetime's worth of issuing demands. Everything within me tenses, my hands going to my lap. My nails dig into my palms, giving all my rage a place to go that won't harm anyone but myself.

"Moi Nachalnik." I give her the respect her title demands, using everything within me to keep my head attached to my shoulders.

The queen might pretend we don't have a mountain of stations separating me and this family, but by the way the queen mother looks at me, I know she will never succumb to such things.

Hedeon's tradition is that when the king or queen hits the age of fifty, their crown is passed down to their heir. It keeps whoever is on the throne young and vigilant. Queen Milena was twenty-one when her father died. He was two years early in passing the throne to her. The power transfer restored some semblance of peace. I don't know much of the Crown's history, but I do know the queen mother was the one running the kingdom for him, even though the throne was her husband's birthright.

"You are the one my daughter is commissioning to write a show for the Arman?" She looks between me and the queen as she talks, signaling Lev with her time-wrinkled hand. Lev dashes to a door on the other side of the room and quietly speaks to someone within.

I nod, not trusting myself to open my mouth.

"Well, go on. Tell us about yourself," she demands, no niceties in her voice.

Servants move through the swinging door with haste, placing plates of salad in front of us. I almost audibly groan. A full-course meal. I will not be getting out of here any time soon. Ten minutes, I tell myself. I start counting in my head.

"I grew up in the Hovel. My parents died when I was young, so I live with my aunt, uncle, and cousin. There's not much more to tell, I'm afraid. The last few years have been rather uneventful."

The best kind of lies are those rooted in truth. I learned that from a young age.

"How quaint." The queen mother looks to the queen with a scowl.

We all dig into our salad, the conversation turning to how everyone's day was. When we finish with the first course, the soup course is set out. We serve ourselves from large porcelain pots in the middle of the table.

"Have you any idea what you are to write about yet?" Raven, Cantrella—I'm not sure what to call her—brings the conversation back to me.

"I was actually painting most of today, trying to get an idea. The Company returns in a week, so I am hoping to have something by that time." I drain the last of my soup, a warm potato mix.

"How exciting! I would love to see your paintings sometime?" Raven almost bounces in her seat at the prospect. Calix sighs beside her.

"What is that?" Raven glares at her twin.

"Not you too, Rave."

Raven sets her spoon down as her bowl is taken and a plate of meat is set before us all. She doesn't even bat an eye at the servant.

"Get off your high horse, Cal. Just because you are too dense to see the importance of what Damira is doing, only means you still have a few things to learn before taking the throne." Raven defends me. I am glad that she is not proving as insufferable as her brother.

"We should be sending supplies to the front lines, moving troops around so they are used optimally. We are wasting money here." His eyes flash with something—anger, hunger, resentment? More troops to the border. More war. More death. Calix can't be serious.

"The boy has a point, Milena. Seems his few years away from Court did him well." The queen mother speaks directly to her daughter, surpassing the third party of her grandchildren.

"If we put all of our coin into sending troops, we might keep our land, but we will lose our people, Cal." The queen talks with folded hands, sending stillness over the whole room. Her wisdom surprises me, but I still don't understand how these can be her words while her kingdom disintegrates under her reign.

It silences Calix.

I don't say anything the rest of dinner, and thankfully, the subject matter is kept from me, except once, when the queen mentions that I will be dining in the Solar with them nightly. She wants to be a gracious host, and that just so happens to be torture for me. No one discusses anything important, and if someone brings up the war, usually Calix, the queen is quick to shut it down. Not because I am here, but because dinner is time for family, and politics has no place at the table. Or so the queen states. The younger two royals tell us about their day, the crafts they made, and what they were taught in lessons.

Once dessert finishes, I excuse myself as the family settles around the fireplace in the far corner of the room. No one objects, Raven even makes sure to mention that she will find me sometime tomorrow so we can talk more. I glance back as I leave the room. These people are supposed to be monsters, unfeeling murderers who pillage and set fire to all things worth loving. But sitting there, children in their laps, laughing and explaining the books they've been reading, it's hard to see them as such.

4

MY HOUSE IS QUIET when I return. It creates an unsteady feeling in my chest. I have not walked into an empty home in all of my memories. Even before we had my cousin, Myla, my aunt and uncle have always taken people in who didn't have a place to go in the harsh winters—and all other times of the year. They've always had a heart for orphans.

As it turns out, my little house not only comes fully stocked with wardrobe, food, and leisure activities—despite its deceiving size—but also a maid. I nearly jumped to the ceiling when I walked into the kitchen last night and found a red-headed woman shoulder deep in the icebox. Her shirt sleeve was pinned to her chest, where her left arm should be. She was just as startled as I was, maybe even more so.

Katiya meets me at the door now, taking my jacket and scurrying off without words or making much other noise at all. A sitting room is right off the foyer, simple bookshelves making way for the windows, with a single couch sitting directly in front of a stone fireplace. I take a book from the shelf and sit in front of the heat, massaging my ankle. The pain that has lingered since childhood exasperated from my fall earlier in the day.

Reading fails. I reread the same page, the same sentence, over and over without any comprehension. My mind is simply too busy.

I grab a notebook from the stack on the side table and start scrawling down a few thoughts. A piece of paper has never sat blank in front of me. I may not know what story needs to be told yet, but words still flow from me. Sometimes I want to paint or draw or write a song, but when I sit down and try to do these things, inspiration never hits. I sit there without an ounce of creativity, but I have never sat down in front of a piece of paper at a loss for words.

Still, the scribbles don't amount to answers, stories too callous for the stage. I snuggle further under the knit blanket. I will not disappoint my kingdom. I will not give in to Hedeon. I will not betray further the home I miss so dearly. I just don't know how to do any of that yet.

A small tap comes from the window to my left, my eyes snap to it. The wind wakes up the beasts of my imagination, all of the things that could be laying on the other side of the curtain. Snow must have started to fall again. The fire in the hearth grows brighter than the small spark it started as. The tap, tap, tapping continues, gaining urgency. I creep to the glass, pulling back the curtain, expecting—praying—to be met with only snowfall.

I jump back at the sight of a face, suppressing a yelp.

Uncle Sumood.

"Faits," I mutter, rushing to hook the curtain back and push open the glass, letting the cold wind in with it.

"What are you doing here?" I beckon him to climb inside, and he does so with a catlike grace.

I will never understand how my uncle makes everything seem so simple. I can't even bring myself to worry about him being seen by the eyes Lev claims are on me. The Network employs my uncle for a reason—he is too good at what he does to be caught.

He hugs me before anything. An exhale is squeezed from me in his soft embrace. I hadn't realized how tightly I was holding my shoulders.

"Do you want to leave?" He holds me firmly, speaking against the top of my head.

I knew he would be coming at some time or another. Not only because I knew the Network wouldn't leave me long without contact, but because Sumood wouldn't let anything stand in the way of making sure I was okay.

"I can be your ears." I beat him to the extending of the assignment. This is what I was made for.

"We can get you out. You don't have to do this, there are other options." His hands find my shoulders, pushing back to look me in the eyes. We both know I couldn't run from this opportunity.

His midnight skin blends into the shadows of the dimly-lit room. He has always kept his hair short, better for going unnoticed in darkness. All of my life, I wondered what it would look like if he grew out the curls, curls that must be similar to my aunt's. Her hair coils in a way I wish my own frizzy brown hair could, though she has been keeping it in braids lately.

"You know as well as I do, I am fit for the job. If it was going to be anyone, it is good it's me." I try to reinforce my assertion with a smile. I'm not sure it convinces either of us.

Despite my upbringing, I am not a natural-born spy. I was not born with the ease to lie and sneak around. It has come from a place of survival, of necessity, and even at that, my instincts are less than my uncle's. He and Aunt Selah are the ones who do all the work—conversating with our Hedeon neighbors and poking around when they get a morsel of information that could help Reine in the war. I pay close attention when people around me speak, but other than that, I haven't contributed much to the Network. Not for lack of wanting or trying, but despite being trained, I am not enlisted in the Network like my aunt and uncle.

I guess not until now.

Up until this point, I hadn't been allowed to join fully. Me, Selah, and Sumood, being one of the families the Network decided to plant behind enemy lines to keep the young kids safe, meant I was sheltered from a lot of the Network's dealings. The Hovel was just one of the many areas across Hedeon that were chosen. I don't know any of the other Network families, but I'm told they're out there. We—now grown—kids are the future of Reine. A space is being carved for us back home. We just have to stay alive until we can return.

I take a few steps back, leaning against the arm of the couch, taking pressure off my tender ankle.

"You really want to be here, with these people? I will not make the choice for you, but think it through," Sumood pleads.

"What do they want me to do?" I am not running from an opportunity to help Reine.

"Nothing dangerous. The Network only needs you to listen, to look around. See if you can find plans for the warfront. Do not endanger yourself, Mira. Hear me when I say that." He pauses.

"I hear you." I fold my arms across my chest.

"If you need to get in touch with us, leave your boots on the doorstep. No one will take notice, but the eyes on you will alert us." His glance darts around the room quickly, making sure this is an acceptable place for me to live. Though, I am not sure anything can be worse than we have it in the Hovel.

"I'll report back anything I find. The Crown has me dining with them, so I am sure to hear things one way or another."

Pity lines the forehead of my uncle, finding furrowed brows to live in. He's gained wrinkles in the past few years, aging before my eyes. If this war had never continued, would he look his age instead of creasing before his time?

"Mira—" he starts, but I stop him.

"I am okay. I will be okay. I am safer than I was in the Hovel. I just need to keep my mouth closed and get through these two months," I assure him. Uncle Sumood is as protective of me as a father would be, maybe even more so.

As much as it should pain me to think, I rarely felt the lack of my parents, not with the love of my aunt and uncle. Maybe if I remembered my parents more, I would feel the hole of their absence. But when I think back to them, they are almost faceless, more a feeling than a picture. Sumood was my dad's best friend. They grew up together and fought for Reine side by side. Sumood never saw me as a burden, even as he had to leave behind the land he loved to get me here safely.

And that's why, when he says, "Your aunt would kill me if I didn't tell you to do as the queen asks. So, write a play that shines the sun on Hedeon. Don't do anything that will risk your life, Damira."

I have to reply with, "Of course, I will be safe," even though I don't mean it.

"They're taking care of us. They've sent someone to fix up the house and provided coin enough for us to feed ourselves. We've used this week's allowance to buy food for the neighbors." Sumood changes the subject, even though I can tell he doesn't believe my words. He knows me too well, but he obliges my attempt to spare him any burden for as long as I can.

"At least the Crown is holding true to their words."

"Don't worry about us. Focus on your job here. I'm not sure who will be assigned to you, but I can't be your Network contact because of our relationship. You do, however, know where to find us. Don't suppress your steps, my love. I'll see you soon."

He hugs me once more, pressing a kiss to my forehead.

"Eyes and ears up," he whispers, climbing back through the widow.

"Ears and eyes up," I agree, pulling the glass behind him and settling the curtains back into place.

5

Portraits hang from the walls of the small room, men and women adorned in crowns and jewels. Each of them holding a scepter that has a golden bat with outstretched wings perched atop.

The timeline of the Hendricks covers the walls from left to right. They all share characteristics, but none look too similar. Women with dark skin like my aunt and uncle, men with bronze skin like my own, porcelain skin like Calix and Raven. Their hair color and texture following the same ebb and flow as their skin tone. A few features stay prominent, a slim nose, tall necks, round eyes.

I wonder about my own ancestors often, people of whom I have no memory. I must resemble them in some way. Someone loved the long nose that I hate, the slim shoulders, the freckles that splatter my body in no apparent pattern. Each aspect of myself drew someone in at one point in time. My doubts about my appearance might be comforted if I could see their faces like these portraits on the wall.

I follow the painted history, each face framed in gold and emerald. Mirrors with stains on them line the ceilings, making the portraits look like they stretch upward forever. The paintings stack in rows, looping back when they reach the end of the room and starting over on the other side. The end of the line hits halfway through the right wall.

Queen Milena is painted very close to her likeness. The silver hair, the almost tan skin, the spectacularly uninviting eyes. She has no wrinkles in the portrait, she hardly has any in real life. I don't know how she's managed to evade them so long, but I am sure it comes with a strict diet of no laughter.

A frame is hung beside hers, empty of its portrait. This one has charcoal running through it as well as the standard gold and emerald.

"It's for the next monarch."

I turn quickly, feeling as if I have been caught somewhere I shouldn't be. Raven strides into the room I've found myself lost in. She wears an easy smile, the opposite of her brother.

"When a new heir is born, they receive a frame crafted by a Za-mak Mezdu. The Divine works through them, creating something that will point to the future ruler's reign. Supposedly, the dark strands in this one signify a shift in the next reign," Raven explains, coming to my side to look at the frame.

Across Hedeon, any religion is allowed, however, the only religious leaders permitted are the Mezdu. The in-betweens. They are trained to talk to the Divine, whoever you believe the Divine to be. They are overpaid chameleons. Because of this, a new religion in itself has been created, one in which obscurity is welcomed and vagueness is the core. The Divine allows Hedeons to do as they please. They send up their prayers, and everyone lives in their beautiful lie.

I miss the belief of my parents, of Reine. The Faits, who brough forth the world from The Three's will. Because they were lonely. Because they wanted a creation to love. I still pray nightly, but perhaps I am just as deceived as Hedeon.

"Told you I would come find you." Raven turns to me. Her hair is swept back today, away from her face, which highlights her high cheek bones.

"What are your plans today?" She glances up to her reflection on the ceiling, absentmindedly fixing a stray piece of hair.

"Just wandering around, waiting for an idea to hit," I admit. My notebook remains useless scribbles, nothing I jot down seems to ignite anything within me.

"How do you usually get inspiration?"

"The Hovel is full of stories. I turn a corner and am met with at least ten. I can't escape it there."

The Zamak is a quiet place, I have yet to run into anyone willing to speak with me. The servants keep their heads down, and when I try to speak with the guards, I am greeted with averted eyes and curt answers.

"I know just the place!" The grin pulling on her face is different from Calix's. Though it resembles his, hers is more inviting.

We wind through the Zamak, down a corridor full of windows and a hallway of mirrors that leads us straight into a courtyard. It's the size of a field, a garden with fully grown trees. A pavilion casts shade in the middle—an unusually sunny day for this late in winter. Relaxed against one of its columns, Calix leans, arms crossed and eyes closed.

Raven marches us right up to him.

I'm not sure if he's asleep or choosing to ignore us, but we get close enough for Raven to kick his outstretched boot.

"This whole courtyard, and you choose to step right on me, Rave?" His eyes open slowly, looking up to us through his eyebrow. His gaze slips from his sister to me, a small tug at the corner of his lips.

"What are you doing out here? It's freezing, Calix. Did you suddenly become immune to our weather in the last few years up north?" Raven studies her brother, hugging her arms tightly to her chest in response to the cold.

Again, the missing years of Calix's life come into question. Up north, the mountain cities. That crosses out him serving on the front lines, but I'm not sure what adventures he could have run into in such terrain.

"The sun is out, and despite the temperature, I realize I have missed the sunlight." He leans his head back again, closing his eyes. I try not to read into his words, but I once heard a whisper that he's been working in the mines the past two years and can't keep it from coming to mind.

"You're going to catch a cold." Raven rolls her eyes, glancing around the garden, squinting against the sun.

"I have three meetings today and two different lunches with delegates. I need some fresh air before I have to deal with the many fires of which you and Mother fanned the flames while I was gone." His eyes snap back open under Raven's unwavering attention. With a deep sigh, he stands, brushing off his pants. "Don't pretend to care about my health, Rave. It's not becoming." Calix pats her shoulder as he passes us.

"He really has become such a pain since he's returned," she mutters. It's an opening to ask where Calix has been, but as I build up the courage, she turns, grabbing my arm again.

"I don't want to talk anymore of him. Let's get back to what we were doing," she huffs, fixing a smile on her face.

She leads us with purpose through the rest of the courtyard, down a few stairwells, and then into a dark hallway. In the rest of the Zamak, gold, iron, and mirrors decorate the walls and ceilings. Paintings and statues and furniture too nice to use. But this corridor is lacking ornamentation, clearly a hallway that few see. I have to force myself to continue walking arm in arm with her. She has no reason to suspect me. I am a guest in their house, but my hair still stands on edge being alone with her.

Oblivious to my hesitation, Raven chatters on about dresses and a ball that is coming up. That I will be forced to attend. She insists we find dresses together. Apparently, she can never get Calix to assist her anymore, a shame because he has a good eye for beauty, she recounts.

We climb a few more steps, toward a door at the end of the hollow hallway now behind us. Raven pushes open the door, flooding us with light. She looks back at me and grins.

"You're going to hate me for this later." She grabs my arm again as we emerge.

"Welcome to Court!" She sprawls her hand in front of us.

Vendors line the walls, the long-domed ceiling a glass cylinder cut in half. It brings light to the strange trees that are planted and grow straight through the tile. The uncharacteristically apparent sun streaks down in a dance, mingling with the particles that float through the air.

Women and men alike meander around the floor, large dresses taking up the space between people. I don't know how no one trips over all the fabric. I look down at my own skirts, billowing and mixing with Raven's dark-colored gown. Sunrise and Sunset. My skirts' hues of yellows and pinks, hers greens and purples. Though, to the observers, we could be cut from the same cloth, two Hedeon women out for a stroll to eavesdrop fresh gossip.

"You must be Damira. I am so excited to meet you." A woman as old as my grandmother—assuming I have one—grabs my arm and pulls me into the flow of meanderers. "You will love being here. My name is Anna, by the way. I grew up in Court and got married right through those doors, just outside the courtyard." She pauses for a breath and points to our left. Raven and I both glance through the crowd of people to the towering double doors.

"I know you won't be here for more than a few months, and of course, you will go on tour with the Company after the show runs its course here. But after that, when the circuit is over, you could find yourself right back here, if you make the right connections, that is." She winks and purposefully aims her rock of a marriage ring to the light, making it sparkle.

"All that is good and the Divine, Anna!" Raven throws wide eyes at her, pulling us out of the lady's grasp and down the row of vendors, skillfully putting the crowd between us.

"Nice to see you, Moi Nachalnik!" Anna calls, waving us good-bye as her attention is caught by something to her right.

"And just like that, you've basically met all the ladies at Court," Raven whispers to me. "Don't worry, we can stay clear of them. They're fun to watch from a distance and poke fun at. Up until a few years ago, Cal and I would come and sit at one of the tables over there and make up stories about the courtiers that would pass us. Then he grew up, apparently, and took more interest in the things of the treasury and the war." She rolls her eyes when she talks of her brother. I nod along, not sure I could ever see Calix sitting here, genuinely relaxed and laughing with his twin. The two come across as sea and shore, only sharing origins. Even their looks are complementary, not identicalities.

We enter one of the stalls around the perimeter of the room, walking through rows of expensive artisan jewelry. Bright gem-stones hang from the ceiling of the small stall, earrings and neck-laces displayed on tables. The sheer amount of coin wasted in this one stall is staggering.

"My mom brought in the vendors when I was young. She thought that if we were going to all gather in court and gossip, we might as well be doing something productive along with it." Raven navigates us back out of the stall and into another with fine perfumes.

"All the vendors are local artists. They make their living from the people here, and thus, they keep making the things we go crazy for. It's an easy system, but one that has taken years to build. A few times a month, vendors from past the sea even stop in to sell their exotic inventory."

"It's all very intriguing," I answer back, smelling the candles that are samples of the perfumes.

"I have never smelled something so amazing." I point a candle at Raven, and she lowers her nose to it. It smells of lavender and a hint of rose. Of home.

"Oh, that's splendid! You need that." She puts the candle back down on the tiered table and motions to the seller who has been keeping a close eye on us. She points to the candle and then holds up one finger.

"I couldn't. I am sure it is worth more coin than I have seen in my lifetime." I have never found an occasion to be shy of my poverty. I am always surrounded by people as down on their luck as I am, but within these walls, my misfortune feels like a dirty secret.

"Nonsense. You simply must have it, and I have coffers I will never see the bottom of. Let me buy this for you as a gift. A welcome to Court and a thank-you for this new friendship." She smiles so genuinely I have a hard time fighting it.

The man selling the wonderful scents comes back with a beautiful lavender-colored crystal atomizer. He packages it in delicate paper and places it in a bag, handing it to me by the ribbons.

"Put it on the Zamak." Raven winks at the man, who hasn't looked as nervous as I would think talking with the princess, but his face falls a little at her words.

"Moi Nachalnik." The expected nervousness rises to the top, asking Raven to stay a moment longer.

"Yes?" Raven raises an eyebrow.

"It's just that, the Prince instructed us merchants to no longer charge anything to the Zamak. He said that if we are to be paid, it will be upfront and in person." The words come out in a stutter. He avoids looking into Raven's eyes.

"He is unbearable," Raven sighs, and fishes out some coin from the velvet purse that hangs off her wrist.

"Thank you." She passes over the coin. He smiles and softly replies his gratitude.

Arm in arm, Raven leads us back out.

"He's always doing things like that to try and save coin. Cal thinks I'll be deterred from spending anything if I have to always have it on me. To his credit, it works half the time, but I would rather die than admit it to him." We walk the outskirts of the vendors, in stream with the rest of Court. Hordes of footsteps echo off the marble floors, chattering and laughter hang above our heads like a guillotine.

"It seems you could never run out of coin here. What is he so worried about?" I ask, hoping she doesn't see it as prying.

The woman in front of us lets out a howl of laughter at something her counterpart said, throwing her head back in a dramatic cackle, and then replies to the man in a hushed tone. Raven giggles slightly, and I have to as well at the animal-like squall.

When we compose ourselves again, Raven replies, "If I am being honest, and I'd like to think I am the most honest in Court, we are not as well-off as a monarchy ought to be. We are draining funds quickly. The war has taken it out of the best of us, though I have been told not to worry, especially with Cal on the job. He is infuriated at Mother hiring you on, but if she brought you here, then clearly, we are not as far gone as Cal exaggerates." She shrugs, throwing a hand to the wind, sealing her ease.

I file away the information to pass onto the Network, but it looks like if I want to learn just how drained they really are, I will have to befriend the prince.

6

I HAVE A FEW hours before dinner and my demanded presence during the Crown's family time. I can feel an idea bubbling inside of me, but it hasn't risen to the surface yet. Between the paintings I am working on, and the ladies I met at court today, I have more and more ammo for the empty gun I was handed.

The cool breeze is welcomed through my open door as I enjoy the sunny day. I sit on the stairs just inside my house, though, to still take advantage of the furnace. My notebook lays open beside me, a start to some kind of story, but I'm not sure where it's going to go. I stare out at the grounds, replaying the morning and finding myself more and more angered. The people here are only concerned with one thing: themselves. How can I ever break down a wall gilded with not only gold, but selfishness? Something even harder to penetrate.

This morning's prance through Court didn't only negatively affect my mood, but my ankle. I roll it out now, having untied the strings of my boot to give it some relief. The muscles throb, somewhere deep, and have for as long as I can remember. Exasperated by standing, walking, using it for any prolonged amount of time.

A silhouette exits the Zamak, heading down the path toward my house. I lean back, my elbows on the steps. His walk is a waltz, the cadence more leisurely than anyone else would dare possess. I sigh, as I await the inevitable.

When he finally reaches my door, he only stares at me, waiting for me to speak first.

"What do you want, Calix?" I stop myself from rolling my eyes.

"Just checking in. Rave told me about dragging you to Court. Wanted to make sure you didn't flee to the mountains and make my life that much happier." He's smug, staying in the doorway, trying to look casual but toeing the threshold.

Three buttons. That's how many open holes line the front of his shirt. I shouldn't care about the muscles in his chest, but I can't help to think the tease is on purpose. His shirt is wrinkled and untucked, but from what I've heard of Calix, he's a rule follower. No matter how much he rebels in these simple ways. From the first time I met him, the air around him divulges that he knows more than he leads on.

So, what is the real reason he is here, staring at me like that?

"Well, I am fine and still here. I can't flee, even if I wanted to, remember? Now, if that's all?" I shoo him away with my hand. I should be making friends with him, but right now is not the time. I am in too much pain, on the verge of an idea, and Calix is the last person I want to be speaking with.

"Have you started writing?"

"I don't need a babysitter, contrary to what you think. I will do the job the queen asked of me, and I will do it with a smile to serve this kingdom." I smile in example, trying to prove I am dutiful.

"Somehow I hardly think that is the case, darling." Calix's eyes focus intently on me, a dark forest of green inviting me in to be swallowed by the shadows. I try to ignore the pet name he won't stop annoying me with.

That first conversation I had with Calix, when I didn't know to conceal my feelings, taints every new conversation we have. He knows how I feel about the Crown, the war, being here. I couldn't lie if I wanted to.

Fine, if he won't leave, then I will. I huff, standing. But as I lift my foot, I wince, not just from the pain in my ankle, but from the lack of support for having forgotten to retie my boot. I sit back down with haste.

Calix finally steps in—toward me with such surety it makes me pause. He bends down to a knee, taking the strings of my boot in his hands. I jerk back, but he holds still.

"I can tie it myself," I insist, but he doesn't falter.

"Just because you can, doesn't mean you have to." He is careful of my ankle, somehow picking up on me favoring it. He is intentional not to touch any part of me, just the laces.

He steps back when it's tied. I stay on the step, looking down at him.

"I stopped by the room that Lev set up for you to paint in. All our coin is going to you to write, and yet, any time I find you, you are sitting around, not writing." He leans back against the door frame, crossing his arms and taking liberties with his eyes, they roam not only me but my space.

"Must you be here?" I stand again, taking the few steps down until we are both on level ground.

He grins as if he's the thing that's broken me down. If only I could tell him that he is a single drop in the well of my rage. I think *I'd* even be surprised to learn how deep it truly goes.

"You put too much pressure on such pointless things." Being royal, his words hold such weight, but he flings them around as if they are light as a breath.

A calm rage washes over me. "Pointless? Pointless! You see no value in what your mother has planned? Your people are falling apart at the seams. Maybe in all your roving the last two years, you failed to see the realities of life without privilege. There is no food, no shelter, no reason to live if everyone is being brought up just to fight and die. Words give them hope. This play has the potential to bring life back to where there currently is none, and you have the audacity to call it pointless."

Calix reddens in the face, dropping the charm and donning the anger that never rises to more than a flicker in front of me.

"Watch how you speak." He takes a step toward me, voice full of iron, in an authority he never earned.

"You have done nothing to gain my respect." I walk out of my house, the words flung from my tongue with little care.

Let me get beheaded, let me get kicked out or killed. I can't stand his arrogance, not when I have seen his decisions play out firsthand.

His boots pad behind me down the path. I don't know where I am headed, but it is away from him.

He doesn't let me get far, staying close on my heels as I turn the bend in the road.

"Mira," he calls, clearly not worried who hears. My feet carry me to the only place I have felt safe on this mountain. He follows me the whole way, up the steps and through the doors.

"I am not going to continue to talk with you unless you apologize." I finally turn to him, arms crossed.

He glances around the Arman Theatre's foyer with confusion, like he didn't keep track of the turns that brought us here. I seemed to have struck his curiosity. He sighs heavily, like a child getting ready to give an apology they don't mean.

"I may have been quick to speak," is all he offers. I don't judge whether it's sincere or not. Instead, I make my way up the grand staircase.

My imagination runs out of my grasp most days, but even on the wildest of chases, I never could have thought up this foyer.

Paintings of past plays live forever on the ceiling, each portrait comprised of so much detail I could spend a lifetime staring and still not absorb all that makes them up. Gold frames surround the portraits, gold curtains make way for golden windowpanes, gold sconces, gold handrails, gold woven carpets. The bones of my people surround the portraits, skin curtains make way for ligament windowpanes, teeth sconces, finger handrails, muscle carpets.

The obliteration of my people paid for this theatre.

It makes it that much easier to hold onto the anger against Calix as he follows my steps to the balcony doors.

The theatre is filled with a sweet melody that caresses my face when I enter the balcony on soft feet, trying my best not to disturb the person playing the pianoforte on the stage. Somewhere in my childhood that I can't remember, I learned to play the piano. I don't know when, but I know that I can play, even though it has been years. I sit in a chair to get off my ankle that is beginning to send shocks of pain up my leg, and lean against the balcony railing. A few seats down, Calix sits as well.

Far below, the boy at the piano closes his eyes as his fingers dance over the keys. He plays for no one, the theatre empty except the three of us. The melody starts slow, rising and falling on beat, but as he quickens, the chords become dissonant, spread apart, and go astray. He bangs on the keys, down to the low notes and then up to the higher ones. Back and forth, the repetition running circles through his hand.

It's beautiful.

The fighting, the turmoil. The composition is full and broken all at once. It brings tears to my eyes. Tears I can't stop from falling, even when Calix glances over at me. I wipe my cheeks, focusing on the boy pouring out his soul, and away from the stubborn one at my side.

The young pianist has felt things I can't begin to understand. He leaves it on the keys, in the sound, in the air. I can't be sure from this distance, but I think tears fall from his eyes too. Silence is abrupt after the thundering that was brought into the room. The boy pants in the silence, arms dropping to the side. His rust-colored hair falls to his forehead, stuck with sweat. I peek at Calix, who studies the boy's face with little more than triviality. I stand quietly, wanting to give the boy his privacy in such a vulnerable moment, but my foot hooks on a seat leg, and I stumble, causing the pianist's eyes to dart up to mine. He fumbles over the piano bench as he stands.

"I'm so sorry," I yell down. I quickly descend the stairs, ignoring my screaming ankle, and head toward the stage. The pianist, frozen, keeps his gaze on me. No footsteps come from the balcony as a telltale sign that Calix has followed. When I glance over my shoulder, he is nowhere to be seen.

"I'm Damira." I climb the steps up to the stage, my voice carrying off in the emptiness of the theatre, the golden bat hovering above and watching my every move. The pianist smiles hesitantly.

"I'm Deacon," he says, as he shakes my outstretched hand.

"That was beautiful. I mean, truly beautiful. Did you compose it yourself?" Standing this close, I can see he is older than I first thought. Maybe a year or so younger than me, sixteen or seventeen. His blue eyes pick up every hint of light, his pale skin brighter in the spotlight of the stage.

"It's not finished yet. I know it still needs work in some places." He rubs his arm as he speaks, avoiding looking directly into my eyes.

"Will you be done with it soon?" I try to conceal the excitement growing in my chest.

"Depends on how much time I have to work on it. I am part of the Arman's stage crew. I came back a few days earlier than the others to attend to some family business. It seems we have a new show to work on, thanks to you." His smile is genuine, though small.

"Well then, Deacon. Do I have a proposition for you."

7

T HE IDEA FLOWS FROM me. All the parts—painting, the piano, walking around Court—come together to make a whole. In the place between being awake and asleep, genius hits. I pad across the cold floor of my bedroom, lighting a candle and sitting at the desk. Ink bleeds onto my hands as I scribble words, and in turn, I bleed a story onto the paper. The sun comes through the windows behind me, but the story doesn't yield to it or to the tiredness in my eyes. Katiya brings in a kettle of tea, and I drink, forgetting to blow the steam away and burning my tongue. I catch my eye in the mirror once, bent over the desk, looking similar to a goblin in children's stories. I straighten my back and continue on.

Two days pass in the same rhythm, with little sleep in between. I even skip dinners with the Crown, my apologies sent through

Katiya. My fingers are stained black, and my eyes sting from straining to see in the dim light.

The play is finished.

Pages of dialogue, stage directions, and a few sketches of costumes and set designs. I don't know how I managed it. It's even more miraculous that I actually think it might be good. I can do revisions with the Arman Company and perfect it as we go, but at least I have something on paper.

I have my reservations. What I plan to do, well, if it's not treason, it is certainly treason adjacent.

Morning comes too quickly after a night of anxious sleep. Today I meet with the actors. I roll over, groaning into my pillows. Katiya opens the curtains, sending me to burrow further into my blankets. I take a few deep breaths, pushing through the nerves pooling in my stomach that make me nauseous.

For Reine.

I can do this—for Reine.

Lev waits for me outside my front door to escort me to the theatre. He doesn't smile when I greet him, hardly even acknowledges that we walk together. I clutch the papers to my chest. Not many people run around the Zamak grounds yet, except those who work for the rich. Including myself. And Lev. Things we both should keep in mind.

"How long have you been working for the Crown?" I ask Lev as we start down the road. He wears the same thing daily, just in different dark-colored variations. Always dull. I'm starting to think it could be a uniform in its own right. Shackles that tell everyone just to whom he belongs.

"My whole life." He grunts, no further explanation.

"Did your parents work for the Crown, then?" I press on, not taking his silence for an answer. I know he doesn't want to talk, for whatever reason, he's been cold to me from the first day he picked me up. But if I don't busy my mind with something, I will hurl my innards up, and I am sure he will like that a lot less than making small talk.

"Yes." He doesn't look at me, his eyes fixed on the path ahead.

"Do you at least like it? Or do you feel as if you have to stay?" If he had wanted to leave, I would think it should be possible to some degree. He's older in age, surely enough that not working could be an option. People in the Hovel or towns alike don't ever hit the stability that comes with age, however, people who work for money sometimes can.

Lev turns to me.

"I don't like you. I won't like you. I know you are hiding something. I knew it from the moment I laid eyes on you. I may not know what it is, but rest assured, I will find out. So there is no need to fill these little silences, just focus on your steps, and I will focus on mine so we can get through these two months easily. That is, unless I can get evidence as to why the queen should have you beheaded. Understood?"

I had not expected his full voice to be so menacing. People have a way of contradicting themselves. Mean features, kind voice. Haunted eyes, charming smiles. This man is all around dreadful, and I find myself wondering whether time or circumstances have made him this way.

"Understood," I mumble.

The air is thick this morning, smelling of fresh snow and bread, I assume from the bakeries down the Krepost. Two months until spring. The dead of winter in Hedeon has always been the worst time of year for me, and it's not just the permanent shivers or the chronically dry skin. Something bad always happens in the winter. Eight winters ago, I was brought to Hedeon. Every winter since then, like a curse, something bad has happened. A friend dying, a flu threatening the health of everyone in the Hovel, new restrictions on food because of perishing farms, the list goes on.

Sometimes the curse is much smaller. I had kept to myself growing up, and when I finally opened up and tried to have friends, my heart was obliterated. Two winters ago, I thought I loved a boy, but he ended up choosing another girl over me. I was left to pick up the pieces by myself.

Mornings like this, when it is so glaringly winter, pinch my heart.

The golden bat watches over me as I walk down the Arman aisle, its eyes following me from where it perches at the top of the stage. I flip on the light switches, one by one. We don't have electricity in the Hovel. Actually, I am unsure of any other place in the whole continent of Nadez that has electricity. It's a fable, a fairytale to tell children to help them dream at night. The buzz settles in my bones with the flicker of each light turning on. Those who grew up here don't seem to be aware of the sound the power makes, but it echoes off the void inside of me.

I set out chairs in a circle but then decide against it and put them back behind the curtain where I found them. My arms scream at the exertion. I take a deep breath, staring at the mess of chairs, debating if I should put them back out again.

"Damira?" A tiny voice asks. I turn around to see a woman, a head and shoulders shorter than me. Her long chestnut hair hangs to her waist, a luxury, a symbol of status. I have never seen anyone like her, patches of her skin lighter than the rest. It's breathtaking, olive brown, but lakes of milky white swirl in negative space. A pond on her face, a river on her arm, all breaking up the darker tone.

"Nice to meet you." I stick out my hand and she shakes it without thought. Not having many memories of Reine helps in lots of instances, but muscle memory never truly goes away. We hug by way of greeting in Reine, never so formal as a handshake, and it was the hardest custom to get used to here. Those in Hedeon are much more reserved. I have never gotten the hang of it and often touch out of turn. Thankfully, in the Hovel, it goes more unnoticed, as the culture there defaults to necessity as opposed to niceties.

"I'm Pasha." The woman smiles widely, teeth shining white. I wonder how hard she worked to get here as opposed to those in Court. I don't know how one becomes an Arman actor, but if their reputation proceeds them, then I doubt they all came from the right parentage.

"I am a background actress mostly, and I work with props," she adds.

The door to the left of the stage opens, and a chatter of people walk in.

"Those are the others." She smiles, turning around and bouncing toward them on such light feet it's impossible to believe she'd have any burdens weighing her down.

Fear grips my throat, threatening to spill out through tears or vomit, I don't know which. I need to go speak with them, but my throat closes, my feet freeze, and my stomach drops.

Just get through the next ten minutes. Deep breaths. The feeling will pass.

The feeling will pass.

The feeling should pass.

But it doesn't.

And so, I do it afraid.

All types of people are sprawled out on the stage, stretching or relaxing, laughing with one another with ease. They look to me as I come before them, fear coursing through my every   heartbeat. People in the Hovel read my stories weekly, but they are never put to the caliber of Court, to being acted out in front of the wealthiest of Hedeon.

"I'm Damira." It's a weak greeting, but it's all I can pull up. I don't have to quiet the group, they all stare at me by their own curiosity.

"I am not going to lie to you all, and it's not just because I am sure you are well aware of my upbringing. I have never done this before. I don't know how to direct a play. All I know how to do is write. So, I wrote." I pause to take a deep breath. A few people shuffle, a couple of them who were lingering in the back come in closer. "The queen wanted something that would instill hope in Hedeon, something that would speak to the state we are in and bring some kind of nationalism to those who watch. Well, I am not sure I have done that, but I do know these words will make people feel. Make people think. I would be honored if you would act out this story that I have put my all into, but I understand if it is not what you signed up for."

None of them move or try to speak. I can't tell if that's a good sign or bad.

"I only have one copy—" I start motioning to the stack in my hand.

"You can get it to a scribe later today who will make replicas." A kind gentleman at the back of the stage speaks up, hair to his shoulders, height similar to the ladder he stands beside. A few others nod with his words.

"Perfect. Then today, I will read it out to you, and tomorrow we assign parts."

The story comes from me with ease, many of the words already imprinted in my mind. I trip over the first scene, trying not to look in their eyes as understanding washes over their faces. My nose stays to the papers, begging The Faits that this rough draft will convey all I mean it to. I finish the first act, and no one screams out for me to stop, so I continue on to the second act, summarizing a few things that I am still working out. The second act ends in a laugh, which launches us into the third and then the fourth, coming to the ending that will make it very clear what I mean this story to be. I take a deep breath before reading the last line, my voice shaking as it comes out. I finish and peek over the paper, taking the moment to look at the horror on their faces.

I want to say more, to tell them that it still feels unfinished and that there is so much room for improvement, but I force my mouth to stay shut. This story is theirs now, they can do with it what they like. That's the scary thing about writing, once it is penned, it no longer belongs to the writer. I know none of these people that sit in front of me, and yet a part of my heart now belongs to them. That is the curse, and the blessing, of the artist.

Silence is suspended between my last words and the Company's first. A few people stand, staring at me with harsh eyes. They leave, the only thing in their wake a swinging door. I barter with myself not to cry. Six people gone. Six people who see how this play could be received. I close my eyes, taking a breath as the fear bubbles up that I have done something irrevocably wrong. My time here is shorter than I thought it would be, but I had to try.

"Beautiful."

My eyes snap open to the man who leans on the stray ladder. He wears clothes just shy of fitting, his height something that isn't accounted for in Hedeon. Pasha starts clapping, applause breaking out from the group. A woman stands, one who sat at the front, staring stone-faced at me the whole time. I do my best not to cower back in intimidation.

"They're too fearful to say anything, don't worry about them." She speaks in raspy words. "As for the rest of us, I think I can speak for everyone when I say that we would love to be a part of this." Her skirts cut through her waist, her stomach full in a way mine never had the chance to be. I admire her curves, the way she takes up space with nothing to apologize for.

Those behind her start to stand.

Deacon, the composer, speaks from the right of the group. "You don't know *our* stories yet, but I am sure you will find them similar to yours, Moi Dramaturg." *My playwright.* A few people mutter in agreeance. I can't smile at the unity, at the terrible luck we all share. We are the same. Hurt. Broken. Betrayed by a kingdom that should have cared for us.

The man at the ladder parts the Company in two as he walks up to me.

"My name is Kolyo." He extends his arm to me, giving what I am sure is his version of a smile. Barley any lift at the side of his lips. "Have all that I am, but I ask you to make it worth it."

"I promise." I drop his hand when he pulls away, but Pasha is quick to replace it with another.

"This is Myka." Pasha introduces the woman who already gave me her allegiance. Myka's hand in mine displays the contrast of our skin—hers a darker shade of bronze.

"I almost wanted to leave the Company," Myka speaks. "Not that that is an option, but I had lost the excitement I used to be so fond of. You're bringing restoration where I thought there was only ruin. I am the Arman's conductor, and I would love to help write pieces for this." I refrain from throwing my arms around her.

I get passed around the group in introductions. The costume designers, the musicians, the stagehands, those who can help with directing, and those who think they will be the right fit for different parts. Because of the six that left, we might have to stack jobs, but everyone seems perfectly willing to do so while assuring me that the lost six will keep their mouths shut. Even if they don't agree with what we are doing here, they won't betray their own. I am one of them now. By the end of the day, we are casting our vision as a group, dreaming of what could be. For the play and for the kingdom.

Rehearsal ends an hour before dinner. Content with the day's work, I stay after, putting the stage back to how it was this morning, shoving chairs aside, rolling the piano back to center stage. My fingers scrape across the keys in my struggle to move it. A few notes ring out through the hall, gliding on the emptiness of the auditorium. It catches my curiosity, forcing me to sit on the bench.

I place my fingers where I know they're meant to be, finding middle C. I can't remember who taught me these things, maybe it was my mom in all the talent I've been told she had. Or maybe it was my dad, even more a mystery to me than my mother is. Perhaps I was just taught by a tutor like most kids my age would have been.

The notes are shy at first, scared of waking the emptiness of the theatre. My fingers move, as if separate from me. They know the keys like they've done this hundreds of times before. Friends in the oldest regard. A song comes out, a song jollier than the one

I witnessed Deacon playing. A song of my people, I think. The familiarity is frightening.

I close my eyes as my fingers play. I can all but see the ballroom, grand and painted in yellows. Women and men dance around each other's arms. Long flowing dresses sparkle under a glowing chandelier. Someone stands at the head of the room, watching the merriment. My memory lingers on the faceless man as if he has something more to offer me than the people in the ballroom.

I falter, the memory falling apart. My fingers switch tunes, switch memories.

The notes come out harsh. A song from somewhere deep in my core, a place of hurt I have left untouched. An open wound I start pushing into as I play. It's a juvenile melody, but bleeding all the same. Anger rises, the anger I try to keep locked close to my chest every day. Anger that burns white hot. My fingers slam against the keys, the notes crisp and sure with each stroke. The sound comes out with precision.

Abruptly, the song comes down, my fingers slowing, the notes becoming unsure and tripping over themselves. It sounds more like what I feel inside. The confusion and careful steps. I stay here for a moment, in the repetition. It is so similar to the repetition I heard Deacon play the other night.

The song moves on, building up, building to something, growing and growing.

A loud noise jolts me and stills my fingers on the piano.

Calix comes swaggering in, one hand in his pocket, his thumb hooked out, and the other resting on a sword. He's undoubtedly come from some kind of training, his curls pushed out of his face with sweat and his clothes casual. The double doors at the back of the theatre slammed in his aftermath.

"Oh, did I miss rehearsal?" He cocks his head to the side and frowns exaggeratedly.

I pull the cover over the keys and scoot back.

"Don't stop playing on my behalf." He puts his hand on his chest. A flair for the dramatic. Maybe he is the one who belongs on this stage.

"Did the queen send you again?"

"No, I am just being a dutiful son." He climbs the steps to the stage. I stand, heading over to my papers sprawled on the ground.

"It went well today, so well I expect most everyone to show up again tomorrow. Thanks for stopping by. Same time next week?" I ask flatly, sitting to gather my papers, and to alleviate a tired ankle.

To my dismay, he sits in front of me, but he doesn't bother to lift a finger to help. I am sure he should be embarrassed of his hands, hands that issue demands like his grandmothers. I am also sure that *embarrassed* is not a word in his vocabulary.

"I just need enough information so that when my mother asks how it's going, I can give her a report," Calix says, cutting to the bottom line and ignoring my dismissal.

"Maybe if you actually showed up when we were rehearsing, you'd have something to tell her."

I stand, a stack of papers in my arms, turning away from him. He jumps up and follows close at my heels. I should give in to what he asks—I don't need him sitting in rehearsal, for fear of what he will think, but I can't bring myself to comply with his wants, especially since he hasn't made any effort to make my life easier.

"Yes, a great point. The only downside, however, is that would require actually sitting in rehearsals." He clicks his tongue in disapproval.

"And neither of us wants that." I lead us down the hall, toward where I was told a couple of scribes can duplicate my manuscript.

"It would save us both the hassle of having to be in the same room together for longer than a few moments."

"I am sure you will figure something out. You seem very resourceful." I glance at him as he strides beside me now. He runs a hand through his hair, flattening the curls that are already worn through from whatever activity required that sword.

"You think I'm resourceful, Mira?" He raises an eyebrow above a smirk.

"You wouldn't like to hear what I think of you."

I turn down the stairs and dead-end in a room with the scribes. Three people sit at the desks, scribbling away on parchment.

"Is it possible to get fifteen copies of this by tomorrow?" I ask the man at the very front.

"Of course, that is hardly anything." He smiles, but then spots Calix behind me and straightens up, wiping the grin from his face in replacement for reverence. He bows at the hip.

"Moi Nachalnik." He breathes quietly, stricken by the prince. Calix's eyes flicker to him momentarily. Disinterested would be an understatement.

"Thank you." I smile and turn to leave. Calix follows.

Back down the hall we go, though I am not sure where I lead us this time. He doesn't talk but doesn't leave me alone either. I need to be making friends with him, but I can't have him reporting back to his mother the subject matter of the play either.

"Fine, Calix. I will help you placate your mother." I stop our walking, turning to him with arms crossed.

"You will?" He lifts an eyebrow.

"Yes, just meet me after rehearsal, and I will tell you whatever you want to know to make her happy. I don't want to be around you any more than you want to be around me."

Once again, he isn't shy about his wandering eyes, from my booted toe all the way to my straying hair. A small grin pulls at the corner of his lip, but I can't find the reason for it.

"Fine," he finally says. "I will see you tomorrow afternoon, darling."

8

MY BOOTS SIT OUTSIDE my door as I wait in front of the fireplace with a blanket and a cup of tea. I am not sure when the Network is going to come, but this is the first I've had time to make contact since Raven told me about the supposed lack of coin Hedeon is going through. Katiya hides somewhere within the house. I welcome her out whenever I lounge in the common space, but she stays confined to the corner she calls her own, despite my invitation. It does nothing to help my loneliness but bodes well for my spying.

A knock at the door sends me to my feet with little regard for the tea mug in my lap. I remember it before it hits the ground, but still too late, as lukewarm tea drips from the bottom of my shirt.

"Faits," I curse, the tap continuing at the door.

I run over to it before Katiya wakes or comes out of her hole. I open the door to a woman clouded in darkness. A cloak hood pulled deep over a face.

"You look a mess." She pushes into my shoulder, past me and into my house.

I close the door behind us, turning around in time to see her pull the hood down. Badly dyed black hair spools out, and she throws it over her shoulder. It's long enough to be a testament to the wealth of Court, but that doesn't explain the hair dye.

"Are you alone?" She takes note of the room quickly, eyes jumping around the space.

"Katiya, the maid, is in her room at the other end of the house."

"Good, then we will make this quick." She folds in her arms. The cloak isn't the only thing that brings shadows, her clothes beneath are just as dark.

"Should you have come in through my front door? I've been told there are guards watching me."

"A bluff." She shrugs, confident even in the little details I give her.

She stares at me, waiting. I then realize it is I who has the information to give.

"Oh, right. Um, the Crown might be draining funds faster than they can keep up. Raven told me that she thinks they're doing alright, but the prince seems pretty on edge, if you ask me. I haven't been able to get closer to him, I mean I have had the opportunity, but he is so aggravating it is off-putting when a chance opens up. But I will try again," I promise.

"Raven?" Her eyes widen slightly, in a familiar movement I can't place. The deep blue pops against the fake hair that is a cheap replica of Raven's raven hair.

"The princess—Cantrella." I clarify.

"Of course, I know who she is. You talked to the princess?"

"I think she thinks we're friends. I have been eating dinner with the Crown most nights. They are treating me like a regal houseguest, or maybe more like a pet." I glance around my private quarters, a spoiled pet, but one with a leash all the same.

Her stare is unwavering, and we do not move from the door. Up close, it is easy to see the freckles that spot her nose and cheeks. Red, unlike her badly dyed hair. She wears scrap cloths all sewn together. She's probably only a few years older than me, but she holds herself with much more confidence than I have found in my own years.

"What's your name?" I ask in her silence, but she lets the question fly over her head as she finally budges and moves to warm up by the hearth. I follow, plopping down on the couch, careful of my tea-soaked hem.

"We didn't realize how close you were. This changes things. Can you get your hands on some ledgers? How much information do you think you can extract?" Her words quicken. The way she speaks of herself as a multiple, she must be higher up in the Network.

I don't know much about how our operation runs. On purpose. The more you know, the more people you put in jeopardy if you are caught. We are a web. Certain people answer to certain people, all intertwined but only occasionally intersecting. There is only a handful, from what I understand, who actually are in the know about the majority of our workings.

"Maybe. I could try, but I won't promise anything. I can do my best and see where that leads us."

I have to get closer to Calix, that path is inevitable, no matter how I've tried to put it off.

"Do better than your best." She stares, and then rushes back to the door, cape and hair flowing behind her.

"They call me Tenny, by the way. If you need to contact me again, you know how. I'll be here within a few hours of the boots being set out. I'll be back to check on you if I don't hear anything in a week's time. Eyes and ears up."

"Ears and eyes up."

She opens the door, the coldness seeping in ever so quickly before the door is latched behind her as if she had never been here.

The doors loom in front of me. Over two weeks of these dinners, and I haven't gotten over the sinking in my stomach when I am faced with entering the Crown's Solar. Lev pushes open the doors, always leading me in.

"Damira, finally! Please tell my brother he is intolerable! He never agrees with me, and he always underestimates my intellect. It's appalling. Apparently, that just coming from my mouth isn't enough." Raven sighs, flung over an armchair in front of the hearth. Calix stands in front of her with crossed arms and releases a heavy sigh. They both match today, only in clothes though, clearly. Calix wears his darkness like the depths of the ocean, and Raven wears hers like the swallows of the night. I wouldn't be surprised if they both wear dark colors so often in order to draw attention to the emerald in their eyes.

"You are intolerable." I stare with little emotion and a lifted brow.

Calix's eyes tick slowly from my head to toe once again.

"It's a good thing I care for neither of your opinions," he assures us and then moves past me to the table, his shoulder grazing mine.

Raven stands, hooking her arm in mine, and sits us down beside each other, across from Calix. Anya and Alek, the littlest royalty, sit beside Cal, and he busies himself with speaking to them so he doesn't have to endure our conversation any longer.

The queen enters late, the servants already starting to place our first course on the table.

"My apologies, everyone, I had a farmer I was dealing with. I am truly famished, though," the queen announces as she sits and starts quickly on the salmon soup.

None of these people have ever felt famished in their life, I know that for a fact. The queen's poor choice of words leaches any appetite I managed to hold onto past the doorway of this room. How easily she throws around comments that hit me so deeply. Does she know that I have seen her citizens die of hunger right in front of me? In the harshest of winters, when we were too late with food delivery, I saw the bodies that waited for reprieve. Why is death the only pardon from this despicable life we never chose?

I swallow my words, sharp and slicing my throat on the way down.

"How was the farmer?" Calix asks, perking up and out of his lazy-boy persona.

The queen doesn't answer him, but instead entertains Raven's questions about tablecloth colors for the Revel. I suppose that when you are queen, you can pick through words like a garden, discarding the weeds for flowers.

"How was the farmer?" Calix asks again, with more force.

"You know my rule, Calix. No business at the table. We can discuss later." She smiles, breaking a piece of bread to dip into the soup. I glance at Calix as I spoon my own soup. His stare at the queen lingers, trying to read which way her emotions are leaning after the talk.

"Mother—" Calix starts. The queen's eyes snap up, daring him to say another word. He doesn't.

"I had a wonderful day picking flowers for the Revel." Raven straightens, interjecting a safe topic and pleasing her mother.

"Why don't you tell us about that, dear?" The queen's squinted eyes turn from Calix and open with delight at Raven. Calix drops his spoon, making a loud noise, but it is ignored by everyone at the table.

Raven chatters on about her day, all the things that go into planning the Spring Revel. The ball, the festival, the meals, the performances. My eyes stray to Calix throughout dinner, watching as he eats in silence, chasing the dumplings of the main course around his plate. He plays the dutiful son well.

The family moves to the lounging area after dinner, just as always. I head toward the door, never wanting to intrude on these moments.

"Damira, will you stay?" Raven looks over the couch, everyone's eyes turning to me. I glance at the queen, who nods her approval.

"Sit with us." The queen motions to where they all lounge in front of the fireplace. I am a mouse in a bat's cave.

I move to sit by Raven on the couch, but Alek hooks his hands around my wrist, pulling me down to sit on the floor by him and Anya. Anya climbs into my lap, leaning her back into me as she stares into the fire. Alek huddles to my side.

"You fit right in." Queen Milena smiles. I wish her words weren't true, but I suspect they think me no more than a new plaything. Maybe in time their curiosity of things below will be quenched, and they will lose interest in me.

"Can we speak of the farmer now, Mother?" Calix asks from the armchair to the left of the queen. She sighs in concession, finally giving her attention to him.

"He is worried about the winter. It is lingering, and he is concerned for his fields. He has had to release more than a few tenders on top of it." She brushes off the words like snow on a coat, but Calix doesn't let her breeze over it.

"What did you tell him?"

"I gave him some coin and assured him all will be well, come spring."

"Mother." Calix sits straighter.

"The advisors signed off on it. I don't want to hear another word." Her eyes go from the fire to him. Her stare pins him to the chair.

"If we don't change how we spend our money, your words will be nothing more than false promises. Comfort our people, but don't let your word become obsolete."

"Calix," she snaps again, this time it yanks the silence out of him, and he resigns to looking into the fire.

Raven sits on the couch behind me. I turn, and her eyes meet mine with a sigh and a small head shake. The kids play for a while, and we sit in silence. Raven tries to bring conversation, but it dies soon after it leaves her lips. Calix is the first to stand and announce he is going to retire.

"I'll walk Damira home." Raven jumps up, prying an asleep Anya off my lap and handing her to a nursemaid. I stand, and Raven leads us to the door that takes us outside.

"Have a good night, you two." The queen smiles softly, staying where she sits.

The moon reflecting off the snow lights up the whole Krepost below. I pull my scarf tighter around my neck, my breath running toward my house before me. Lev waits by the door to escort me like every other night.

"No, it's okay, Lev. I can see Damira to her house tonight." Raven relieves him softly. He steps back with his hands folded behind his back as we continue down the path. I glance back at him, Lev throwing threats with his squinted eyes.

"Usually, we are a bit more fun as a group, but tensions have been high lately," Raven explains.

"Does your mother always dismiss Calix like that?" My house is on the opposite side of the grounds, so we have a winding walk.

"For the most part. I hate to admit it, but he does have good ideas. Cal is smart, the smartest of us all. Mother doesn't take advantage of it as she should. She puts all her stalk in the advisors who are so scared of her, they always agree with whatever she asks." Raven confides in me as if I have done something to win her trust.

I may only be a new toy, but the Crown treats me with such empathy, I don't know how it's possible that so many freeze in the streets far below us. I may be stuck in the Zamak, but my mind is continuously in the Hovel, with the people I am much happier to call my neighbors than these.

"I feel sorry for him, always trying to improve the kingdom and then just being shut down like that." Even though I am just prodding Raven for information, I'm not sure how much deception is in these words. It makes sense why Calix postures himself as thorny, how else can he be heard if he doesn't stick in the queen's side?

A few courtiers pass us, making their way to the gates, gawking at Raven and whispering to each other when recognition of who I am sets in. Raven doesn't seem to notice, doesn't let on that she does, at least. How strange to grow up with such devotion from people just because you were born into a certain family. It has never made sense to me.

"He will prevail." She assures me with a shrug. "It's Cal. He always does."

The snow has been shoveled from the path we take, but still it is stacking tall, as it has begun to fall again. We finally reach my house, but Raven stops me before I can ascend the porch stairs.

"Do you have any siblings?" she asks.

"My aunt and uncle have a new daughter, Myla. She is the closest thing to a sibling I have," I lie. Some things I couldn't bring myself to include in my new identity. The only images I have of my brother are tormenting. I know I loved him, I know that we were close, if not in age, then in friendship. He slips from my grasp as I try to save him. I see him most in my nightmares—flashes, feelings, nothing more.

"A shame. Brothers are terrible, but Calix is the other half of who I am. I wouldn't know what to do without him," she thinks out loud, staring off a bit.

"You said he hasn't always been that severe, that opposing with your mom?"

"That's right. We used to have fun when we were younger. I still find myself missing him a lot of days, even though he is now just across the hall. I can't remember when exactly it happened, or what caused the change, but it has only been exasperated by his time away."

"It must be a lot of pressure to be in the position you two are in."

"You would think so, yes." She speaks gently, still her stare fixed down the path.

"Goodnight, Damira." She smiles and walks back toward the Zamak, the snow crunching in her ascent.

9

THE ZAMAK GROUNDS ALWAYS have more to offer. Some days, during our lunch break, everyone eats together, huddled in a circle, laughing about jokes I don't fully understand. Other days, everyone goes their separate way for the hour, getting business done or taking a quick nap. Today is one of those days. My body is still used to the small portions of the Hovel, and I have even more been at a loss of appetite hearing of how the Crown speaks of the war. So, I wander around the Zamak, exploring the secrets it never gets to keep.

To the side of the sprawling castle, a large, windowed building stands among the snow. It caught my eye quickly, but today is the first day I have had time enough to venture to it. It's like my greenroom, or the greenhouses of home. Foggy windows from warm breath, a beacon in the tundra.

As I slip the door open, heat kisses my face, wrapping around me and pulling me in for a long-awaited embrace. Instead of rows of plants as I had assumed, potted trees line the windows, all giving way for the magnificent fountain that sits in the middle. It is all open space, the door not obstructed from the rest of the room.

It gives me no shelter to hide from the prince lounging on the fountain's edge.

He lies on his back, completely undisturbed except for the one eye open and his head tilted in my direction.

"Seeking refuge from this miserable excuse of a day?" He closes his eye and turns his head back toward the domed ceiling.

"I thought you'd be used to it, from your time up north," I bait him, unable to drop the curiosity.

He chuckles, opening his eyes again and swinging his feet around to face me.

"Would you like to sit, darling?" he asks, and because I am supposed to be trying to be his friend, I oblige—pushing past the fight I want to pick with him.

As I approach, I can see that the water in the fountain is more of a pond than only a water feature. It houses bright orange fish of different shadings, plants that sprout straight up from the water, and the most magnificent smelling flowers. The statue in the middle of the fountain is a bat on its hind legs. Hedeon in all its glory. The menacing face of the bat is incongruent with the peaceful nature of the room.

I glance to Calix, who sits quietly at my side, looking up at the ceiling. He is in his usual wrinkled attire, dark colors and grossly overly-draped with jewelry. His shirt always unbuttoned at least one button more than what could be considered proper. In all his charading around, Calix always forgets to tell his eyes of his deceit. They never seem as uninterested as he's trying to be. He turns back to me.

"You don't know where I truly was these last years." He raises an eyebrow, looking at me with a tilted head.

"I've heard the stories. Calix Hendricks, Hedeon's youngest commanding general, the savior of the north, the echo of his grandmother." I parade the names in front of him, the whispers that have carried on the wind.

He laughs lowly, shaking his head and rubbing the back of his neck. "An elaborate part I play. I would think you would know a thing or two about that."

I know he knows nothing of my true identity, but my heart still misses a step, down the cliff of my rib cage, falling to my stomach. I take a deep breath, but it is clear his remark wasn't pointed, as he stands, walking to the clouded window with his hands clasped behind his back, studying a leafy plant with torpor. I turn with him, shifting on the ledge, my heart making the slow ascent back to my chest.

"Court believes I am somewhat of a legend, rumors I am sure the queen started, and I am commanded to keep up the ruse. I am something to everyone and nothing to all."

"So where have you truly been?"

He squints at me, squaring his shoulders as his stare follows the lines of my face. Whatever he's contemplating, he picks a side, and starts speaking.

"Mother sent me away to the Koloniy in the mountains. I have been learning from the best generals, lieutenants, and captains Hedeon has to offer, all while staying out of the way of my mother. So, I am afraid all of the stories and tales you have heard fall rather short of the truth. I am nothing but a nuisance best dealt with by being forgotten." He laughs, but it doesn't reach fullness. I wish I could take credit for how he is opening up to me, but something tells me the prince would have spilled all of this to the first listening ear he was given.

"The Koloniy?" I ask, not having heard of such a place. He looks away, toward another plant to his right. He stuffs one hand in his pocket, and with the other, holds a leaf between his finger and thumb. Again, he pauses before he speaks, combing through words.

"Only our best soldiers advance to the academy. It is an honor to have been committed." His tone is flat, the words practiced to be repeated. "From the academy, the graduates proceed to be spies, or upper command, or in my case, king." His countenance hardens, the words pulling him away from whatever shred of emotional insight he decided to share with me.

"That is, if there is a kingdom left for me to govern after all of these frivolous hobbies my mother demands to fund." He turns in my direction—that smug, arrogant prince I have had the displeasure of knowing returns.

I stand with a sigh. "Here I thought we were finally moving past that." I don't have time to argue today, nor the emotional capability to defend my very existence. Besides, lunch hour is nearly over, and I should be getting back, instead of engaging in useless quarrels with stubborn princes.

"Rehearsal is about to resume." I look him straight in the eye, not feeding whatever need he has to fight with me.

"I will be by later to check on you all," he nods, letting me leave without dispute. Even after promising to help him pacify the queen, he hasn't bothered to stop by yet, so I take no weight in his hollowed threat.

I trudge back through the snow, mood tempered by the cold that makes a home on my cheeks. How am I to make friends with Calix when every time he speaks, he brings up how much he despises that I am here? He is intriguing though, I will give him that. The part he plays is so well rounded, I wonder if he even knows who he is anymore. Against all odds, it seems he and I have something in common. For all his boasting about wanting to run the treasury, for loving a sword over the stage, he didn't seem too happy to have had the privilege to learn at the Koloniy. I surely won't be able to figure out his contradictions if he can't even do it himself.

All thoughts of Calix dissolve when I walk into the Arman to see the Company spread out on the stage, laughing with one another. The theatre operates according to different laws than Hedeon. The actors fall over themselves, all leaning on one another or laying in each other's laps. There is no space for prudishness in acting, not when many of the parts require being so close to one another. It punches me in the gut, reminding me of the shape of home.

"Okay, who's ready to assign parts?" I clap as I walk on stage, all eyes turning to me. We have all but assigned parts in the prior week, everyone already knowing their strengths and where they belong among us, but there are still a few smaller roles that have yet to be claimed.

I sit among the Company, no one bothering to sit on chairs when the floor is so readily available. "Calliope and Anoki are our two leads, as we have already decided," I start, pointing to the pair who sits on opposite sides of the circle from one another. Calliope has often played a leading role in the past, and it is no wonder why. She demands attention, the beauty of her dark hair and the depths of her dark eyes pull any onlooker in. She is porcelain with hard angles threatening to shatter even herself. Anoki is tall, towering, with brown hair that is cut short. He is handsome, boyishly so. I have only heard him talk once, but the others swear the part was written just for him. I took their word for it.

"Pasha has already said she would take the part of city goer #1 so she can focus on building props. Raise your hand if you are on the prop crew with her." I take note of the five other people who will be building our set. "Perfect. Myka is our conductor. Deacon is helping her with composing. Kolyo is stage crew as well as dead man #1. Ira, you are Cosette. Dilean, you are the newly betrothed." I nod to each person as I address them, proud that I have managed to learn everyone's name in such a short time.

I continue through my list, the background characters always a second job to something else, to make the show run smoothly.

"Let's start running the first act."

Everyone moves into motion, jumping off the stage and into their places around the theatre. Calliope starts downstage, amidst a crowd of people, when Anoki enters the scene. They hold the scripts in their hands as they speak, but to my surprise, they already have most of the words memorized. The crowd disappears as the first scene transitions into the second, leaving only Anoki and Calliope. At first, I had just assumed Calliope's beauty was what brought attention, but she has a way of speaking, of positioning herself, that makes you want to hang onto every word she lets slip from her mouth. Every word is a question, and you listen closely so you can hear the answer whispered.

Anoki walks with Calliope, around the make-believe garden. We haven't spoken of the choreography for the scenes yet, but the two are so natural that they already know where to stand and where to walk. Anoki's voice carries through the rafters, weaving through the chandelier. I wonder if the grandeur of the theatre is jealous. These two are so encapsulating when they perform, it leaves no other attention for the splendor of the room.

Calliope calls to where I sit in the velvet chairs a few rows from the stage, "Moi Dramaturg, do you mind if we change this line here? I think it will flow better if we break Anoki's line in half, let me interject, and then let him finish the thought."

"Yes, of course. Let's try that, starting from your line, Calliope."
I flip the paper back over in my hand, following the words on

the last page as Calliope recites them. I write the new assembly of words onto the paper, and we continue.

We run the scene twice more before moving on. I interject every once in a while, putting in my vision for how the stage will look or where they could be standing. Act 1 is the easiest of the acts, so we breeze through it relatively smoothly.

Calix snuck in at some point. I only glanced back to ask a question to Nikita about the spotlights, but was greeted with Calix's head drooping as he let sleep overtake him. By the end of the day, he's gone without a trace. We are careful how we rehearse anyway, being intentional not to mention a few names, and leaving out some details from the script. We will add them in eventually, but for now, we play it safe, even though rehearsals are private affairs.

As the rest of the Company clears out, Kolyo has found some wood and is nailing pieces together. He and I talk about the vision I have for the first act, and while it is hard for me to see that these two pieces of scrap wood could ever be anything, I have no choice but to trust him.

"Are you not heading home?" I ask Kolyo between his hammerings. He wipes the back of his hand over his brow, looking down at me. He towers over everyone, in height, but he is also a few years older than the majority of the Company.

"Nothing's waiting for me at home," he murmurs, not stopping his hammering. He doesn't talk much, and when he does, his accent is thick and almost hard to understand. I'm not sure where he's from, but it's not this region. Somewhere in the mountains, perhaps.

I don't know what to say. I could agree with him, nothing is waiting for me at my new house either. I could ask if he'd like to share the meaning of his comment. I could agree with the things he doesn't say—that this life we have to live is so infuriating, all I want to do is hit things with a hammer too. But all I say is, "I'll see you tomorrow, Kolyo," and walk out of the Arman with only his grunt of a goodbye.

I head up to the Zamak, wanting to get some painting done. The sun has lowered on the horizon, casting golden honey throughout its hallways. I linger in the sun beams, soaking up the warmth they bring. As much as I want spring, I can't help but beg The Faits to put it off just a bit longer. A chill that even the warmest day on the beach couldn't thaw, courses through me at the thought of opening night.

I lean against a wall in the corridor that leads to my greenroom, giving my ankle a little rest. Through the window, the snow melts, dripping from the trees, a blade of bright green grass spears through the slush. If I had all the time in the world, if I wasn't at war with everyone within these walls, I might set up a canvas right here and paint that blade. Refusal, I would call the piece. It reminds me of what Uncle Sumood told me days ago. Don't suppress your steps. The grass doesn't shiver away because of the snow, or because he is the only one standing upright. He makes himself known.

It was an odd thing for Sumood to say, considering all our lives here, we have been conditioned to not bring any unwanted attention our way. Sometimes I wonder if this is all worth the fight when our reality is so bleak. What are we truly fighting for if our life is one long cower from those who will always instigate war? I'm not sure what Sumood meant when he said not to suppress my steps, but here, staring at that persistent blade of grass, I am taking the advice as a means to stand for what I believe in.

This play.

This story.

This truth.

People need to hear these things. If anyone can stop the war, it is not me or Selah or Sumood, or even the Network, but the Hedeon people fighting back. The people not suppressing *their* steps. The Crown has no power if we take it from them. I just need to start a conversation, to get people talking about these ideas.

Ambitious dreams I am sure I will never see actualized float through my mind, shiny lies that draw my attention. Footsteps jerk me out of my reverie. I shift my focus from the sun heating my face to where the hallway bends in a corner. A soldier stands, grey uniform with a black stripe down the side. He's frozen looking at me, eyes twitching around the ends of the hallway, in front and behind him.

"Damira?" he asks, but already has the confidence that he knows who I am. I nod, turning fully to face him, repositioning my large skirts. My arms fold in front of me, keeping the warmth close to my chest. I look at him, waiting for him to speak, but he just stands there, fidgeting and on high alert.

Finally, he speaks, quietly, barely even qualifying as a whisper. "I'm with the Network."

The surprise grows on my face, jumping from my gaping mouth to my widened eyes, and then to my raised eyebrows. In the staring, I realize who this soldier is. He's the man always planted outside the Solar room doors. He doesn't wear the hat that accompanies the uniform, instead, it's in his hand and pressed to his side. That is why I hadn't recognized him immediately.

"I have been meaning to talk to you earlier, but there hasn't been a good time." His eyes continue flickering between me and the hallway. "I just wanted you to know. You have an ally in these walls—I'll keep my eye on you."

"How long have you been in Hedeon?" I ask, taking up his habit of surveying the hallway behind him.

"Since I was fourteen, eight years ago. I was smuggled over with a family during the Battle of Cotea. That is all I am at liberty to say." He is cut from the fabric of Hedeon soldiers. Short hair close to the scalp. Clean shaven. His intimidating stature probably moved him through the ranks quite easily.

"I came after the battle at the capital too. I was ten." I speak just as quietly as the man. Footsteps echo behind me from the long hallway. I glance back to see the queen mother at a far distance. He bows his head, taking a step back. We have spent all the time we shouldn't have been given.

"My name is Kover," he quickly throws out before walking past me and down the hall. And we both go about our day, pretending we didn't both just get a small taste of home.

10

Practices continue through the week. Each day, reading parts, composing with Deacon, trying to figure out the designs for the costumes and set. At one point, Pasha got sent home early because she spoke the name of a certain pervious play on the stage, and apparently, that is an action coated in bad luck. Every night, I get back home after dinner with the Crown, completely drained and lacking much more information for the Network. Calix has barely bothered to show up for rehearsals, and when he does, he broods in the back, nodding off most of the time and escaping before it's over. I don't know what he's telling the queen, what information he could possibly be gathering when he sleeps through it all. It's an act of mercy from The Faits themselves.

We worked a few hours extra today, so I will not be moving from my bed tomorrow or the next day. The queen instructed us to take two days a week off so that we don't get burnt out in our efforts to obey her orders. No one argued, the exhaustion clear on everyone's face. I wander through the Zamak now, heading toward the greenroom. Dinner was canceled tonight, as the queen is away for some kind of appearance across the plain, and she won't be back for another few days. An ease has settled over the hallways, everyone a little less upright, now that her presence doesn't linger around every action, awaiting judgment.

I have finished three paintings over the past few weeks, having gotten an idea that will add to the emotions we are trying to evoke. Six weeks until opening day. I'm thankful for Calix's disinterest in paying attention to me. I am not sure he would allow us to continue if he realized what we were doing, though I wonder how obvious my motives truly are. We are showing hope, but the queen never specified the type of hope. A loophole that might get me beheaded, but it's all for Reine. I will walk to the gallows with loud steps and my head held high.

Staring at the painting, at the faces of my friends in the Hovel, makes me miss them more than usual tonight.

I stand before I can stop to think about what I'm doing, shoving a few papers in my pocket. I layer on my coats and a cloak. Snow hasn't fallen in days, and the last heavy fall is almost completely melted because of the sun that has been making unexpected appearances. If I hadn't lived in Hedeon most of my life, I would think spring is nearer than it is, but I know this is a trick, the weather as cruel as those who own it. Cold temperatures will linger for another month, more snow undoubtable. We will barely see reprieve by opening night.

My greenroom, luckily, has a door that leads directly outside, backed right up to the sliver of forest that lines the eastern end of the palace. Everyone is quiet, resting until the queen gets back. No one is paying attention to my whereabouts. Lev went with Queen Milena, and as a result, I have felt the few and inconsistent eyes on me relax even more. I pull my hood up, tucking my hair behind my ears. I will never get used to the chill that wraps around my bones the moment I step outside here. Reine is warmer in all corners. I was not born with ice in my bones like the Hedeonites.

I rush to the tree line. The space between the back door and the forest is open land, a space to be easily caught. No one yells at me though, so, unseen, I slip between the fullness of evergreen and oak trees. The noise of the Zamak above and the Krepost below are muted by the trees, a blanket of silence in a city that doesn't know of such a wonder.

The Krepost is steep most of the way down, but there are little valleys, clearings, that let in the moonlight. I stop, in the middle of the trees, taking a deep breath, forcing myself to listen to this certain kind of quiet I haven't heard in some time. The vastness of the night sky above is dizzying, allowing for the caress of wind and pricks of cold against every exposed part of me. How can we live in a world of war when peace like this exists? If only we listened to the trees more, to the forest animals, to the wind that finds a way to coexist with the silence. If we stopped and looked up into the stars more often, would we realize how small we are, and that there is more to life than artificial borders of land?

Reine is nothing now because of this war. We may not get much information from home, but we know this. Selah and Sumood can't tell me how the capital is still standing after the raid that sent us here, or even who is holding the lines, but I have been told of the destruction.

A snap of a tree branch cracks behind me! I whip around, lowering my face from the sky and back to the trees. Calix stands at the edge of the small clearing. Like two magnets repelling one another, the night light bends around him. He couldn't bring his shadows out here; the moon wouldn't allow it. It betrays him, showing every detail of his face. The greenness of his eyes that pierce me, the slope of his nose, the lines of his cheekbones, the sharpness of his jaw. I am stunned by the way the moon loves him.

"What're you doing?" Calix's voice crawls out, unsure of what to say, what to ask. That look lingers between us before I shake it off and glance back up to the stars. They aren't as bright here as they are in the Hovel, not with the pollution of light from the Krepost.

"Getting some fresh air." This is where we could change the tide of our relationship if I am careful. I wish I hated the idea of spending time with him more than I do, but something about how one corner of his grin tilts up when he talks, makes me want to see if I can get both sides to raise. A challenge I am too stubborn not to accept.

He laughs. "At least when I lie, I decorate it, add a little embellishment."

"We're not all born liars, Prince."

I bring my eyes back down to this world. They crash into his.

"What are you really doing out here?" He's challenging me, his eyebrow raised, and that stupid half grin.

"Can I show you?" I challenge him right back, opening my stance to the way I was heading. He thinks through the question, but after a deep breath, he concedes.

"I think it should be noted that I am classically trained in combat. Just want to put that out there before heading deeper into the forest with you."

I turn around and lead us away from the Zamak, taking that as a yes. He comes beside me, walking with his hands in his pockets. He glances up to the sky and then back to me.

"Can you read them?" he asks after a few breaths. He evaluates every word uttered to me, taking a moment every time to contemplate before speaking. The weighing of scales, balancing one word for another, fixing the equation, and trying again before he allows any to pass his lips.

"Growing up in the Hovel didn't allow for much stargazing. Everyone was too focused on surviving the things below. Only the rich have time to glance up and make stories of things that are abstract." I don't mean to make my remark pointed, but I'm not sure it came across the way I intended.

What I don't tell Calix is that I knew the stories of the stars back home. The legends that Reine came up with and passed through generations. I see the same stars here, continually repeating the tales in my mind since I got to Hedeon. My memories might be gone, but these stories have always stuck with me.

"That one there is my favorite." He points to a cluster of stars to our left. I know it as the stars of the Forgotten Head, but I try to see it differently, try to figure out what story Hedeonites could have made from it.

"What is it?" I humor him. Or so I tell myself.

"The story of the Hidden Apple. The tale goes, once there was a wealthy old man. He was dying, and he knew it. So, in order to figure out which one of his five adult children to give his legacy to, he hid a golden apple in the mansion they all lived in. He told them that whoever found the apple would get the inheritance. The kids looked high and low to find the apple, turning every book and lifting every paper weight." He pauses, staring ahead into the stars.

"Who found it?" I am forced to ask.

"No one. That's the thing. The old man died before the apple was found, and he didn't write anyone into his will. The money was donated to a local village."

My eyes widen as I take him in, his straight lips suggest he's not joking. His voice is softer than I've heard it before, as if the forest doesn't just have a calming effect on me, but on him as well.

"Did they ever learn where the apple was hidden?"

He nods, his dark hair eating up the moonlight. I climb down a little cliff, Calix following as we descend the hill that is the Krepost.

"It was in the ice box in the kitchen. The most obvious place for an apple to be, so obvious that nobody bothered to look there," he recounts.

"What a strange story."

"I think the old man knew exactly what he was doing. The kids were spoiled, they probably didn't even look in the kitchen. He wanted to help the village, but didn't want his kids to feel as if he didn't love them."

Calix leads us down a few boulders. I absentmindedly hold my hand out to him, asking for assistance. He hesitates, and I realize my misstep. The bareness of our hands, the way we are alone, everything about tonight is inappropriate in his world of Court. I am full of foolish decisions.

I keep my hand stretched, unsure if I should pull it back, and lower myself down the cliff without help. We both stare at the treaty between us. He raises his hand slowly, stopping right before it connects with mine. I think he might turn right past me and run back up the hill. His eyes flicker over to mine, the moon behind him creating a glow around his silhouette, an aura of white light.

His fingers are cold when he finally decides to gently place them just beneath my own. I am too aware of how hard, or not hard enough, I grab onto them for balance. He leads me down steadily, bringing me to the same level he's perched himself.

We're face to face, close as only the ledge allows. He keeps my stare, keeps his eyes locked on mine, not wandering, as is their tendency. Our hands are still clasped between us, a brief reprieve from the cold, being this close.

So close.

Too close.

I tear my eyes from him, taking a step down to the next level of gravel and grass that flattens out to the valley.

"There are more ways to show love than coin." I bring back the conversation that was buried by our ill manners, shaking off the tingling in my hand.

"You have no stick against which to measure the greed of coin, darling." He shrugs, placing back that impenetrable mask of equally easy going and uncaring.

After a bit more of a walk, we emerge from the trees, onto a side road. From here, the Hovel snores as one, the breaths of the night almost visible. Inhale, a floor creaks. Exhale, someone shouts. Inhale a bottle is broken. Exhale, a baby cries.

I pull my hood back over my head, not wanting to be noticed, though at this time of night, the only people who are out will be drunk or asleep. I still am taking no chances.

I turn to Calix. "Keep your eyes down and watch where you step. Do not speak to anyone, and keep your hood over your face. The last thing you would want is someone recognizing you, especially with me." I grab the hood of his cloak and pull it securely around his face. His stare holds my hands around the hood. His eyes shimmer, his breathing becomes faint. For someone who talks so boldly, one touch and he is undone. It would be comical if he didn't have me similarly affected.

I shouldn't be this close to him. Shouldn't offer a touch with such ignorance. That's the second time tonight. I know better. I turn around and make my way down the dirt path that branches through the Hovel. The houses, if they are even worthy of such a name, lean on each other. I'm pretty sure that is the only reason they are still standing. They would have nowhere to fall. Wood rot weaves through the air, but to Calix's credit, he doesn't wrinkle his nose at the smell.

We turn a few corners, weaving under clothes drying on lines that have been long forgotten. Calix doesn't bother to keep his head down, gaping openly at the height the houses have managed to steal from the sky. With each breath from the wind, the buildings creak, swaying, if you look close enough. A house of cards, just waiting to be swept away with a gust.

I stop on the threshold of our house, only to silently beg The Faits that my aunt and uncle don't have anything incriminating lying around. The door is unlocked, always unlocked, because crime is low here. Everyone is equally as bad off as their neighbors.

The main room, the only real room of the house, is heated by the fireplace, ushering us in to join in its warmth. It bathes everything in the color of embers and shadows. Or everyone would be more accurate to say. Not many things reside in the house other than the people. Selah and Sumood stand in the middle of the room, hovering over a table. A few people sleep in corners, tucked under blankets and knit hats. It's significantly warmer in here than outside, but a chill still hangs in the space.

My aunt spots us first, eyes widening, as a smile overtakes her lips. She rushes over to me with open arms.

"Damira," she breathes, wrapping me in her warmth. She is honey dripping over toast. The physical embodiment of affection. The sun's rays that linger in the late summer evenings.

My uncle joins us, wrapping me under one of his arms, baby Myla strapped against his body. She sleeps with her head supported by the fabric. I place a kiss on the top of her head. Only after we all take in everything this moment has to offer, does Selah notice Calix.

"And who is this?" she practically sings. Her hair is in twists, different from the braids it was in weeks ago. It feels much longer than a few weeks. I have never been apart from them for this long, from the sounds of it, even in Reine, we were always all together.

Calix stays silent, Aunt Selah staring between the two of us.

"I've been instructed not to speak," Calix leans in and whispers to her with that grin. I refrain from punching the prince. I do, however, obviously roll my eyes.

"Cal," he amends finally, stretching his hand to her. Aunt Selah has taken to as many customs of Hedeon as she needed in order to not be suspicious, but one habit she could never shake was hugging. I take after her in many ways. Selah surpasses Calix's hand and wraps him in a quick embrace. He stiffens, Hedeon virtues like a board straightening his shoulders, but doesn't say anything against it.

"So nice to meet you. I am Aunt Selah, and that's my husband, Uncle Sumood." Selah gives him the names everyone in the Hovel has taken to calling them. They are family to us all. Uncle Sumood shakes Calix's hand, sparing him any more awkwardness.

"We are just finishing up for the night, would you two like to help?" Sumood leads us back to the table that has all kinds of supplies spread out. The makings of care packages for those that can't find shelter. Blankets, snacks, hats, gloves.

Selah arranges us into a line, assembling things in order. I pull up a stool to sit on. Calix takes note of it with his observant eyes.

"Seems you all have your hands full," Calix remarks, but not a single complaint.

"It'll start to slow down soon. Winter is always busier than any other time of the year," Uncle Sumood says at the end of the table.

"He says that about every time of year," I lean in and inform Calix.

"It's wishful thinking that there would be a non-busy time of year," Sumood chuckles.

"In my loving husband's defense, we don't have our Mira's extra set of hands, so we are busier than usual right now." Selah places a kiss on Sumood's cheek.

"Well, hopefully, by the end of the night, we can help catch up on what *our* Mira would have done." Calix grins at me and moves a bit faster in stuffing the bags.

Aunt Selah points a smirk in my direction with knowing eyes. I brush her off, but she has never been able to let anything go.

"So, Cal, what do you like to do in your free time?" Of all the questions Sumood could ask, I suppose this is a rather disarming one.

"In the limited free time I get, I like to read."

Sumood lifts his eyebrow, eyes flickering to me above a small grin. "What types of books are your favorite?"

"Biographies, mostly. I'm not much a fan of make believe." Cal's eyes also flicker to me. The blanket in my hand suddenly becomes the most interesting piece of cloth I have ever seen.

"Damira, could you help me in the back room?" Selah grabs me by the arm and pulls me with her. I glance back to Calix, who is answering another one of Uncle Sumood's questions, so neither of them take much notice of us leaving.

I close the pantry door behind us, Selah turning around quickly with a wide grin.

"Damira!" she squeals.

"He's the prince," I blurt out, needing to squash any false beliefs she is holding onto.

"Oh, I know." Her grin doesn't change.

"Then why are you acting like that?" I push her shoulder, walking to the shelf behind her. It's stocked full, thanks to the Crown, no doubt. They've kept their word to provide for my family. I pick up a jar, a green vegetable preserve that I can't distinguish. I scrunch my nose at the sight and put it back.

"Because he is cute and, so far, kind. We shouldn't judge people based on their families, Damira." She plants her hands on her hips, a mother teaching her child a valuable lesson.

"His ancestors killed our people." I turn to her, head on.

"But has he made any commands that incriminate him?" she asks, eyebrows raised. My aunt has always been more forgiving than I could ever be. She saw my parents massacred by the Hedeon Crown, but she still believes in giving everyone a chance.

I had thought Calix was a trumpet of war speech, a mouthpiece to what his mother and grandmother believed, but have I ever heard him speak of the war besides asking to keep their soldiers alive? I tuck the realization away, planning to think more about it later.

I stare at her, knowing she has more to say.

"He seems different, that is all I am saying. I know the Network asked you to get close to him, to spy, but don't forget that he is an individual person. That he could be more than the sum of his parents."

"I am not more than the sum of my parents!"

"You are more than you realize, and your parents would want you to be more. You had amazing parents—it is good you are like them—but that doesn't mean Cal is like his."

"You have too much faith in the people who killed ours."

"The prince's family might have killed ours, but I'm sure your ancestors have killed plenty of his as well. Protect your heart, but don't build walls so tall that no one can scale them. Life is a balancing act, full of grey, Damira."

She pulls me into a hug, the familiar smell of spices from spending many hours in the kitchen, trying to make something out of nothing.

"Are you being safe?" she whispers into my hair.

"I am." The lie is easy because we both know the truth of my position, even if we don't talk about it.

"Don't be stupid. Be kind but be alert. Eyes and ears up." She lets me go, looking into my face.

"Ears and eyes up," I reply.

We return to the main room, just in time to help finish the supplies. Calix and Sumood stand facing each other, the supplies in their hands all but forgotten as they stare.

"You can't be serious," Sumood gapes at Calix. My heart leaps to my throat, pulling every nerve and muscle up with it.

How could I have been so naive to bring the enemy here? Of course, Calix would start a fight. I jolt, regaining control of my body. I take a step toward them, but Selah grabs my arm. I turn back to her, to see her studying her husband. I'm about to pull away, but then Calix laughs, causing me to turn around and study the wonder in Sumood's eyes.

They aren't arguing. They're joking around!

"I swear to the Divine. I flew halfway across the yard, the man was so large. I broke my arm and still have a scar to prove it." Calix rolls up his sleeve past his elbow, showing Sumood a thin line on his bicep. Sumood's hearty laugh fills the room, and I exhale.

We all join in on the laugh as Cal recounts the story he just told Sumood. We finish up the last of the bags, and all too soon, I am hugging Selah and Sumood one last time, Calix resigning to shake their hands. It's late, and we all need to be getting to sleep. The Hovel is still when we reemerge into the cold. Calix tries to take the lead back to the forest, but I interrupt his step.

"There's one more stop I have to make," I tell him, catching myself before grabbing his arm to steer him the other way.

We trace the familiar path through buildings, parting just enough to allow travelers to walk through. Safler leans against the wall, asleep and covered almost completely. Her mouth hangs open, revealing her partially toothless smile, the gaps similar to the broken windows of the building she lives in front of. Safler can't walk, doesn't ever move from the corner, so I always make an extra copy of my stories for her. She keeps them stacked under a rock beside her limp leg.

I pull the papers out of my pocket, pinning them under the rock with the rest of them. I hesitate for a moment, watching the mound of blankets lift and fall as she breathes.

All my treasonous efforts are worth it, no matter the consequences, for my kingdom. But also, for her.

11

THE TREES BEND TO hear our words. The scandal of the century—Prince Calix visiting homes of his peasants. Hopefully, the gossip won't make it back to the courtiers.

"May I ask you something?" Calix asking permission catches me off guard, as we climb back up all the ledges we had climbed down just hours ago.

"Go ahead." I had figured we wouldn't get out of this without an explanation of some sort, for a myriad of things.

"What happened to your parents?" He is gentle in his question, more aware of my feelings than I thought he was capable of being. Silk covering the iron. I pause, looking at him, waiting for the joke or jab, but he just comes up beside me, waiting with soft eyes.

"They died when I was little. I don't remember much, their faces fade with each year, but it doesn't make missing them easier. My aunt and uncle took me in and have raised me as their own." I keep the answer short, but enough to allow him to feel as if I am letting him in. None of this is real, I have to remind myself, I just need to get my hands on the ledger.

He doesn't respond. I am not used to empathy when I speak such words, and he doesn't ruin that streak. I am not a tragedy. We have all lost. Our world is built upon the bodies of those who once loved, by the ones who still love. We walk in silence for a bit, but he has found another question before long.

"Have they always done that? Allowed people to sleep in their home and give what little they have to those who have less?" His eyebrows furrow when he glances at me.

"Surely you've known how bad the people have had it under your family's reign." Calix is not ignorant. In all his contention with his mother, surely, he has an idea of what exactly he is fighting for. But he still has a look of disbelief, of a realization that has hit him so hard he didn't have time to brace himself for the impact.

"Knowing and seeing are two different things, darling." His words are lost in the breeze, barely mumbled, so I am not even sure I've heard him right.

"That is the reality for many across Hedeon. Selah and Sumood have been fortunate, I have been fortunate, to have a place to live. So, they give back what they can. It doesn't make much of a difference, but to a few people, they are a lifeline."

"And what was your part in all their helping?"

"I wrote stories. I gave our neighbors the will to live so they stayed alive long enough for Selah and Sumood to help them."

"Did it work?"

"Sometimes—I'd like to think so, at least. There was a man once, who lost his family as a child, grew up in the streets of the Hovel. He started reading my stories and, one day, after a month of planning with my aunt and uncle, he was able to leave. I'm not really sure where he went, and it was a blessing from the Divine itself that he had the health to begin the journey, but he had the hope of finding somewhere better because of my words. It was an anomalistic instance, but one I had a little help in making."

Like the sea running from the shore, he laps back into silence. All the way to the Zamak. We turn out of the woods and onto cobblestone paths, winding the way back to my house. Maybe it was a mistake to bring him to my home, to introduce him to my aunt and uncle. Maybe it didn't draw him closer, but instead, pushed him further away. Maybe what little redemption I thought I was seeing in Calix was a trick of the moonlight.

I am not cut out to be a spy.

I turn to him when we hit my front porch, planning to apologize and try to salvage whatever I can from this evening. Instead, he picks up my hand, holding it in his own. I stare down at them, just as he does. I'm not sure which of us is more surprised. His thumb runs races around the top of my knuckles, igniting the laps of my own heart.

If we were in Reine, I wouldn't think twice. But we are in Hedeon, and he is the prince. To hold someone this way—hand-shaking is cordial, acceptable. Even earlier in the woods, it could have been argued that it was only for sake of help that he reached out to me. Holding hands like this is intimate, a sign of trust. He stares down, as if trying to solve a riddle, and my hand is the clue.

"Calix," I look up into his pine eyes, not really sure what words I planned to follow the plea.

"Thank you, for showing me your home." His voice is stripped bare of any pageantry. Somewhere in the woods, he lost his coat of spectacle. Now he stands without armor, without a fake grin to hide behind.

Just weeks ago, he stood this close to me when we first met, stared at me as intently as he is now. I didn't know who he was then, didn't have a reason to hate him. I do now. He is the heir of my enemy. Everything I was born to hate is all he was born to be.

And we are standing with my hand in his.

I pull back quickly. I might need to get close to Calix, but I do not need to be this close.

"I'll see you at rehearsal when the new weeks starts," I tell him, turning around and walking inside without another word.

"I just can't get the last run," Deacon murmurs, fingers floating over the keys in the same three notes, a variation in the fourth. I sit beside him on the piano bench, watching.

Behind us, the stage crew prepares props and scenery. In groups around the theatre, actors and actresses practice their lines. The light overhead dims and relights as Nikita and Feliks work on the sequence of lighting for different scenes.

"I think this is my favorite," I tell him, running through the four notes myself. I keep my eyes in front of me, trying not to focus on the prince napping in the back row of the theatre.

"Maybe we should just change the whole thing. We are going up, but maybe we should be going down, to make it more dramatic?" Deacon whispers the question more to himself than to me. He runs a hand through hair that is getting almost too long for him to see past. He pushes it back continuously when he's hunched over the piano.

His hands cross over me, going to the left, instead of where we focused on the right. He plays a few notes, running different variants. He hits a run that causes us both to straighten and look up at each other.

"That one!" we say in unison. He plays through the full piece, landing on the low notes to end it.

"A masterpiece," I whisper, truly having never heard anything like it.

"Is that for Act 3? That's amazing!" Ira perks up from where she's sprawled out on the floor with a paintbrush. She's a small thing, in a different way than Pasha though. Ira has chopped, ash blonde hair, and wears oversized clothes most of the time. I don't think it is for any other reason than it is what seems to be the least maintenance. She is soft-spoken and kind, while usually keeping to herself.

"I'm going to run through the whole thing," Deacon tells me, my cue to get up and find someone else that needs help.

Pasha works with the prop crew today, her few lines memorized early on. She's halfway up a ladder when I find her, paint smothered on her forehead and knotted in her hair. She is a Fait-crafted portrait.

"Did you get the swords worked out yet?" I ask. The biggest feat for the prop and costume crew has been figuring out how to secure or make the amount of swords we need.

"Almost." She takes careful steps down the ladder, jumping when she's a few rungs from the ground. "We found some lovely old ones that will cost almost nothing, plus a few hiding in the bowels of the closets. Now we've moved onto the shields. We need to find a way to make the emblems believable, but hopefully, that won't be too hard." She pulls a cloth out of her back pocket and wipes her hand, though the rag is stained and doesn't appear to be doing anything to clean her.

"Excellent, and that—" I look up to the set she was painting, which doesn't look to be more than a few scrap pieces of wood nailed together, with abstract paint lathered on.

"Don't worry, Moi Dramaturg. It looks unpleasant now, but it is all a part of the process." Her genuine smile allows me to believe her.

The theatre clears out at the end of the day. Calix escaped at some point, leaving quietly enough that I didn't notice. I flip off a few lights, the lighting crew having labeled the switches for me, as I can never remember which is which. I am not sure if it was out of kindness or so I will stop messing up whatever they're working on for the play.

Someone knocks on the open stage door from beside me, as I stoop over to pick up paintbrushes discarded everywhere except where they belong. I turn back to Tenny standing in a gown. An elegant, long, and frilly gown. Her hair is waved and tied up intricately, in a way that hides how terribly dyed I know it to be.

"I told you I would check up on you if you didn't contact me." She smiles like a feline. I know it's not a threat that I am the one helping her, but her words are haunting.

"I'm working on it," I whisper, though she hadn't bothered to.

"We are running out of time." She comes closer, taking in the half-finished set discarded chaotically across the stage. She lifts the hem of her skirt with each step. Tenny doesn't belong in such a nice dress. She is made for pants and running and swords and freedom. Not the suppression of corsets.

"What do you mean? What happened?" I ask, standing straighter, a shiver forming at the base of my spine. I pull my hair back, as if fidgeting will make me less anxious.

"They are starting to march toward the Battlement of Cotea again. We need something, anything, that will help us stop them. If they take the capital, the war is all but over." Calix is like iron, but Tenny is steel. I am not a metal at all. I fold at the first wind that is blowing the wrong way. I am clay, moldable to a maker's wanting.

Tears rise, but I hold still.

"We don't believe they will do anything for weeks. They are still far off and don't have any sort of camps set up. This is early intelligence, so it might not happen, but we all need to be prepared for the realities. Find what you can and report back. Soon." Her words a prophecy foretold. She turns and walks back toward the door, her skirts swishing with each step.

"Eyes and ears up." She nods before she gets to the hallway and then exits.

"Ears and eyes up," I mutter, and then she is gone.

I finish cleaning the theatre, but have nowhere to go, so I wander the Zamak hallways aimlessly, trying to kill time before dinner, but not having the capacity to do anything. This news, a sword on a string above my head, waiting to be cut down. I turn down a few hallways, stopping in a room full of paintings larger than life itself.

In the middle of the room, sitting on a cushion bench, is Raven. Her head angles up, as to take in the entirety of the monstrosity framed on the wall. She glances at me as I walk further in.

"Damira." She pats the bench beside her, pulling her large skirts in so I can sit.

On days I am in the theatre, I wear slimmer dresses, with muted colors and much easier to walk in. Sometimes I even push my luck with trousers. I always wear my boots with them, despite what's proper in the Zamak. I sit beside her, folding my hands in my lap, and looking up to the painting.

A dozen men and women, covered in blood, wield swords. Some lay slain on the ground, spilling with gore. All the figures are dark, shaded, even the sky looks like a thunderstorm is rolling in. The soldiers grimace, clearly hating the battle, though they still fight. A city in the background burns, tongues of fire lifting from spires. Smoke whorls into the sky.

"Isn't it devastating?" Raven asks, rawness in her voice she can't cover.

"What war is this?" I'm unable to take my eyes off the child that lies in a pile of other bodies, haphazardly discarded without care, bent in ways only achievable by a corpse.

"The sad thing is, this war happened centuries ago. It's not the one we are currently fighting. Isn't it funny that no matter how much we evolve, one thing remains? This painting could be of the current war, or the one a century ago, or the one a millennium ago. It is always the same picture, the same desperation," she thinks aloud. I pull my stare from the anguish and look to her, tears lining her eyes. She glances at me, huffs a silent laugh, and wipes her cheek.

"You probably think me silly." She tries to smile, but the pain is so clear on her face.

"I think you are exactly what this kingdom needs." I want to grab her hand, to tell her just how much I understand. I am still unsure if my aunt's words ring true about Calix not being like his parents, but sitting beside Raven, I see no resemblance to the monarch that slaughtered my family.

"Tell that to Cal. When the time comes, it's just assumed he will take the throne. He is the one who can lead. He thinks me too emotional." She wipes the last of her tears from her cheek and shrugs as if to say *he's right*.

"Maybe he is the one who is not emotional enough to lead," I assure her. "How does that work, since the two of you are twins?" I had assumed it would be Calix, as it seems everyone else does, but Raven continues to prove herself just as capable—in my eyes at least.

"He was born two minutes before me. So, by the law of Hedeon, he technically has first rights if he doesn't abdicate to me. Which he never would. Though I could petition my mother, technically, since we are twins, but she would never give me the crown I so long for," she explains, not looking away from the painting looming over us. "Can you image painting something of this proportion?"

"I could never wish for so much talent," I breathe.

"I like to come in here to think. Being around the art makes me remember I am a part of something bigger than myself. That my steps could affect future generations. I always feel terrible for this painter in particular, though. What a terrible job artists have, always having to come behind the tragedy to immortalize it." Astonishment coats her whisper, sacred words in a sacred place.

"There's a statue cemetery in the lower level of the Krepost. I used to go there too, to look at all of the history. It might be a burial ground of sorts, but nothing there is truly dead. Can you imagine if no one painted or sculpted these things?" Raven continues. "There'd be no memory of the lost. But more than that, art has a way of making you feel things you weren't aware you had the capability to feel. Even the darkest of paintings, like this one, gives me an empathy I thought I was immune to."

She holds her chin up. Usually, when the Crown holds their noses in such a position, it is to look down on those around them. When Raven looks up like this, it is in reverence, in the humility of being smaller than the world in the painting.

Calix would march on Reine himself. Raven has reserve in such finality. Maybe that is why I can stomach being her friend without feeling treasonous to my kingdom. She would be different if she were on the throne. She sees what her brother cannot.

"Enough of this talk." She brings her stare back down to me. "How are you? Would you like to walk to dinner with me?" She glances at her wristwatch and paints a smile on her face. The hopelessness from a breath ago dropped, but by the haunting in her eyes, not forgotten.

We walk to dinner, arm in arm, smiling and laughing as much as two women destined for more than this Court can. Everyone waits for us in the Solar. I hadn't realized it, but I think we've managed to arrive late.

Kover stands at the side of the open door, grey uniform, black stripe. I take in his face, though he doesn't even glance in my direction, just stares at the wall in the distance. We don't know each other. He is a guard, and I am a guest. But I still wish I could acknowledge him, reach out to him in some way. He is a piece of home that centers me in a den of monsters.

"About time," Anya whines, hanging over her brother when we make it past the threshold. They race to the table, Alek reaching his seat first. Calix saunters in after us, not even darting an eye in my direction.

Good. Hedeon is marching on Reine, and I can't begin to unwind the complicated tapestry that is what happened between Calix and me last night. I hate him. And it will stay that way because I have no other choice. I will not betray my kingdom like that.

I sit in the seat that has become labeled as mine, right beside Alek and next to where the queen mother would sit if she ever deigned to show up. I have only eaten with her one other time after the first night. At least, that is one less thing for me to be distracted by.

"How are rehearsals going, Damira?" Queen Milena asks me halfway through dinner. She cuts into her chicken with a gold knife. I had to stop myself from gawking when I saw them placed beside our dinner plates.

The poor shall starve, and the rich will eat with golden utensils.

"They're coming along well, I think. I'm not sure exactly what I am doing, but the Company and crew have been so much help along the way. They truly are all the talent. We would be fraying at the seams if it weren't for them," I assure her, shoveling some spiced rice onto my fork.

"I am sure you are contributing more than you give yourself credit for. Cal speaks very highly of your talents." She looks between him and me.

I glance at Calix with a raised eyebrow, and he throws that deceivingly charming smile my way, adding a wink. The queen doesn't notice, as she and Raven ramble on about the coming Revel. The play is the finale to the week of the Spring Revel. The ball is the start. I am condemned to be at both.

As soon as the plates are cleared, we move to sit around the fireplace. Alek sits in my lap tonight, while Anya sits on the couch I lean on, braiding my hair. More like knotting my hair, but I let her, without complaint. The smile on her face is worth the extra time in front of the mirror brushing it out. Calix and Raven mutter to themselves, the queen just observes her family.

In moments like these, it's hard to separate myself from the job I am supposed to be doing. It is all too easy to look at them and only see a family.

And how easily I fit into it.

12

"I will not be wearing this." I stare at Raven, who is most definitely having more fun with this than I am. She has me in a wafting raspberry-colored dress with ruffles around every tier. I look like a pastry.

I made the mistake of running into Raven after rehearsal today, and I haven't been able to escape her claws since. We paused only to eat dinner and then found our way right back here.

"You look gorgeously uncomfortable." Raven flips through dresses hung on the many racks that pollute this room. She pulls two more gowns and shoves me into the dressing room to change. Through the open door, the tailor, named Port, discusses something, laughing in harmony with Raven. I catch myself smiling, even though none of the dresses are to my taste.

The ball is weeks away, but apparently, this is one of those things you have to plan in advance, because as we get closer, the more booked everyone will be. Or so Raven has explained. I have hardly had to lift a finger, as she enjoys the planning, and I know nothing of this world.

I slip on the next dress, leaving the back untied for lack of flexibility to do it myself. No one gasps as I come out. Raven suppresses a laugh by piercing her lips. I step up on the pedestal and am met with three reflections of myself staring back at me.

It has always felt unnatural, looking at myself in a mirror, and I have often felt that the flaw in ourselves is that our outward reflections are so readily available. It creates people too obsessed with their looks, with wanting to fit into a certain standard of beauty. Court has only proved my theory further. Mirrors everywhere, lining the walls, the ground, and the ceilings. Places to catch your reflection, to make sure you are finely composed, that every hair is lying in its supposed position. Everyone is so obsessed with their own looks, they fail to see the guises everyone else has put so much effort into crafting.

Seeing my reflection as often as I have these past few weeks, has started to make me pay more attention, to see if I look like someone I'd want to see staring back at me. And now, in this room full of gowns and reflections, I can't help but take in the entirety of myself. To think that I am pretty. A dangerous thought. Beauty is drawing attention. Beauty is calling out to say that you exist. I teeter between wanting to fade into the background and not wanting to suppress my steps. It is a precarious balancing act.

"I don't think this is the one," Raven calls from behind a stack of fabrics, pulling me from my thoughts.

"I am not sure any of these fit me well," I tell both Raven and the man who is making the clothes. He stares at me, tracing me up and down, measurements flying across his eyes. It's how I assume I look when studying a blank sheet of paper.

"Go change back into your clothes, I have an idea." He shoos me with his hand and looks back to Raven, taking off his thick-rimmed glasses and pinching between his eyes. They share a few more words as I dress.

We spend the rest of the evening envisioning a few evening gowns for me. The seamstress's hands float over the paper, sketching the specifications Raven and I imagine. After looking and feeling fabrics, testing lengths and taking measurements, Raven whisks off as the tailor and I finish up, with promises to see me tomorrow at dinner. I stay behind a few more moments to put finishing touches on a few designs.

"Thank you for helping me and Raven today," I tell Port, as I prepare to delve into the cold night air, wrapping my shawl securely around my chest.

"My pleasure." He folds some fabrics and stacks them on a table in the corner.

I don't know why I linger, but something makes me stay for just a beat longer.

"Have you been designing long?" I ask, trying to mimic my uncle in the way he asks questions with no opportunity for offense.

"I actually only found the talent in my later years. If you would believe it, I didn't think I had much creativity within me growing up." Port has not yet hit middle age, but he is still passed the age that one would think could easily pick up a new skill.

"How did you realize you could design?"

"Accidentally." He finishes with the stack of fabric in his hands and turns to me fully. "I was mending a pair of trousers, which I learned in childhood, and all of a sudden, I saw it as a blouse. I cut it up, and the next morning had a nice shirt for my sister. A few people asked my sister where she got the blouse, and she directed them to me. They came with their own fabric, and I started a business before I knew it."

"Blouses are much different than ballgowns."

"Indeed. Once my imagination started up, I couldn't quiet it down. I got better at the craft, worked my way through Court, and eventually, my name became known, and the princess wanted me herself."

I hesitate at my next words, but I have to ask them, to see if I am the only one who feels this way.

"Do you ever think being that ambitious was a mistake?"

He leans back on a worktable, taking his glasses off to clean them with the hem of his shirt. He takes a deep breath and places them back on his nose. We can both see each other clearly now.

"Yes."

Our art has diminished to the demand of others.

"I am sorry."

"As am I."

We share the moment for all it is, and then I nod my head to him, exiting without anything else to say.

Down the hall from the room we were occupying, there is a door that exits to the grounds. The field around the Zamak calls to me. I linger in the night air, instead of heading to my house, the warmth from inside still clinging to the folds of my clothes. The last snow but a memory, the moon full, no breeze to bother.

The mountains behind the Zamak are free of pillaging, strangely bare from the rest of the maximal adornments of the Krepost. The pinnacle I stand on looks out on the trees and the emptiness that spreads to the horizon. The moon seeks out the remaining patches of snow between the trees, light bouncing off in radiance. I sit in the grass—standing in front of such beauty feels blasphemous. My tired ankle thanks me for it.

Hedeon and Reine alike have more land than they can fill, and yet, Hedeon still insists on infringing on our border. It will never make sense to me. What happens when one conquers the whole world and is still hungry for more? Uncle Sumood says that power is an ever-hungry beast. Perhaps the victors will turn inward after conquest, crumbling until they turn against themselves, and more war breaks out with people they once called family. Is that how we got here now, once being family with the people we so hate? The piece of art Raven was studying haunts me now, all war looks the same.

Light footsteps come from behind me, timid enough that I know they are not from the Crown. I glance back to see Deacon walking toward me in the same uncertain way he does most things.

"Good evening, Deacon." I turn with him, as he comes beside me and sits down, crossing his legs in front of him.

"What are you doing out here?" he asks, pulling his open sweater more tightly around himself. The lack of breeze hasn't completely suffocated the chill in the air.

"I was just watching the trees."

A flock of birds flies overhead, chirping in beat with the flap of their wings. When I was first misplaced in Hedeon, I found it odd that so many birds stuck around for the winters here. They are made of an admirable resilience. A stray from the flock lands just in the distance, hopping a few times before stilling. Her head and body, golden, glowing, her wings as dark as the night. She chirps, head twitching back and forth, singing a quick song before flying back to her family.

"There will always be birds," Deacon whispers beside me. I look at him, his copper hair sticking up in all directions. He pulls on it when he gets frustrated or lost in a train of thought.

"What was that?" I ask, unsure if I heard him correctly. He takes a deep breath, bright eyes glancing up, and then quickly back down to the forest, as if the sky is too vast a freedom, and he isn't worthy to even look upon it. He turns away, fidgeting, just like the bird.

"It's something my dad used to say. There will always be birds. He moved around from village to village when he was younger, his parents often moving wherever the harvest was plentiful. He said, in those times, he would always listen to the birds chirping and their consistency. Then, as he got older and had a family of his own, he became more stable, but the world around him was the thing to change. The war, the disappearing coin, the Crown demanding more work than we could give. In those days, he listened for the birds again, hearing their comforting songs. The worst could happen, the world could be falling apart around him, but there would always be birds."

"There will always be birds," I repeat after him.

"We could hardly afford a gravestone, but we scraped up all the money we had, just so we could write those words on it." He keeps his stare ahead, tears in his voice.

"What happened to him?" My question so quiet, it could get lost in the breeze.

"He worked himself to death. Or the Crown worked him to death, really. We had a farm. The fields were good for a while there, but if we didn't reap the capacity the Crown thought we should be able to—he worked tirelessly to make sure we harvested all we could from the fields. It was his death. The fields fell into disrepair, the Crown sold the land to someone who could nurse it back to health. My mom, brother, and I had to find somewhere new to live, with nothing to our name. By chance, I learned that I could play the pianoforte. I played in taverns until I was approached by someone who worked for the Crown, and I was recruited to the Arman."

I don't know what to say to him. He is past the need for comforting, the rage in his far-off stare telling me everything I need to know. The softness I have come to associate with Deacon has thawed in the heat of his anger. He turns to me, looks me straight in the eye.

"The Crown never did anything for me. Or my father. I am just one story, one person, but all of the people I love can say the same thing."

This is the reason he is composing for me, wanting to be a part of this play that could be the downfall of us all. But there will always be birds. And if the birds can sing, despite the harsh winters, then we can continue to sing, no matter what the Crown throws at us.

"Thank you." My resounding gratitude is something I could never verbalize in its entirety.

His smile is pressed to thin lips.

We sit in silence, in each other's company, until the cold gets to the both of us. He walks back down the front of the mountainside, and I walk back through the Zamak to collect my notebook from the greenroom.

I find myself in a part of the palace I haven't explored yet, having taken a wrong turn, it seems. The ceilings and walls drip in more décor than in the main wing. I wouldn't be surprised if I stumble upon the ballroom where the Spring Revel will be held. It would be a waste to not have it in such extravagant quarters.

I open a few doors, peaking in to see empty rooms and storage of a random assortment of furniture. I should retrace my steps, find where I made the wrong turn, but I keep forward, peering through the hallways that vine off the main one. Double doors tower at the end of the chamber, and I have to crane my neck to see where they touch the ceiling. As I near, murmurs reach me, my heart becoming louder than my slowing footsteps.

The voices come from a room beside the grand double doors, through a much more decent-sized opening. I slide against the wall, sneaking toward the murmurs.

"You are being ridiculous," the queen's voice huffs, anger snapped and unrestrained.

"No, Mother. You are. You are going to spend us into a hole, and it seems no one minds besides me."

Calix.

I stop at his voice, freezing unwillingly. I take a few silent breaths, forcing myself to push forward. Mirrors line the walls opposite me and the door. I can just see the reflection of Cal's back. I don't move any closer, not daring to be caught in the reflection if either of them moves too far to the right.

"I am still your queen," Milena argues, red in the face.

"Not for long, if you keep this up." Calix is unwavering, unflinching before the queen, but I am afraid for him. His words—even with his title, he is flirting the line of punishment. I push back into a curtain draped along the wall, partially covering myself in case I need to hide quickly. My stay at the Krepost is just one extended hide-in-plain-sight.

"You think me stupid. But let me remind you that I was running this kingdom for eight years before I gave birth to you, and I have been doing just fine since. You think you have such a good idea of what our people need, but you have hardly spent time with them, child. When I was younger than you, I was sent to live in a village for two years while my father was in power. I worked, ate, and struggled with our people. I was being merciful to send you to the Koloniy." The queen paces a few steps in the reflection, and then she continues on. "This is what our people need. Hope. A ball. A reason to believe in us. We do not show our weakness by pulling back on the extravagance they expect." The ice that freezes all over Hedeon flows through her veins too. One and the same as her kingdom.

"I understand, Mother. I do. But I have been studying the books, and it just seems like we need to make certain cuts if we want to continue keeping our troops. The elements will kill them if Reine doesn't. The conditions aren't as they once were. We are gaining speed toward Cotea, but if we are to try and seize it in three weeks' time, as you so lovingly planned, then something needs to change."

My heart goes from beating out of my chest to quieting so fast, I think I might pass out.

Three weeks.

Three weeks to get everything prepared so we will have a chance against Hedeon soldiers. I have to stop myself from sprinting away to find Tenny.

The queen sighs, composing herself with deep breaths, mastering the anger.

"We will be just fine, I assure you, honey. I will look at the numbers if you get them to me, but the advisors seem to think we will be fine. We are making cuts in other places, so the troops won't suffer. I appreciate you watching your sister's spending habits. We can all do well to follow your example." The way the queen talks doesn't sound like a mother to a son. She uses diplomatic language, building him up with compliments, even when she gives the bad news that she won't be acting on his advice. I have eaten a meal with her every day for weeks and have never heard the steadiness, the calculation in her voice.

It must drive Calix crazy.

"Thank you, Mother." Calix's iron voice screeches from him. They are done talking for now, but the conversation is not over. The queen's heeled shoes echo off the marble, and I secure the curtain around me.

I wait longer than necessary, just to make sure I won't get caught. I peek out slowly, when I know they are both long gone, and am greeted by an empty hallway.

Three weeks.

I have to tell Tenny. I have to get those ledgers from Calix to see just how broke Hedeon is, and if there is a chance they will be too stripped of funds to march.

Perhaps my life has been crescendoing to this moment. Perhaps I was made for this. But all I can think about is how, if I fail, more of my people will die. I wish to hide behind the curtain until the war is over, but I know I have to face all that is coming.

Three weeks.

13

T HE BOOKSHELF SHAKES, AND I close my eyes as there's no stopping it. It crashes to the ground, the books flying like birds escaping a predator.

"This can't be right." Tenny looks at the shelf she just knocked over. To be fair, it hadn't seemed like it was on purpose. She just let her frustrations get the best of her, and her punch packed more than expected.

I squat down to start piling the books up, in hopes that we can get this cleaned up before Katiya gets back from the grocer. Tenny doesn't bother to help, she just starts pacing.

"You are sure he said three weeks?" She glances at me, hand running through her loose hair.

"Hedeon might not be my first language, but I've been speaking it for enough years to be quite confident in my fluency of small numbers." I don't bother to feel bad about the annoyance in my voice. I dread my quick tongue enough during my normal days, but I don't bother worrying over it in front of Tenny.

"We don't have enough troops, we don't have Cotea protected enough." Tenny starts a train of thought, but stops it quick, eyes snapping to mine.

"I know I am not supposed to hear whatever you were about to say, but is there one encouraging thing you could tell me of home?" I sit back, momentarily forgetting the books in my hand, to look up at her.

Tenny sits on the couch across from me, and I turn to keep an eye on her.

"What exactly do you remember of Reine?" Tenny sits with a straight back, hands in her lap. Looking at her posed like this, it'd be easy to forget she just struck a bookshelf down in a fit of rage.

"The fields of flowers mostly. Every once in a while, I'll have a dream that I assume is from my childhood, but it's hard to keep the thoughts in my grasp when I wake."

"Nothing else? I was told you suffered from some memory loss, but I had thought you'd be able to recount a bit more than that." She is nothing if not honest.

Maybe I should feel shame for forgetting the details of my homeland, but if I am taking Tenny's lead and being honest, I haven't made an effort to remember much. There is a reason my mind has blocked those memories from me, a reason I can't remember, and I believe it is self-preservation. Why should I search for something that will only bring me more pain?

"I still know the feel of the love I have for my people, my family. I think that is enough, at least for now." I start stacking the books again.

Tenny stares at me, leaning forward on her elbows.

"What part of Reine did you grow up in?" I ask, for hope that she will stop studying me like a hunter looking for prints in the snow.

"Cotea." The fact that she answers at all surprises me, but her answer surprises me even more.

"I— "

"I'm not at liberty to say more." She quickly stops my questions.

I stand and start to pull the bookshelf back to standing. Tenny jumps up to finally help. I reshelve the books, not completely sure where each had lived before the quake, but do my best at guessing.

"The Battlement of Cotea can stand against Hedeon forces, Damira. We have done it before and expect to do it plenty more times in the future. We just weren't prepared for it to happen this fast, so we will be scrambling until the attack. Keep looking into those reports, anything you find that could stall their forces, would help." Tenny gathers herself, helping rehome the last few books.

One shelf broke entirely and hangs at a slant now, so we have to pack a few of the books on top of each other.

"I need to go and make others aware of this news. I'll be around, though, if you find anything else." Tenny clasps on her cloak and looks at me one last time, studying me in that same way she did earlier, looking for something I can't give her.

Something out the window catches her attention, and she steps back out of view quickly.

"Katiya's coming, mind if I use the back door?" she asks, but doesn't wait for my answer, as she already heads to the back of house.

"Be my guest," I mutter.

"Eyes and ears up," she calls to me just before she's out of view.

"Ears and eyes up."

The back door in the kitchen closes with a click behind her.

I sit down on the couch with a deep breath. Three weeks until Hedeon marches on Reine. A month until opening night. Everything seems to be racing to a pinnacle, to one catastrophic moment when the charred remains of my life will be reduced completely to ash.

The front door opens, letting in the chill. Katiya scurries in, bags in her arm. I rush up to help her, grabbing the majority of groceries so she can take off her scarf and unbutton her jacket.

"All that is good and the Divine, what happened to the book-shelf?" Her eye immediately goes to the fallen shelf.

I laugh her off, leading us to the kitchen. "My clumsy self. Bumped into the old thing, and the next thing I knew, half the books slid off. I'm sure it won't take much to fix."

"I'll call someone first thing in the morning."

I place the bags on the table in the middle of the kitchen, and Katiya promptly shoos me away so she can put everything away in peace. I head up to my room, to sleep off the effects of this horrible day.

The Company had an appearance on the other side of the Krepost today—something to do with a past show—so I got an early start to my off-days. The play is coming along. The actors and actresses know their lines without papers in hand. The orchestra is still having some issues with the last few songs, but I can hear the progress every day, even if the frustration corrupts their view.

I would truly love this life, if circumstances were different. I find myself lost in the moment, at times throughout the day, enjoying myself, and forgetting about my people suffering back home. All while I am here playing dress-up in a life to which I do not belong. Everyone is just as juxtaposed as I am. All loving this life they have found themselves in, but hurting because of the war, because of the lack of care the Crown has shown for their people. Everyone is suffering, their families barely hanging on, just like mine back in the Hovel. In Reine. The queen speaks so highly of her people, of the arts, but she doesn't show it in any tangible way to the people I work with day in and day out. It makes what we are doing all the more real. The play is coming from a place of deep pain, of longing for change. It is evident in the tears that are shed in Act 2. The actors are talented, but the tears are not fabricated, they fall, the truth of our world wrapped in salt water.

I lean against the couch now, as Raven plays with my hair. The younger royals are on a trip with their grandmother this week, so dinner was delightfully uneventful. My head rests in Raven's hands as she massages my scalp. Calix and his mother recline in the chairs across from us, a book open in Calix's lap. The fireplace to my left weaves heat through the room, though the weather is turning a corner, so we won't need to warm up by the hearth for many more weeks.

Opening night is looming, and there are too many feelings circulating in me, I can't quite figure out which one to feel. I am a walking contradiction. Paradoxes hang from my fingers, enigmas chase each other through my mind, ironies warm my blood, absurdities wrap themselves in my hair.

"Your dad used to love that book—*The Tale of the Lone Spaceman*." Milena ruins the silence that was safe and not demanding anything from anyone. Raven's fingers halt behind my head. I glance from the queen to Calix, who sits as still as his twin, with the book in his hand.

"Oh, don't look so surprised, you two. I do talk about your father, sometimes." Milena rolls her eyes, staring back at the fire.

"I have heard you mention him once," Raven says behind me. I sit up straighter, turning toward the chairs.

"Twice." Calix raises the glass in his free hand.

"That's one more than me!" Raven gasps.

"You two, honestly." The queen rolls her eyes and takes her feet down from resting over the arm of the chair, to face us head on.

"Your father," she meets Calix's and Raven's eyes, "loved to read. Gerek was always working through a novel and could hardly be found without one in his hand. Especially at Court functions. He got into trouble many times by the ladies at Court, scolding him for not paying attention to them or to me. I never had much problem with it, but looking back, maybe I should have." She laughs the way a person does in the wake of loss. Halfheartedly and with many regrets.

"Now, kids. I think it is time we all go to bed." She stands, sighing heavily and clapping her hands together. "Everyone, sleep well. I will see you all tomorrow." She pats each of us on the shoulder as she passes and smiles softly. We all sit in silence for a moment.

"What happened to your father?" I ask Raven and Calix, twisting so I am properly facing them both. They share a look, and Calix shrugs to give Raven the go-ahead.

Raven turns to me. "He left when we were little. We have few memories of Gerek. Mother explained it once after it happened and then never spoke of it again. He had enough of life at Court and just ran away. I don't think he even told her as much, though. She was completely devastated, and I think blindsided. I've never heard her say anything else about him. He broke her." Raven speaks quietly, as if the queen still might overhear. Calix nods in agreeance to her words.

I sit with the new information, turning it over in my head, letting it sit in my hands, staring at it while small things start to make sense with this new information. We all knew the king left, everyone poking fun at him with the nickname *Runaway King*, but the details were never made known.

"I should go to bed too. I have to get up frightfully early." Raven yawns and pads out on socked feet, throwing a wink in my direction, obstructed from Calix's view.

I glance at Calix, who stares hollowly at the ground, lost in a thought. Neither of us moves to follow the others out. His eyes glance at me, and I quickly look at the fire. I clutch the warm cup of tea to my chest, and suddenly feel cold in the absence of the others. Finally, I rise to his challenge and bring my stare to him. He doesn't flinch or flicker his eyes away. He lets me look at him, and I let him look at me.

"It was a few weeks after my dad left." Calix keeps my stare. "The second time I ever heard my mother talk about him. I went to her room because I hadn't seen her in a few days. I walked in, and she was in bed, in the darkness. She screamed at me to get out. She said I looked too much like him, I reminded her too much of him. Raven had been in there day after day, lying with her and keeping her company. We were eight. I didn't know what to do, how to fix myself to look less like him," Calix whispers, the same as Raven did. I add this to the short list of similarities between the twins—their voice in quiet moments.

"Calix—" I start. He shakes his head, jaw tight.

"I've hated him most of my life. Not because of how he left us, but because of how he left her. Just woke up one day and decided he didn't care for the promises he made anymore. But to know when my mom looks at me, she sees him—" He shakes his head, the pain glossing over his gaze. I get up, before I can think better of it, and sit in the chair beside him, putting my hand on his. He flinches at the soft touch but doesn't pull away.

What am I doing?

"She loves you," I whisper.

"I know she does. But that doesn't change the fact that I look just like him." With that, he stands, beckoning me to follow. He doesn't hesitate, but I do. I hesitate because he walks through a door I have only ever seen the Crown exit through. My mind returns to where it belongs in my head, reminding myself that I am just here to spy on these people, not to be involved in their lives, not to be close to him like this.

Once I remind myself of my true intentions, I follow him.

A hallway opens to the outside, a courtyard. The cold doesn't bother creeping to me slowly, it clings like a child to its parent. I wrap my arms around myself as I take in the extravagant breeze-way. Tall columns, granite benches, tiles intricately laid in pastel patterns. Calix moves quickly, through a door at the other end.

I catch up to him, staying silent at his side as we walk back inside. I have to squint, adjusting my eyes from the moonlight to the interior of the chamber void of much light. Everything is dark wood, pulling the shadows to it, just as Calix does. A few sconces lead the way through the hallway that turns off the foyer. These must be where the Crown's rooms are.

Calix doesn't glance at me as he walks easily through the halls, turning and weaving until we stand outside a wooden door. The lackluster, in comparison to the opulence, begs to be ignored. I don't know what lies behind the door, but by Calix's stalling, it is easy to tell he is contemplating all of his actions up to this point. If I thought it would make him feel better, I'd tell him that I am too. With a breath, he commits to his decision and opens the creaking door.

Dust covers all the furniture in a layer. Chairs, books, a desk, lamps. This is an office. The only thing that is immune to the dust is a portrait that Calix now stands before, staring at it. A family, smiling and perfectly posed. Familiar faces, Raven and Calix, not more than five. The other two siblings not born yet. They were sired by another man, long gone, though I know even less of that story.

The man that stands behind Calix, beside Milena, looks as much a twin to Calix as Raven does.

"Dogs don't make cats," I whisper, gaining a slightly confused look from Calix, from the saying that I guess doesn't translate to the Crown.

"You look just like him," I clarify, taking a step closer.

"This was my father's office. I'm pretty sure my mother isn't aware that I know it exists. Raven doesn't know either. She has always taken after my mother, always hated him to her deepest core. Raven can be scary when she puts her mind to something—never wavering in her feelings toward our father, but something in me remains for him." Calix studies the portrait, though I am sure he has sat in here and stared many times. Unlike him, the painting is the least of my concerns.

"Why tell me this?" I ask, taking a few steps back to look around the room. He turns to me, fidgeting with a ring on his middle finger. He purses his lips, as if thinking, though I know he already has an answer. He is too calculated to not know why.

"It's impolite to ask why someone gives you a gift, darling." His laugh fails, falling off before it can be categorized as a laugh. His eyes, downturned, say more than his words.

I cross my arms, leaning back against the desk. His eyes watch my purposeful movement, briefly flickering to my ankle. "I think your mother sees you for who you are now, you don't have to try and prove yourself to her."

"I wish it were that simple."

"Why can't it be?"

"Pain is the underbelly of the monster we call Court. Without it, we would simply stop functioning. And the queen is the instigator of it all. She indulges in everything that catches her eye, to mask the hurt, and everyone follows her example. She clings to the hidden pain, and in turn, I have to prove myself to her over and over again."

Calix has inched closer, so slowly I hadn't noticed, until he is standing right in front of me. I don't know how, but in the past few weeks, Calix has stopped hating me. And I, well, as much as I hate to admit it, he isn't what I thought he was.

"I find it hard to believe that your treasury is so depleted you can't fund a play, maybe letting your mom indulge without so much pushback would help your cause." I ease the words out. I regret them as soon as they jump from my tongue, free falling too fast to scoop them back up. Exploiting someone when they are being vulnerable is not who I am, even for my kingdom. He takes the bait though, and I don't know if I am glad for it or not.

"I know. But it is bad. Our troops are suffering, weakening because we can't keep them clothed or fed. My mother says her advisors aren't worried, but I fear she just isn't hearing them. If it gets worse, we will have to call our soldiers back when they've already suffered so much to get where they are. I can't back down from this fight, and the queen already winces when she sees me, so why not continue to be a nuisance?"

"Your life motto, it seems." I roll my eyes, backing off out of pure shame. I find it hard to believe he can't see the guilt behind my poorly constructed lies. "We all wear masks, Calix. Don't be too hard on your mother because she is surviving the only way she knows how." To him, it might look like I am defending the queen, but all I really am doing is warning him of the harsh realities of our world. Of my world. Of me.

"And what mask are you hiding behind, Mira?" He smirks, taking a step, all vibrato, but I know the minute I reach out to him, he will freeze.

If only he knew how many masks I have layered over the girl I was born. I haven't seen her in years. I'm not truly sure she even exists anymore. I am the compilation of all the things forged in stratagem.

"We should get some sleep, Prince."

But neither of us move. Again, we are standing too close, but I can't manage to understand why it keeps happening. He takes a shaky breath and then finally drops his stare.

"Of course," he nods, obliging me with mischief in his eye. To my surprise, he slips his hand to the small of my back and gently steers me to the door.

Maybe he wouldn't have frozen.

Calix leads us back through the Crown's suite, through the hallways and courtyard, back to the Solar. He leaves me here with a small bow of his head and a "Goodnight, darling."

Lev greets me, as usual, just outside the side door of the Solar. His face grim as he leans against the stone wall of the Zamak. He doesn't move, just stares at me for a moment too long. I open my mouth to ask what's wrong with him, but he pushes off the wall and stalks toward me, pointing a finger in my face.

"Where were you last night?" His glare daggers, cutting me apart like torture in an interrogation. My heart stops, the years of lying and being quick on my feet saving me from showing the horror on my face. Where is this clad demeanor around Calix?

"Why?"

Flashes of the conversation with Tenny last night, the broken bookshelf, the books fluttering like birds through the air. No one but Katiya could have heard that, but she was most surely out.

"Answer the question. Where were you last night, Damira?"

"I went back to my house after rehearsal, and I was in bed shortly after," I explain, sticking close to the truth and throwing my words frivolously, doing my best to seem intimidated by him. It's not that hard to pretend.

"I have no proof that you are the one who stole those outlines of our western base, and that is the only reason I haven't gone straight to the queen." He inches closer, getting in my face in way of a scare tactic. He isn't doing half bad. "I care for those people in there. I don't know who you are, but I am certain you are not who you pretend to be. I see how you talk to the prince, how you pretend to be friends with the princess. There is no veneration in your eyes. Keep up your little charade all you want, but I am not the only one who sees through you. If you step a toe out of the expected line, you won't live long enough to warn whoever helped get you here," he whispers, his words as dark as the sky above.

"Threats are useless when they don't have purchase to land." I keep the scared tone, the confusion in the furrow of my brows.

"Say what you must, Damira, but you don't breathe without someone reporting it back to me." He leans back, crossing his arms.

I can't resist myself. "Then why ask where I was last night?" I regret the taunt immediately, but Lev has continuously told me there are eyes on me, and yet I've managed to house Tenny and Sumood without any suspicion. If Calix's fears and Tenny's nonchalance are true, then I'm assuming the Hedeon army is spread too thin to spend a few extra guards on a lowly playwright.

Instead of waiting for the punishment for such words, I turn around and head down the stone path by myself, cursing my howling ankle. I leave behind a very angry Lev, wishing his stare could shoot bullets through my back.

14

I SIT WITH MY legs dangling off the front of the stage. Calix sleeps in a chair at the back of the theatre, completely oblivious to anything being said on the stage. The Company and I have managed to work out all of the hitches in the first two acts, but going into the third has proven more difficult than I would have imagined. Nothing is lining up correctly. The Company is tired, and the orchestra is having difficulties playing the music Deacon still can't finish. The creating of props is slowing, the first act grand-staircase set becoming more of an issue than it originally was supposed to be.

Everyone is tired and emotionally drained.

Especially me.

The Company clears out as rehearsal ends. I stay sat in place, paralyzed by the weight of what my life has turned out to be. Someone places a hand on my shoulder, and I look up to see Myka smiling smally. She sits beside me, shoulder to my shoulder. She lets out the breath I have been holding all day.

"What if this all just turns out terribly?" I ask her with a shaking breath.

"I think there is *only* a terrible outcome for all of this. That doesn't mean it's not worth it."

I shrug. "I don't mean it in that sense—I mean, what if we put on this play and no one understands what we are trying to say? What if my words are not good enough?"

"Dramaturg, you are an artist. Whatever you have to say is worth saying."

I want to agree with her, but what if the trouble with the third act, the trouble Deacon is having with his music, is because I am not good enough—because I did not create something worthy of the magnitude it is to be displayed?

"I can't fail at this. Sometimes I fear this story deserves more than I can give it."

She sighs, the silence between us allowing Calix to stay asleep far in front of us. Myka lifts a fold in her brown skirt and picks at a loose thread with her thumb. Her dark brown hair is secured back today, the length hidden in a bun.

"I am just a conductor," Myka finds her words again. "I couldn't compose a song if my life depended on it. I take what others have made and give it life in my own way, but you are the one to create life in the first place. Both are beautiful and both are needed, but there is a reason you were given this gift."

"And if no one understands it?"

"Do you create for yourself or for others?"

Her words stop and make me think. If this play doesn't strike the chord we are aiming for, will it still be worth it? Even in the few weeks we've had together, I can confidently say yes because it changed me and the Company. It has made us better. I want this to be enough, but I am not sure it is.

I don't answer her question outright, still wrestling with what I believe on that matter. So, instead I say, "I want it to be more than entertainment. It is one thing to be changed by what we are creating ourselves, but I don't want it to be something easily consumed and even easier discarded. I just don't know how my words could affect someone in the way I want them to."

"Those who are meant to understand it, will understand it. I promise you that. It is a very good play, Damira. Stop fretting over these things."

I grab the anchor she throws at me, clinging to it for dear life.

"I will try," I agree halfheartedly.

She laughs, not believing my words. "You have looked too closely at this play—have seen all the places you have left your fingerprints. I have fresh eyes, and I am telling you it is good. If you can't see it clearly, then trust me to tell you the truth."

She is right. I know she is right, but I still have these troubles buried deep within, that this play is tarnished somehow because I am the one to have written it.

"Thank you, Myka. I will try."

"I'm around whenever you need the reminder." She gets up with a small grunt. "Have a good evening, Dramaturg."

The stage door swings behind her as she leaves. I look back out to the chairs, the invisible crowd that watches our rehearsal each week. Calix still sleeps in the back of the theatre. Usually, he is gone far before we finish practice, so I don't have to bother with him. But instead of just leaving him to his nap, I cross the rows to him. I sit in a chair in front of him, purposefully making enough noise that he begins to stir as I settle down.

"Did I sleep through practice again?" he asks, looking around and wiping the sleep from his face.

"Weeks ago, you asked me to help you ease your mother's thoughts that you are indeed showing up to rehearsal, but we haven't spoken about it once since, and you sleep through the time you bother to show up. What could you possibly be telling her?"

"Enough that she is happy with my work," he grins, sitting up from his slouched position and clearly not wanting to speak about such matters. I don't press the issue for sheer fear of having to answer questions I can't—this subject is dangerous territory.

"What do you need that sword for?" I nod to the jeweled beauty that is thrown on the chair beside him.

"Practice," he says, as if it's no big deal.

"Do you expect to fight?" With all of queen Milena's heroic stories about Calix, I am only now realizing that I don't know much about what is expected of him when it comes to participating in the war.

"Mother would never allow it, but it makes me feel a bit less helpless knowing I could."

"I'm not sure a weapon could ever offer me the same comfort."

"Do they not?" He leans forward with his head cocked to the side.

"No. I do not need to know I can kill someone to find comfort."

"You just need to know you can emotionally manipulate them?" He doesn't say it as an insult, not an accusation of any kind, but despite the grin on his face, it still feels pointed.

"Excuse me?" I balk, leaning back from the chair.

"Is that not what you are doing here? My mother asked you to write a play that manipulates our people into feeling hope, or something of the like. Is that not just as dangerous as my sword here?"

"I'm advocating for hope, not violence. A sword's job is only to maim."

"Or to defend," he raises an eyebrow.

"One wouldn't have to defend themselves if no one raised the sword at them in the first place," I counter.

"That's an idealistic view of the matter, darling. We must defend what we believe in."

"I agree, but that doesn't mean we have to resort to violence."

"And if the sword is the only way?"

"It never is." Because if I thought this wasn't true, then I would have no basis to stand on. I would not create if I didn't think it could somehow, eventually, someway, result in bringing peace to our people. There has to be an alternative to this war, to all this death. I wouldn't know how to live in a world where this isn't true.

"Then let's agree to disagree." He stands, brushing of his pants, grabbing his sword and securing it back to his waist. I stand too, having other things to get to today.

We stand cautiously close, the silence not quite comfortable. I put my hands in my trouser pockets, for I don't know what else to do. A part of me wants to linger here, to hear what else he has to say on matters of war and art and anything else that can help me understand who he is, but the other part knows what a dangerous wanting that is.

"I should be going." I take a step toward the door.

"Oh, yes, me too. Mother wants to take a walk around the garden with Raven and me." We enter the silent foyer, our steps louder than our unsure words.

"Tell them hello for me."

"Of course."

We depart the theatre in our separate ways—Calix goes back up to the Zamak, and I follow the road down the bend.

To my knowledge, there is only one temple in the Krepost. I pass it on my way to the flower shop, but something within calls me to slow down. I walk up a few steps of the ancient building, stopping to read the plaque on the wall. The temple was built for and dedicated to another god in another time, but just as everything with the Divine, the religion invaded and took ownership around the time the most recent war started.

I peak in, the pews mostly empty, except for the queen mother and a Mezdu standing in the middle of the room beside the pyre of sacrifice. Pews surround the pyre in a square, all empty except for the lone shadowed figure sitting in a back corner, watching the two women speak—Lev. I sneak through the cracked doors and hide in the shadow of a column right by the entrance.

"Did she say how much?" The old queen's voice shakes with age.

"Just enough to get her and her family out of the Krepost. She lives on the lowest end, hardly any money to her name anymore," the Mezdu recounts.

The queen mother nods her head, solving a puzzle I can't see. Lev watches silently, leaning in with his hands clasped between his knees. The queen mother turns to Lev swiftly.

"Take the money and evict the family. If they want to leave, we will let them, but there is a price to pay for everything."

Lev nods but does not get up to leave. The queen mother turns back to the Mezdu.

"I will see you next time."

I hide further in the shadows created by the pyre and column. When all my lies inevitably come out, will the Crown be shocked by all the ways I hid in plain sight? The queen mother walks right past me, none the wiser to my existence and future betrayal. The door slams behind her. I can't leave now, not without drawing Lev's and the Mezdu's attention to the door.

The Mezdu approaches Lev, where he still hasn't moved, just has shifted his gaze from the queen mother to the pyre of sacrifice.

"Staying around a little bit longer this week, Lev?" the Mezdu asks, sitting beside him in the pew.

"It's been five years to the day since my wife passed." It is stated as a fact, no mourning behind the words as there should be.

"Would you like to make an offering to her?" the Mezdu suggests.

Lev laughs. "If I thought she was somewhere in an afterlife, an offering would be the last thing I'd be tempted to do."

"So, you don't believe in an afterlife, and yet you speak with me most weeks after the queen mother's visits. What do you believe in, Lev?"

"The Crown."

The Mezdu seems to be just as annoyed with this answer as I am. There has to be more to Lev than his duty, but he has buried himself so deeply in his devotion, I'm not sure anyone could dig him out again.

"How did your wife pass?"

"I don't believe it much matters. All that does matter is that she is gone now." Lev pauses, but clearly there are more words he has to say. The Mezdu lets the crackling of the fire be enough conversation until he manages words again. I have never seen Lev so unsure of himself, so—human.

"I used to be a lot like her," Lev finally says.

"Your wife?"

"No, she was far too good to be compared to. The playwright we hired—I used to be a lot like her, in my younger age."

My heart stops at the mention of me, catching in my throat as if I have been found from my hiding place. But Lev keeps his eyes on the pyre, and the Mezdu keeps her eyes on Lev.

"In what ways?"

"I was a poet, but sometimes poets must turn into soldiers. I was prepared to fight against the Divine itself if I could have just kept my wife. That is how our playwright is—I've read all her stories—she sees the injustices around her, and she is ready to declare war on the Divine."

"Your proof?" I thank The Faits for this Mezdu asking the question I almost blurted out. Perhaps they do consult with those above, after all.

"That she is going to turn our world on edge? None. Just a feeling—it's what I would have done once. The queen has forbidden me to go near their rehearsals, as she is trying to teach her son responsibility, and I can't find any evidence that the playwright is in league with any of our known conspirators. Perhaps I really am as paranoid as my wife once claimed."

"Do you still write poems?"

"Not in five years."

The Mezdu nods, turning to face the pyre. They both sit in the silence for a while longer, but before long, Lev stands, turning to where the Mezdu still sits.

"I will see you next week." He nods his head to her and then leaves to the door. I push back into the shadows that don't feel anywhere as dark enough as I want them to be, but Lev still doesn't see me in my hiding place. He exits, leaving the door open behind him. The Mezdu gets up and follows a hallway deeper into the temple.

I leave after a few more breaths, back into the sunlight. The queen mother is using the Mezdu as spies, and Lev once was a poet. I'm not sure which piece of information I am more shocked to learn.

15

S OME DAYS TRUDGE ON like a soldier through mud. Slow and with little progress. Two weeks until the march on the Battlement of Cotea is supposed to happen, and I have found nothing else that will help Reine. Tenny's getting restless. The Company is still struggling, and I am once again being torn in multiple directions, always caught in the in-between.

I recline on the couch, my notebook propped on my knees, trying to create a way to boost morale. So far, the page is blank as I stare off into the fire. The most frustrating thing about art is that it cannot be forced. It can't be rushed, as it takes its time to manifest in full, wandering and meandering until it is good and ready. The fatigue of the Company is a testament to that. It is just something we have to work through in order to come out on the other side.

A faint knock pulls me from my thoughts. I push the blanket from my lap, the knock continuing to taper weakly. Katiya is out for the night, dinner with a friend, I think. She wouldn't have need to knock, though.

I open the door on silent hinges. Tenny leans on the frame, blood dripping from her forehead—arm cut and leg dangling in an uneasy way.

"Faits," I mumble, frozen at the uneasy sight.

"Some help would be lovely," she grunts, hopping on her one good leg.

I quickly give her my shoulder, pulling her inside and closing the door behind us. No one is around, and somehow, she managed not to leave a trail of blood up the steps.

"What happened?" I rush us down the hallway.

"Help first, talk later," she manages to get out, her breathing labored, wheezing between words.

I take her back to the kitchen, clearing the table in the middle of the room. I sit her down, carefully, needing to clean the cuts that flay her body. She grunts with each small movement, deeply breathing when she's laid back.

I grab a mixing bowl I've seen Katiya use a few times and go outside to scoop up snow. The medical supplies are kept in the bathroom. I take all of them. No doctors live in the Hovel, everyone with enough money to get that kind of an education never deigns to care about those who are far beneath them. We have had to take care of ourselves. For the first time in my life, I am thankful for that.

Tenny probably needs stiches in at least three places. I thank The Faits for the fresh snow that just fell this morning and will help numb her. Her clothes are tattered, I can't even fathom the strength it took her to get here.

After peeling the fabric back and having to cut a few pieces of her shirt, the extent of her injuries are displayed. She's in bad shape. Even with the lightest of contact, she winces, breath hitching. I pack the snow on her. The scrapes on her face, the gash in her forehead, the gaping cut in her arm, and the wound on her leg.

I start with her leg, the biggest cut through her calf. I stitch her up with a sharp needle, weaving the thread back and forth. Mechanically, I move to her arm, less stitches there. Then her forehead, repeating the process. I am nowhere close to good at it, but I am able to close the gouges.

The cold air takes my sweat as I get more snow. I pack it onto her bruised side, wrapping it so it will stay pressed tightly to her. More snow. Wrap her arms. More snow. Wrap her stomach.

After at least an hour, I am able to pull up a chair and take a moment to sit and catch my breath. Tenny is clean and relatively properly stitched. I'm not sure she can tell, having schooled her features into a scowl the whole time I poked at her, staring at the ceiling. Only the few winces she surrendered told me she was still conscious.

"Tenny—" I start cautiously. She lets her head fall sideways to look at me, flinching at the small movement.

"There's a compound not far from here, a whole lot of soldiers. One of the Hedeon army's home bases. I was poking around, trying to get more information about the attack on Cotea," she winces with a deep breath, needing more air than her lungs will allow. "I was caught. Or almost caught, I guess, since I got away. It wasn't an easy getaway, I had to fight my way out. You were the first safe place I came to because I was out west." She whispers, not because of the sensitive information, but because she physically can't speak any louder. Out west—the plans Lev accused me of stealing.

The front door takes this inopportune moment to open, and Katiya enters on soft feet, but not soft enough that she goes unnoticed. We hide behind the kitchen door, Tenny holds her breath. The kitchen is a mess, blood and bandages discarded on the floor. There is no way of getting Tenny out of here without Katiya seeing her. Tenny and I hold each other's stare. Helpless.

We have no other option but to await this fate. Down the hall, Katiya's footsteps slowly grow closer. I run through my mind to find any excuses I could possibly use.

I find none.

Katiya swings the door open, a hum breaking off in the middle of the note.

"By the Divine!" she breathes.

"Katiya," I open my mouth, hoping some excuse will fall out, but I just look like a fish out of water.

I glance at Tenny, but she offers no help, hardly able to speak herself, let alone formulate a lie that could absolve us both.

Katiya looks from me to Tenny, waiting and mortified. From my understanding, she's been a maid her whole life, most likely never having seen this kind of abuse. Except if—

"Tenny's a maid at the bottom of the Krepost," I grab Katiya by the arm and lead her out of the kitchen. "Her employer beat her, and she came to me for help. We knew each other as children," I whisper, as if I don't want Tenny to relive the traumatic situation.

"The poor thing," Katiya shakes her head, but I'm not sure she fully believes me. She glances behind her shoulder to get one last look at Tenny as the door swings behind us.

"I got her stitched up and will have the kitchen cleaned up by the morning, so you don't have to worry. I know it's getting late." We stop in front of the hallway that leads to her chambers.

"Oh no, I can help," she tries to step past me, and I let her, stopping myself from jumping in front of her and seeming more suspicious.

"Katiya."

She stops and turns back to me.

"She's been through a lot and doesn't take well to strangers. I can clean up and will get her back home, or to somewhere safe. Get some rest, really, it's okay." I try a pitying smile.

Katiya wasn't raised to question her *superiors*. At least not to their faces. She nods her head, keeping her eyes down, and moves past me to her room. She turns back right before closing her bedroom door.

"Thank you for helping her." And with that she disappears.

I return to Tenny, where she remains staring at the ceiling. I have never seen her so beaten down, so small. Her badly dyed hair is matted, tangled with the blood and agony. The eye below her gash is swollen, the clothes she wore when she arrived virtually nonexistent after I took scissors to them. Her labored breathing clouds the room, hanging like a storm in the air.

"I think we can stop the attack," she can hardly get the words out. My eyes snap to hers, digging for more information. She readjusts herself just slightly, but still, it takes everything within her to do so, her breaths quickening and labored.

"I learned where they've made camp." I think that she smiles, or she thinks that she is smiling. "If we ambush them first, we might have a chance. If we surround them, they might surrender on sight. I've already sent word to General Kabosik. I don't know what he is going to do with the information, but this could be very good."

I let out a deep breath, sinking into a chair.

"Have you found out anything more from Calix? If they'll even have enough funds to continue the raid?" she asks, as I stare off, taking in the news.

"No, but if you learned all of this, you don't need me to try to do that anymore, right?" I am grasping for a way out, wanting to stop this reckless mission for purely selfish reasons, so I don't have to exploit Calix and Raven anymore. I am a traitor.

"We still need you to do your best. If we can learn how quickly they're running out of coin, we could wait them out. Then we wouldn't have to engage and put our men in danger. That information could be crucial if you can get your hands on it," she ends the sentence with a grunt instead of a period.

I nod. More lies I have to craft.

"You should get some rest. I'll clean up this mess, and then we will have to figure out how to get you out of here. I told Katiya you were an abused maid at the bottom of the Krepost."

More lies and more lies.

I stand, busying my hands.

"Thank you, Damira." Tenny closes her eyes and takes a deep breath that makes her wince again.

I absentmindedly clean up the kitchen while focusing on the news Tenny shared. I do not envy those who are pawns in the armies, forced to kill, over and over again. I could never do what they do, but all the lies of my life have piled up, creating a mound of dishonesty that I couldn't climb my way out of if I tried. And I am utterly exhausted by it.

I've been staring at the ceiling for hours, unable to sleep because of what haunts the backside of my eyelids, and yet, still unable to get up. But dawn is nearly here, so I pull myself from under my warm sheets. Getting dressed takes longer than usual, we are venturing out of the theatre for rehearsal today, and thus, I have to wear full skirts. I need to be presentable for Court. I know they already talk about me enough.

Raven has mentioned the gossip, though I've never heard anything said to my face. I guess that's the construct of gossip in general. To my face, all of the women at Court offer up other women's grandsons, in order for me to keep cashing in on my good fortune. Behind my back, they whisper that my luck will come to an end, eventually. They criticize the clothes I wear and the company I keep. Even though the Arman is highly prestigious, most of the Company were found on the streets, and Court does not forget such things. I sidestep their glances most often, Raven keeping me away from the worst of the men and women.

The theatre is filled by the time I arrive. Even though I'm not entirely sure I've slept at all, I still manage to be a few moments late.

"Good morning, everyone. I am glad to see your beautiful shining faces so bright and early." I grin to the mostly asleep Company. They lay over the chairs, leaning on one another, a few snoring.

I clap a few times, getting everyone's attention. "Come on, everyone up! We have places to be and things to do." I lead everyone out of the theatre, down the road of the Krepost.

No one is awake this early, barely even those who serve at Court. The sun is just starting to cast soft hues of the new day. Everyone in the Company walks in a stupor, the only sound our shuffling feet and the birds whistling above.

"I haven't been awoken before the sun in quite some time," Dilean grumbles, interrupting the silence.

"Dilean, just the other day, you drank Otbrosy Road dry and didn't return until dawn the next morning," Nikita reminds him.

"I said *awoken*. I haven't been *awoken* before the sun in some time."

"Not even to be kicked out of a Courtier's bed?" Pasha bumps Dilean's shoulder with a grin it is too early to be wearing.

"Surely he misspoke," Myka agrees with a nod.

"It is far too early to get into this with you all," Dilean grumbles once more.

"You started it." Pasha wraps her arm around his waist in a hug, but Dilean pushes her off, not ready to be friendly at this hour.

The group quiets, watching the sunrise ahead of us.

The idea came to me the other day, after all the commotion with Tenny. Since we've all been struggling with Act 3, I thought a change of scenery would help. No one asks me where we are going, we just walk until we are halfway down the Krepost. As we descend, the close proximity of buildings becomes less and less. Fields of crops and livestock stretch to the back of the mountain, houses planted on the front side. I turn through a gate, leading the lot of us on a stone path swimming in the grass that is starting to wake from winter.

Just like the waking grass, the Company is beginning to rise behind me.

"Where are we, Moi Dramaturg?" Pasha comes up beside me, grabbing my hand in hers and bouncing along. I delay answering, walking us around the bend of the mountain.

Statues broken and fallen over in the middle of the green yard. The ones that are still intact have moss growing up the side of them, sending cracks through the once-supple stone. Most are statues of men, some women, and a few animals from fables long since spoken.

"What is this place?" Pasha breathes again from my side.

"This," I turn around to face the Company who has gathered in a group instead of a line now, "is where art has come to die." I take a few steps back, beckoning them forward.

Raven told me about this place once, offhandedly, in the middle of a different conversation. It called for me to come see it, and what better way to climb the wall we are all scaling than to use art that has been long lost to boost us up?

"It's dreadful," Deacon whispers.

Everyone takes off in different directions to look at the statues.

"It's a graveyard," Pasha mumbles.

"Why are we here?" Kolyo puts the size of the statues to shame.

I look up to a carved man who stands on a pedestal. His face chiseled, his brow set. He looks to the horizon ceaselessly. A sword hangs at his hip. He is the only statue in the graveyard that points to war. A couple stands on their own pedestal to his left. Wrapped in each other's embrace. The young man's hand digs into the woman's waist. It is stone, but the way the marble bends and curves looks the same as flesh and bone. The two gaze deeply into each other's eyes, with an emotion that lacks no warmth.

Romance has never been something I have thought to envy. If I didn't have the privilege of envy, I sure didn't have the privilege of romance. I have read it, and I have observed it in paintings, and in my aunt and uncle, but that is as close as I thought I would ever get to it. As much as dread fills my every breath, like sand dripping through an hourglass, I have to admit, the moment I was taken in that carriage to the Zamak, the things I thought I would never reach, have suddenly felt within my grasp.

I keep my eyes on the two lovers, but start speaking to the group that scatters around the yard. "When I was little, I saw a statue of a woman. She was on her knees with her arms sprawled forward. On the ground behind her lay a kingdom, a city reduced in size. At the tip of her finger, a sword cut into her. It defied everything I thought I knew. She was defending the people behind her, not with a sword or shield, but with her body. With the only thing she had." I turn my gaze from the statues and look at the living around me. The Company has turned their faces to me, all waiting for my next words.

"Where is that statue now?" I ask, meeting the eyes of the people I now call friends.

"Sold to the Crown's hoard?" Myka asks.

"Used as another body at the front lines?" Dilean interjects, getting a few sad laughs at our reality.

"Burned in a siege?" Ira breaks the silence.

The wind answers when theirs stop.

I take a deep breath, the morning air reviving something asleep within me. Spring is coming, whether we like it or not. Whether we are prepared or not. I just have to trust The Faits that we will be ready.

"Where is it?" Calliope finally asks in her soft voice.

"I have no clue," I admit, shrugging and taking a few steps through the marble crowd. "But does it matter? I don't know where that statue is today, but I think about it constantly. It changed something in me, made me see the world differently. It could be broken in two at the bottom of the Aadria River. It's the feeling that rose up in me that makes the difference. Our performance won't last more than a few nights at each place we travel, but the show bows in the shadow of the feeling that we evoke."

I glance back to the statues surrounding us. Sometimes art evokes art. The need to create comes from seeing the created. "We are not merely entertaining people, we are pulling action out of them, we are pushing them past the limits they thought they knew. We are calling them to be more."

The Company stares back at me. I have become a leader, forged in the fires of demand, and nothing else. Pasha and Deacon nod along, their faces turning from contemplation to something I can only describe as hope. It's small, barely a spark, but I think it's enough to draw us back together, and give us the final push through the wall that stands between us and perfecting the third act. As the words set in, Anoki straightens, nodding his head. Kolyo's eyes soften, no smile, but a gentle nod. One by one, the Company changes—pulling their shoulders back, holding their heads higher—it's small, but enough for me to know they've heard my words.

There will always be music and singing and words and paintings and art. Even in the dark times. Especially in the dark times. When the storm is loud, or the night is long, that is not when the arts stop, but when they persist. That is when it is important to sing or speak or shout even louder. We can't stop the war on the battlefields, but we can change the spirits of those who are together in the trenches.

With new breath in our lungs, we return to the Arman Theatre.

16

Men in grey uniforms with a black stripe down the side march toward me. I'm huddled in a closet, some small cubby I thought I could hide in. I bury my head in my arms, curled up in hopes that if I can't see them, they will disappear into thin air. They cornered us in a room downstairs. Blood-soaked and scared, I ran. I didn't know what else to do. So, I ended up here, limping and trailing blood. My ankle snapped when a soldier tried to grab me. I haven't looked down, too scared of what I will see.

Something in the side of the closet moves. I would have jumped if I was just playing hide-and-seek with my mom. But I have no space to give myself away. Out of all the times I have hidden here, I have never seen the back panel move.

"Sera," Linc whispers from the other side. I throw my arms around him, and he whisks me away from the bad guys.

And then we run.

Linc carries me through our home, through the field, over the river that I always splashed through in the summer, and finally past the wood. Linc never let's go of me, quickening our pace as he nervously glances behind us.

Selah and Sumood wait in the distance, urging us to come faster, not daring to call our names.

Linc puts me down, telling me to run. I don't question my big brother. I glance back, but he isn't following, he's turned with his sword drawn. I try not to cry out as I almost crumble over with pain in my ankle. Selah and Sumood are close enough that I can hear them chanting my name in a quickened whisper. Horses at the ready.

Sumood grabs my arm, picking me up when he notices my limp and the tears that stream down my face from the pain. I look back just as grey uniforms with a black stripe down the side over-power Linc. I start shrieking, wailing even more, pushing against Sumood, who trudges forward with me flung over his shoulder.

"You have to be quiet, Seraphine." Sumood's voice is calming, petting my hair and pushing my head down, trying to stop me from looking back. But I fight him, peering over his shoulder.

Linc falls to the ground, his sword forced from his hand. A solider hits him on the side of his head with the hilt of a sword. His body goes limp, but he doesn't fall completely to the ground, as he is being held up by the arms. One after another, they beat my brother senseless.

I jolt up, screaming, unable to catch my breath.

Katiya lets herself in, a mug in her hand. She hands it to me, sitting on my bed and kindly rubs my back. I have these nightmares often enough that if Katiya hears me stirring, she brings in tea and sits with me until I stop shaking. She never asks what I dream of, or why I sometimes vomit because of it. Compared to normal, that one was rather subdued.

The few memories I seem to have only find me in nightmares.

I am thankful for Katiya's manners in these moments. I couldn't explain myself if I tried. I hardly remember my family, but I remember their deaths. I hardly remember my brother, but I know exactly where he was beaten down by Hedeon soldiers.

"I will start on breakfast," Katiya whispers cheerfully, after my breathing has returned to normal. I nod, not able to even manufacture a smile.

All the emotions I find during my days are misplaced until I can process them, feel them, and put them on the canvas. Faces as familiar as my own spread out through the greenroom. Paint mixed with tears. I don't often like my work, but these—these came from a place in me that I wasn't sure I had. I cut myself open, and this was my blood, just like when I put pen to paper. Painting has never come as effortlessly to me as it has while painting these. I didn't have to think or plan. They just trickled from me, and I stood back and watched as my hand drew the familiar lines I memorized long ago.

I wash the paintbrush in a jar of water, wiping it dry on my smock. Three weeks until opening night. If I focus too much on it, anxiety rises in my chest and threatens to spill through my mouth.

It's hard to capture the desperation I am trying to portray, the one permanently mixed in their eyes. I haven't been able to get it right in Safler's eyes. Her downturned grimace has been staring back at me for days. I have broken down in tears twice. They threaten now. I am not sure if the tears are from frustration or from the project itself. Raven's words strike me, running circles in my head today. *What a terrible job artists have. Always having to come behind the tragedy to immortalize it.*

Just once, I wish I didn't have to wait until tragedy struck to do something about it. All my life, I have been fleeing the wake of misfortune and being too late to do anything about it. Merely another curse of the artist.

"All that is good and the Divine, darling," Calix breathes from behind me. I turn around, paint-stained and on the verge of tears. The look of awe is wiped from his face quickly.

"This is a lot of material you're wasting," he sighs, remembering he shouldn't care.

It is hard to know which Calix I will get when he finds me. Sometimes he's petulant about my presence, and other times he's showing me his father's office. It leaves me completely at a loss as to how to behave around him. But at least for today, I know I need to be friendly, to get information about the ledgers. I release the anger in my fists, trying not to let his entitled words get the best of me.

He pokes around, pulling canvases turned backward against the walls.

"They are good, I admit. But what use do they have? We could be putting the money that it takes to supply your hobby into more important things. Like the wellness of our soldiers who are actually making a difference." He's angry today. At me or the world, it's hard to say, but it's evident. Something has happened to set him on edge.

Deep breaths. I take deep breaths.

"What are you doing tonight?" I ask, ignoring the bite in his words. He shrugs, turning back to me.

"Meet me outside the theatre, in an hour."

He doesn't answer, just holds my glare and walks out. I take it as a yes, though I'm not sure I should.

An hour and an outfit change later, I wait inside the Arman doors, the foyer buzzing with people and me horridly under-dressed. I changed out of my freshly painted-on clothes, but not into a nicer dress, just a different pair of trousers.

Maybe Calix won't come. I wouldn't mind, but somewhere deep in me, deeper than any thoughts of him should have al-lowance to be, I want him to understand why these things are important. Why this play is needed. Why my existence is not in vain.

"If I had known we were coming to the symphony, I would have dressed better," Calix comes from behind me, still in the same plain dark clothes he was wearing earlier, his collar open a few buttons and the hem untucked in wrinkles. His face is not as set as this afternoon, the previous iron mood softened with time to cool off from whatever had him reeling.

Just as I'm about to tell him that no one will see us, Anna comes in from the chill outside and makes a beeline toward us. She bows to the prince and then turns to me.

"Damira," the old courtier sings, grabbing my hand and raising it into the air, her eyes following my arm to my outfit—permanently paint-stained trousers and an oversized button-up blouse.

"Always one to be innovative, it seems." She glances again between me and the glamorous dresses of the other people wandering into the Arman. She then lifts an eyebrow to Calix, not to criticize his own casual appearance, but if to say, *Why did you let her come looking like that?*

"Oh, these are some of my closest friends," Anna waves over a group that is just walking in. Each wears contradicting colors from the others, purple and red and orange, all mashed up like pieces of a jigsaw puzzle that are forced to fit together, the picture lost in coercion. They take turns bowing to Calix and then shaking my hand in introduction.

"Are you two joining us for the symphony?" a man with long whiskers twisted into points and named Jero, asks Calix and me in a tone of suspicion.

"Oh, of course not. Clearly, she is not dressed for the show. Could you imagine?" A woman, who I didn't catch the name of, laughs. She only mentions my lack of dress, nothing about Calix's.

"Oh, no, we will see you in there." I smile a toothy smile, unable to resist.

The nameless lady gives a look of horror, Jero full of unbridled disgust. Anna looks at me sympathetically. Anna and the nameless lady bow to Calix and then give me a pointed glare before leaving.

"If you ever want something nicer, I am sure I can spare a few things in my closet," Jero whispers to me, patting me on the hand before following the others.

I let out a laugh when they are out of ear shot, and to my surprise, Calix shares the small chuckle.

"You would have thought I showed up with no clothes on at all."

"It's not your fault, anyone who stands next to me pales in comparison to my charm, darling." He flashes his teeth.

I let my eyes take a stroll down his outfit. "Yes, charm. That's what it is."

I turn quickly, leading us down a less-elegant hallway, away from the foyer and grand staircase. I turn beside the stage door, into a small closet of a room.

"Up we go." I smile back to Calix, up the rungs of a ladder. I shimmy onto the thin catwalk that hovers above the seating in the theatre.

"Hope you're not afraid of heights," I add, quickly realizing the possible fault in my plan.

Calix looks just as comfortable here as on solid ground. It's hard to imagine him scared of anything. His will is too strong, he could just wish any fear gone, and it would cower away, tail between its legs.

I sit down, folding and refolding my legs until I find a way comfortable for my ankle. Calix settles in beside me, feet dangling down. He leans back on his hands, glancing around the ceiling, the other rafters around us.

As the crowd is allowed into the theatre, their chatter wafts its way up to us. A few laughs stick out against the rest, a couple of words here and there uttered so loud I can almost make them out. Calix leans forward to watch the people who are now in their rightful orientation to him—below.

"I haven't sat through a symphony since I was little and was forced by my mother," he complains.

"Well, maybe that is your problem."

"I doubt it."

Lights on the walls flicker, the crowd takes their seats with a shuffle, silence being sat as they are. The curtains swing open below the hovering golden bat, revealing a full orchestra, all dressed in white, holding instruments much nicer than they have any need to be. The conductor walks out in dramatics, her jacket the length of a dress flowing behind her in a vision. Applause erupts. Bai Margaux. One of the most famous composers of our time. The orchestra is made of musicians collected from all over Hedeon. All sought out, no auditions. The Crown finds them.

Bai Margaux raises her hands. A collective breath, and then the first note graces the air. I scoot closer to Calix so he can hear me over the melodies.

"Pay attention to the composer. Watch the emotion she wears so easily on her face."

I have read every article on Bai Margaux and her orchestra. This is my first time seeing them, hearing them. A lifelong dream, and while it happens to be the best seat in the house, I am next to Calix Hendricks, with little ability to focus on anything other than his knee so close to mine.

"She's just waving her hands around obnoxiously and looking a little out of breath. She actually might need to go to the healers and get that checked out," he squints, faking concern.

"Look closer." I turn my attention back to the stage, unable to look at him without seeing red.

"I am tired. I've been training all day and then had to sit through two incredibly alarming meetings," he readjusts, settling back with his dangling leg resting against my bent one. I am not sure he notices. I tell myself that my racing heartbeat is from the mention of his alarming meetings and not the proximity of our seating.

"You are a child. Leave if you want," I snap, not giving him anymore attention if he is going to act like that. I thought it a good sign he showed up, but perhaps he truly is as dense as Raven claims. Though I can't bring myself to believe that.

He takes a clearing breath, leaning forward, arms through the railing.

What Calix thought was Bai Margaux needing a physician, was actually her working through some kind of hurt. The redness in her face, the uneasiness of her breathing. The orchestra comes out with a full sound. Starting with the pain, with the noise, and slowly it becomes deconstructed, soloing each instrument, reducing it to one melody.

"She's upset," Calix mutters lowly.

I nod. "Look at the horn player," I point down toward the middle.

Her eyes are closed, swaying ever so slightly. Her eyebrows furrow as she works through the cautious melody. I glance at- Calix, eyes fixed on the hornist. His face has fallen, the mask of who he must be slipping. His mouth purses at whatever thought was provoked by the hornist. His eyes flicker to me, quickly, not taking much time away from the orchestra.

"Stop staring, darling. Pay attention."

I turn back without retort, thankful for the dimly lit rafters.

The music slows, the continuing of the dismemberment of harmonies. Bai Margaux becomes smaller, softer, deep breaths between each note. Lament. The losing of who one once was because of the tragedy we just worked through. Each note in opposition to the one beside it, though the melody is softer, daintier, not gentle but broken. Bai Margaux heaves with her movement crumbling.

Something about this part in the song brings up a forgotten memory from home. A man spinning me around, my feet planted on his shoes as we sway back and forth. An orchestra of our own plays behind us. The faceless man bends down, moving me from where I stand and placing me beside him. He crouches, my height when he is on bended knees. We watch the music, and he whispers to me, pointing at which musician to watch, each one displaying more emotion than the last.

"This is why they are important," his voice is almost as formless as his face, but I hear the words.

"There is no greater truth than from an artist in the middle of their craft," the voice whispers. I look up to the man and wrap my arms around his neck, something in my heart made a promise in that moment. A promise that I would find the truth the man spoke of. And I wouldn't stop trying to show others the importance I learned in that man's arms.

A crescendo brings me back, a tear escaping my eye. I wipe my cheek, the orchestra finding redemption, the melody coming together as one. The instruments cry out, though tender, a newness comes forth. No more confusion in the large sound, no more deconstruction, but a firm identity of faith, a new dawn on the horizon.

I stand as the applause raptures. My claps adding to the sound of praise. Calix stands beside me as well, a look on his face I can hardly read. I nod to the door behind him, and we exit just as quietly as we came. I follow Calix away from the theatre, the symphony will continue on without us. He leads us through a door, into the cool air. It is welcomed after sitting in the stuffy rafters.

"What did you think?" I ask, arms folded, as we walk through a garden of hedges planted behind the Arman.

"I think you cry easily." He boasts his indifference, not looking at me as we pace forward on the cobblestone. I stop abruptly before a turn in the garden walls, causing him to do the same. I stare for a moment, under that impossible expression staring back at me.

"I will not apologize for being soft. Not in a world that holds bitterness and hatred above all else. I have earned the right to cry in this life, whenever and wherever I feel like it. And when I see something beautiful, I will cry. Because we are robbed so often of such things in these harsh times." I look him up and down, knowing he is a lost cause, but still, I find myself pathetically trying to show him the why.

"Go on," he breathes.

"Those people in there have sacrificed their lives to play music. To give people something that helps them process emotions and gives them a sense of purpose or belonging. You might not be able to hear the music the way others do, but that does not make it insignificant. You are not the judge of importance."

He contemplates again. Calculating. Searching the Arman Theatre behind me. I glance too, can't help but give the building the attention it deserves. The back is a reflection of the front, tall pillars and the wraparound steps. Steps I have spent my whole life imagining I would one day get to walk up. Steps that have become as sacred as The Faits or the Divine.

"I heard it."

My head snaps back to Calix, his words quick as he avoids looking me straight in the eye. He stares off anywhere else, to the hedges, to the theatre, to the stars. He has changed back to the soft Calix before my eyes, the act of circumstance melting.

"Calix Hendricks, did you just say you understand what I am talking about?" At the use of his full name, his eyes snap to mine. He takes a deep breath, running his hand over his face.

"I heard it. I did not say that I understand you, I said I heard it. When we were sitting up there—" He pauses, shaking his head, opening his mouth and closing it, his jaw feathering.

"What?" I take a step closer. He sighs, his breath visible in the air, swirling with silent melody.

"When we were up there, I glanced at you, and you were somewhere else. Lost in the sound, and there was a look on your face. You were at peace, but your brows would furrow, like you were following in conversation. I have been around Court my whole life, but always at a distance, removed. Even if I could have seen people's reactions to the symphony, no one in Court wears their emotions as easily as you do. I heard it then, the depth, the something more that I am still not privy to. I don't understand it, and I still think this all—" he motions behind us to the theatre, "a waste of money in the extravagant way we spend it, but maybe it is not all for nothing."

"Calix Hendricks," I breath again, in awe of his honesty.

"Darling, I'd really prefer it if you'd stop calling me that." He adjusts his shirt cuff from beneath his coat. His eyes link arms with the shadows of the night, skipping over to look at me.

"It's your name, isn't it?"

"Just Cal. Just call me Cal."

I don't answer, unsure of the proper response. He stares at me, fighting for words too. We start walking again, through the hedges and starlight.

"Why do you favor your ankle so much? What happened to it?" Calix finally asks.

"I broke it as a child, and we didn't have the supplies to care for it properly."

"I have never known such want," he admits, as if it's something he has pondered and had to reconcile before.

"Perhaps that is why my world—painting, the Arman, writing—is so hard for you to grasp. When you're rich, you have no need for the arts, you see no lack of empathy in yourself. You don't need to be assured that you're not the only one suffering." He isn't defensive at my words, he just nods and thinks over them.

We stop walking again, having made a small circle around the garden and back up to the theatre. He turns to me, jaw feathering.

"Yes, but just because I have money doesn't mean I am not suffering."

He lets me look at him, doesn't try to hide behind his words, as he tells me he does with most everyone else. I'm not sure how I earned this, but if I think too hard about it, it makes my stomach hurt.

"Then, perhaps no one gets out of life without such plagues."

"Though some bear it better than others." His grin isn't the leading kind, but instead almost—pure. Could such a word be used to describe the prince?

"Careful, that almost sounds like a compliment."

"You don't have to say that as if it would end the world if it was," he laughs from deep within, so genuine it pulls a laugh from me as well.

"Not end it—maybe halt it for a few moments while processing the anomaly."

"Well then, I should start to make a habit of passing out compliments, if only so when they come around, I don't cause a catastrophic event."

"Do you really foresee yourself finding need to pass out more compliments?"

"If you continue to stick around, then yes."

I falter. He laughs.

"I should be getting to bed—I have an early morning tomorrow. Would you like me to walk you back to your house?"

"No, I have a few things to do backstage before I retire."

"Goodnight, darling." He nods slightly and then leaves me alone in the gardens.

I hate everything Calix represents. So why do I want nothing more than to follow him?

17

“**Y**ou all are amazing,” I smile as Calliope and Anoki run through the final act.

Tears are brought to the eyes of all those who stopped their jobs to watch. Even mine. I never thought that my words could be more than written on a page. Sure, the people in the Hovel loved my short stories, and I don't discount the difference it made in them, but I think any writer, any artist, secretly dreams of their work making a difference on a large scale. It was my most pointless dream, one I would never utter aloud, not even to myself.

The Company brings to life my words in a way I didn't even know to hope for. I can hardly breathe, hardly think, when I see the things I scribbled become living in front of me. My characters speak, cry, laugh, coming off the paper and to the stage in front of me. Daily, I tear up at the fact that though this is a horrible place, and I am being forced to do this, this is the very thing that makes my life worth living.

In the back of my mind, I always feared the thing I loved so much would never love me back. But then, Anoki speaks, and Calliope sheds a tear, and Ira cracks a joke. All following the lead that my words prompted. Telling a story that has been brewing in me since I stepped over the border of Hedeon.

We run through the second half of the play once more before we've exceeded our time for the day. Some string quartet has the stage for a dress rehearsal tonight, so we have to clean up quickly and evacuate. Most of the Company is going out for drinks, and by twisting my arm, or more literally, linking arms and dragging me with them, I agree to go.

The Krepost is buzzing tonight, rest-days upon us and everyone abandoning what little responsibilities Court has. We are so far down the Krepost that the Zamak stands as a moon in the distance, calling the tides of Court back and forth at its will. Pubs and taverns line both sides of the road, people fill the sidewalks and street, so busy that no carriages dare pass through. Court lovingly refers to this part of the Krepost as Otbrosy Road. The word confused me the first time I heard it, but the closest way I can translate it into Reinen is *the remnants left at the bottom of an ale barrel.*

A man shouts from a doorway of a pub, waving us in, a boyfriend of one of the actors, but I can't keep straight who. Humidity drips from my skin the moment we enter the pub. So many people cram into the small space, hardly any room for breathing remains. Women sit on the bar top, and men stand with arms around each other's shoulders. The perfume of sweat and alcohol dance around us, just as the revelers do. We follow behind the boyfriend in a small line, my hand wrapped in Pasha's, so I don't lose her as we squeeze between drunks.

A booth waits for us at the back of the room, an alcove cut into the wall. The ten or so of us slide in, a waitress quickly placing mugs on the table. Someone passes out cards, and despite the noise in the tavern, we start a round of Daruuk.

"Who wants to put money down?" Kolyo asks. Most of us shake our heads, hardly having money to sustain us, certainly not enough to just gamble away.

"I'll take you," Myka rises to the challenge with a lift and chug of her glass.

"Are you sure that's a good idea?" Pasha puts her hand on Myka's arm.

"I have had a terrible week and want to blow what little I have to my name. So, if it's alright with you all, I am going to take you." She firmly holds Kolyo's stare. A grin grows and he nods, putting some coin down too.

I understand the feeling of wanting to take back control, because that is a word that hardly exists anymore—it belongs to the Crown, just like everything else.

Kolyo deals six cards to each of us, flipping over the final card and placing the deck on top of it. Deacon plays first, moving the defense onto me. I can't raise his attack, so it moves to Pasha. She defends.

We discard, deal, and repeat time after time, the money going back and forth between Kolyo and Myka. I have no luck in cards, have never been very good at them. Almost humorously bad, actually. But no one is paying attention to me, instead, we are all joking and laughing and hardly considering the cards in our hand. It's the first reprieve I've had in days, in weeks even.

When any part of the Crown is around, I process myself through their eyes. Caring too much about how they see me, wanting every action to come across the right way, every word landing exactly where I mean it to. I am a curated version of myself, primped and preened, and as well-mannered as I can be, though I admit I fail often around Calix. But when I fail, I am still worried, still assessing myself and dwelling on all the ways I could have acted better. Sitting here with the Company, I am myself, with no need to care how I look to others. I live without imagining how I look to someone else. For this rare moment in my life, I forget myself.

"Don't bring up that show," Myka whines, finding better spirits, as the night removes the weight of those prior.

We've all abandoned our cards for mugs of ale, forgetting that anyone put coin down in the first place.

"I will be long dead before I ever stop bringing it up," Kolyo chuckles in his deep voice.

"It's embarrassing."

"You couldn't help yourself, and you didn't know he was a duke," Pasha pats Myka on the back as she buries her head in her hands.

"A duke?" I balk. "What happened?"

Calliope is the one to answer, in her soft voice, the blow is lighter. "After one of our shows up North, we were invited to a ball being held in our honor that we hadn't been prepared for. Myka was walking across the ballroom when she spotted a young man—"

"He was just so cute!" Myka interrupts her, burying her head even further.

Calliope continues, "Attack would be too strong a word for what happened—"

Dilean cuts in with a laugh, "Attack is exactly what happened! I was on the other side of the ballroom, and I saw it all play out. My drink came through my nose! I spit it all over a girl I was talking to, but honestly, it was worth it."

"I have horrible luck. Always have," Myka adds from her folded position.

Calliope resumes the story, "She was heading toward the man who we all now know is the duke. Myka was planning on just talking to him, offering him a drink. She had two chalices in her hand and was walking with that confidence I so admire. Well, the heels she was wearing weren't hers, and therefore, were slightly big. She tripped, right in front of the duke, and sent both her drinks through the air, drenching him from head to toe!"

The snickers the Company were trying to hold, break from their restraints. The sounds of the pub are covered by their laughter.

"They were not small chalices," Dilean grabs my arm and bursts with another laugh.

"We all told Myka it was a bad idea, that she should have waited until he was done talking to the noblemen he was surrounded by," Pasha adds.

"The company he was keeping should have been a clue to his identity," Ira says quietly.

"Oh, Myka. That is horrible!" I try to comfort her. She lifts her head to me, finally showing her face.

"He was so sweet about it in the moment. It made the whole thing so much worse. And these fools," she motions to the Company around the table, "were all huddled together giggling. Everyone saw, and now I am no longer allowed to show my face in Sevar ever again."

I can't contain my laugh, "They banned you from the whole of Sevar?"

"They banned *all of us* from the whole of Sevar," Deacon confirms.

That sends the Company into another fit of laughter.

Before I know it, last call is shouted, and everyone is staggering out, finding some other place to drink or somewhere to sleep. Pasha drags me along, begging me to continue with the rest of them.

"You have no duties tomorrow morning, come on. I think we are going to go to Myka's apartments, and aren't you just dying to see what those look like? We are going to play some marble game that the lot of them won't stop talking about. It will be loads of fun." She rambles in the kind of intoxication that can only come with a lack of sleep. She, unlike the rest, didn't have much ale, nevertheless, she blends in with the crew.

"I wouldn't be able to make it through the game, Pasha. I am much too tired." I pull out of her hand slowly, walking backward up toward the Zamak.

"Fine, then. We will see you in the new week," she waves. "Everyone, say goodnight to Damira," she yells behind her as she walks backward, arms out, grasping toward me. Everyone yells their goodnight, smiling and waving and so full of life.

I stumble home—well, not home—more from tiredness than ale. My head spins with all the laughing I did tonight, and I can't shake the grin that has found permanence on my lips. I'm not sure there was a time I have ever laughed so hard. The Hovel has a way of dampening the sound, quieting it before it even starts.

The air of the night is almost as intoxicating as the ale, freshness that I gulp down in excess. It's a pleasant walk, all the way up, and through the gates. I enter the house on quiet feet, the fireplace lit, a figure sitting on the couch in front of it.

I still, not reacting fast enough. The shadow stands and turns to me.

Uncle Sumood.

I exhale, near crumbling.

"Sumood, you gave me a fright," I exhale in a whisper, walking over to hug him.

"Katiya." I look past him, toward the back of the house.

"She's been asleep for hours, didn't hear me come in." He walks me over to the fire. I unclasp my cloak and jacket, discarding it to the couch behind us.

"Why are you here? Is Aunt Selah alright? Myla?"

"They're fine. We're fine. I wanted to come check on you. Tenny hasn't heard from you in a while, and though I can't take an official report, I wanted to make sure my niece was doing alright." He smiles, pulling me into another hug.

"How is everyone else?" I ask, sitting on the couch when he releases me. All the curtains are drawn shut, we will hear Katiya long before we see her. We are free to speak. To hear Reinen on each other's tongue.

"Better since you and Cal came. We've been receiving a mysterious amount of extra shipments from the Crown. Food, clothing, and coin. Your aunt and I are under the impression it is from your prince." He smiles, sitting beside me, close enough I could draw into him if I wanted. When I was a kid, I would have, even a few months ago I might've, but whatever small amount of innocence I was clawing to keep, has been stripped from me since becoming a spy for my kingdom in the palace.

"Calix? Has been sending you coin? That is highly unlikely," I laugh, looking into the fire.

"See the good in people, Mira." Uncle Sumood puts his hand on my folded knee.

"When they have done something to deserve it, I will," I stubbornly retort. I'm not entirely sure I even believe my own words. I'm just so tired of being constantly asked to give more than I hold.

"None of us deserve it. We are all sinful people, in some way or another. But we push on, trying to be better than the day behind, hoping those in our life will give us the benefit of the doubt. How many times have you been forgiven when you didn't deserve it? That is what we give back to others. People are not as wicked as they might seem—we are all just doing what we think is best."

My mind flashes to lying to Calix, trying to get the information about the coffers while he was showing more of himself to me.

Perhaps we all do need some forgiveness.

"I do want to see the best in people," I admit.

I wish to be forgiving, in spite of the unkind life The Faits have dealt me. But, at the end of the day, I think I am shamefully just as hardened as one would expect in my circumstances. I don't know how Aunt Selah and Uncle Sumood do it. I don't know what secret they've managed to uncover, while the rest of us sit in our bitterness. Even when they have seen the horrors of the Crown, of people in general, they still choose the kindness that has not been awarded to them in life. It's otherworldly. It's hope I wish to have.

"Have I ever told you of the time your father and I found ourselves on the wrong side of the border?" he asks, leaning back onto the couch. I shake my head.

"We were riding, almost a day away from Cotea. Your father had just had his heart broken. Little did he know, your mother would come around a few weeks later and make him forget anyone else had ever existed. We knew we should have turned around, but your father kept asking for a little more distance, a little more time away. So, we rode. Nightfall came, and we were a great distance from home, though we weren't sure how far. Thierry never admitted it, but we were lost. Right after sunset, we came upon a small hut, not much bigger than this room. We knocked, hoping to seek shelter, and an older couple welcomed us in and let us stay the night. It was in the chatting that we discovered we were in Hedeon. And you know what the couple did?" He pauses for my answer.

"Kicked you out and gave you that bullet wound?" I poke his upper arm, where I know a scar is gouged. He never would tell me that story.

The southernmost part of Reine used to be its own kingdom, before a war in Sumood's youth united the two. I always have assumed the scar came from those times, the times he never talks about. He was young and claims Reine has been a better home to him than the kingdom he was born under. Such an answer has never satisfied my curiosity.

"No. We continued talking and laughing, and then they fed us and gave us somewhere to sleep. They said the war was between two kings long ago, and they had no skin in the game, therefore, they could care less what color our flag waved. At some point, Damira, we must stop fighting wars on behalf of those long dead. If it doesn't end with them, then let it start with you." His words are dangerous, not because they speak of treasonous things—we always speak of dangerous things—but because of the righteous indignation flaring in his eyes.

"I'm not sure I contain that much forgiveness," I concede, readjusting my ankle and turning back to the fire. This forgiveness Sumood speaks of is what I have been trying to convey in my play, what I have been trying to show the people of Hedeon, but how will my audience learn these truths if I can't learn them myself?

"You contain multitudes, ma lumière principale."

My leading light.

A pet name, but something more. An honor. A Reinen name of high calling reserved to only those you would follow into the darkness.

He forces me to look him back in the eye, meeting me with a soft smile.

"I need to be getting back, I'm sure your aunt is worrying already." He stands, walking to the door. I follow, wrapped in a knit blanket.

"What were you doing out so late?" He pauses in the open doorway, turning to me with a grin.

"I made friends," I smile.

We don't talk about the play, he knows better than to ask me, because then I will have to lie or tell him the truth. Either way, worrying will come about. We are on a need-to-know basis, just like the Network condones.

"Good for you, Mira." He kisses me on the forehead and dissolves into the night.

Sitting in the pub tonight, laughing and playing cards with the Company, I understand what Sumood spoke of, putting an end to a war that was started long ago. That's what I want too, an end. But, unlike the elderly Hedeon couple, I can't go quietly. I do have skin in the game. And lots of blood.

The blood of my people.

My family.

My parents.

While I do not know if I contain the multitudes Uncle Sumood is so sure about, something in me thaws at the thought of a certain prince giving food and coin to a people I thought he cared so little about.

18

T HE DOUBLE DOORS ARE unlocked, so I take that as invitation enough to let myself in. Even the maids are scarce today, as everyone is resting on their off-day. I've never had the opportunity to rest, and I am still unsure of how to sit still. So, when the hallways are quiet and I can't stand to paint anymore, I wander.

Which has led me to this part of the Zamak. The hallway is darker, flat black wallpaper with shiny black patterns, with only small windows breaking it up. I close the door quietly behind me and wind through the hall. The carpet under foot silences my steps. I have never been told I couldn't roam the grounds freely, but I am still cautious in all my exploring—my searching for information. Lev says there are eyes on me, but the Crown must be confident in their outside security measures, because there are not many guards around the inside of the Zamak.

I turn a sharp corner, rooms appearing on either side of the hallway. A small song starts at the end of the corridor, growing in confidence as I get closer. A violin. The melody is flowing out of a room to the left, carrying on the air, washing over me. In my experience, violins are a tricky instrument, only allowing themselves to be played by those who have the softest touch. I never tried to master the fickle things. Despite the challenge, whoever plays has understood the instrument so intimately.

I stall by the doorway, listening before I look in. The song grows like the wells of a sea, rising and dissolving. Each note pulls the other, like two kids holding hands and spinning in circles. The melody runs down the sidewalk, skipping and jumping in a summer breeze. It runs back up with arms out, pretending it's flying through the wind. The song slows, becoming a bit less confident. It's not because of confusion necessarily, but fear maybe, apprehension.

I peak past the doorway, mindful to stay hidden in the shadows. I trip myself at the sight, staggering in accidentally. Calix doesn't look as surprised as he should—as surprised as I feel.

"You shouldn't spy, darling, it's rather rude."

If only he knew.

He removes the violin from under his chin, the bow dangling at his side. I move entirely into the grand room full of instruments. The decorations are similar to the Arman, everything gold and accented by gold. If the sight of an instrument in Calix's hand didn't already make him stand out against the light colors, then the all-black outfit he's wearing would.

"You play the violin?" I gape.

"I did, when I was younger. I haven't picked it up since I was seven or eight." He leaves his statement open for questions, but all I can do is stare.

Calix, the prince who had a hard time sitting still for the symphony. Calix, who has had nothing but disdain for what I am doing. Calix, who falls asleep during rehearsals. Calix can play the violin, not only play, but has an expert's understanding of it for a kid of seven or eight.

"You're a prodigy."

An even bigger surprise. How much do I actually know about Calix?

"That word has been thrown around, yes," he shrugs, as if the title is just as easy to gain as being prince. He softly places the violin down next to the stand that holds the music he was playing, and I laugh. Out loud.

"Why did you stop playing? Why did you pick it back up today? Can you teach me how to do that?" The assault of questions flings themselves from my mouth.

He laughs to himself, shaking his head. "One thing at a time, Mira."

Calix motions to the pair of chairs off to the side, and I eagerly sit, not just so I can get answers, but because the rain outside has caused my ankle to flare up and welcome the reprieve. A porcelain tea set is arranged atop a table between the chairs, a story of some kind painted in figures along the side. He disregards the finery, propping one foot up on the table. I wait for him to settle before I pick a question out of the storeroom in my mind.

"If you haven't played since you were young, what made you pick it back up today?" I ask.

"You." The fact he states isn't filled with shame, there is no bruising of pride in his admittance. He leans back, both arms spread on the sides of the chair that encompasses him. To the credit of Calix, he always has a way of saying what he is thinking. He is not shy of his emotions or thoughts. The boys I grew up with always put on a front of impenetrable armor, pretending they never felt anything. It makes me a degree more partial to him.

He waits for me to speak. Of course, I need to speak.

"I made you pick up the violin again?" I mean to say the words with smugness, with an air of inevitability that I would get to him. But they come out with confusion, uncertainty in his meaning.

"Ask me your other question," he nods slightly, lifting his chin to me.

"Why haven't you played since you were young?"

"My dad was the one to teach me. Or at least the one to get me into playing. I tried to play after he left, but it made me feel as if I was trying to be like him. And I didn't want to be anything like the man." He keeps eye contact with me as he speaks, pulling the words up from somewhere deep and dusting them off to show them daylight for the first time in a while. He exhales, running a hand over his face and leaning forward.

"And then you happened. I heard you play the piano that day in the Arman with all of that emotion, you showed me the symphony, you talk about how important these things are, and I got curious. I wanted to know I wasn't the only one suffering."

A silence lingers between us as I try to understand all of these new fragments of information presented to me. He heard me play the piano, he didn't think the symphony was useless, he's actually listening to the things I say, pondering them.

"I've heard you've been sending supplies and coin to my family," I change the subject, but not entirely because these things are connected in my mind. Calix sending coin, Calix playing the violin, Calix not being the monster I thought him to be. I am putting together pieces of a new man in my mind.

He straightens a bit, like he's been caught sinning against the Divine.

"Why would you do that? You have been pestering your mom to stop spending coin, and here you are giving it away?"

"I've been asking my mom to stop spending it so thoughtlessly. The people in the Hovel need the coin. You heard the queen scold me. She was right, in a way. The soldiers' fight will all be for nothing if they return to a kingdom filled with only bodies. I have heard the tales from my grandmother's reign, the war she amped on, the lives she took out of sheer cruelty. I used to see the Cassis massacre in my nightmares. I will not reign like that. I will take care of my people."

How did these rumors stick about Calix being the echo of his grandmother? Just as ruthless and more than half as cunning? The more I learn about him, the more these perceptions are shattered. He is hardly anything like the grandmother I have met. The front he has put on for years to protect the tales his mother spreads, has certainly been convincing. He always weighs his words when he speaks to me, and I am only just beginning to catch on to the fact that, perhaps, for some reason, he trusts me enough to not lie like he does to everyone else.

"Thank you." I've only ever seen Calix as the prince, not the future king. It is only now that I see the possibilities of his potential. That he is more than the son of the queen. I wonder if that is why he tries so hard, because the women who have come before him cast such great shadows. He must be something bigger altogether to merely be noticed.

"I wish you wouldn't be so surprised by such a humane act of kindness from me, darling," he whispers. It wretches my breath from me, but I am not sure if it is from the statement or the purpose in his gaze. Or the fact that this is the first time he has called me "darling," and I am not annoyed by it.

"Will you play something else?" I ask.

He stands, picking the violin back up, so naturally placing it below his chin and rattling off a quick rhythm. I lean over the arm of the chair, watching this prince who is an enigma wrapped in a bow of mystery.

The melody he chooses is different from the one I overheard earlier. This one is solemn, cold. Broken pieces making a stained-glass mosaic. He closes his eyes, dipping and rising with the rhythm. The melody reminds me of the song we are stuck on in the fourth act of the play. Confusion and careful footing. Deacon and I had written the final moments of the play to be a big fanfare, the confronting of the main characters, the orchestra building up to a crescendo. But what if it is this? Cautious steps, soft words, and unsurety. Flames can't start without a spark. And how wavering are sparks, after all.

The melody dies slowly, a candle blown out. He opens his eyes, stalling for a moment, tracing me. He removes the violin and offers it in my direction. "You said you wanted me to teach you."

I move across the room to him, grabbing the instrument and pulling it up to my shoulder, the small neck awkward in my hands.

"Here. Pull the end pin up so your chin is in the rest correctly." Calix stands against my left shoulder, gently pulling my hair out of the way, tucking it behind my ear. A chill goes down my spine, and by The Faits, I hope he doesn't feel it. He grabs the end of the violin, hand covering my own, and pulls it closer to my neck. My fingers must be wrong on the strings—how could they not be on the wrong strings with his distracting presence—so he moves them, showing me how much pressure I need to put down. He then pulls my shoulders, pushing the small of my back to correct my posture. I can't find a breath.

Hedeon morals are out the window.

He moves in front of me, the phantom of his heat lingering at my back.

"Bring this elbow up more." He gently places his hand below my elbow and pulls up, stepping back to admire his work. "Beautiful." He smiles softly, genuinely, contrasting the sharp lines of his face.

He doesn't wear such a smile often, so it surprises me how easily it finds its way there.

I push the bow, creating a shrieking sound that attacks our ears.

"Keep the bow up and then down," he instructs with a laugh, moving my fingers so my pointer finger lays correctly on the bow, my thumb barley touching my middle finger. He pushes and pulls my hand so I can get the feel of the strokes. It's a lot like painting, back and forth, light and controlled.

He comes back around to my side, repositioning my left wrist. I pull the bow back across the strings, sounding slightly better, but still bad enough to cringe at. His laugh is beautiful when he forgets he's trying to be someone else.

I look up at him, across my shoulder. He already stares down at me, our eyes slamming into one another's. His hair hangs over his forehead, his bright green eyes rimmed with flecks of gold. His head leans in, just slightly, hesitantly. The corner of my lip pulls up, urging him that this is okay. Or at least, I think this is okay. I shouldn't be this close to the lineage of my enemy, shouldn't be letting him get closer. I should be trying to get information from him. I am a spy. Horridly unprepared and untrained, but still a spy in enemy territory.

But I let him lean in.

Our foreheads touch, our breath the same air.

"Mira—" Calix breathes, a beginning of a thought he can't finish. My name belongs on his tongue, never sounding as right as it does than when it comes from him. I don't move, and neither does he. Our noses touch, our lips so close I don't dare flinch. It takes all the strength in me to not reach out further.

He makes a fluid movement, but instead of pressing in further, he takes a stride back. I blink a few times, dropping my hands down, the violin and bow dangling at my hip.

"I need to be going." He jumps back in haste, bending at the hip in aptness, and turning to leave without another word.

19

R aven insisted we start our morning with a walk around the yards. Arm in arm we stroll, eyes stuck to us when we pass anyone. The gown Raven picked out for me pinches my waist, demanding slow steps as to not work up a heavy breath. Just as everything is not as it looks in Court, a walk isn't simply a walk. It is a show for onlookers. Another play with different actors.

I haven't seen Calix in a few days, as he has been mysteriously missing from dinner and rehearsals. No one even mentions his name. I don't dare ask where he is, for fear of the answer. I have pushed the incident from my mind, forgetting it ever happened. No matter what I thought I felt for the prince, he is a prince and from Hedeon. Nothing could have, should have, realistically happened. It doesn't make it feel any less like there's an anvil sitting in my stomach, though.

"You have a final fitting in three days, and after that, we can talk about your hair and makeup. Can you believe we are just a week from the Revel? It has rushed up so fast. Wait until you see the silks and flowers I've chosen to decorate the halls. The whole Zamak will be transformed in a matter of days. It is truly my favorite time of year." She uses her free hand to gesture as she talks. Raven, unlike Calix, is full of information when she talks to me.

Opening day is in two weeks. The second week hardly counts because we will all be preoccupied with the festivities leading up to it, like the ball. Even more than the thought of Calix, the coming of my doom weighs heavily.

"I am just thankful for the warmer weather," I admit, only a light cloak on my shoulders today. The sun is out and warming my face for the first time in months. The air is cleaner up here than in the Hovel, and all I want to do is sit in the grass and breathe deeply.

"Spring in the Krepost is so wonderful. Just you wait until the middle of spring when—" She starts, but trails off, I'm sure realizing I won't be here in the height of the season. Three weeks, and I will be on tour with the Company, if everything continues as the queen plans. If I don't end up in the cells for my questionable crimes. Months on the road, and then my future stops at the will of whatever Milena demands.

"Well, I suppose you won't be here, but when you return, it will be autumn, and oh, how I adore autumn!" She hardly misses a beat, moving on without confronting the truth. Raven speaks in absolutes I have never been able to match. When I return. Not if. Under different circumstances, I might have been allowed to stay when tour is over, but we might not even get to a tour in the first place. Though no one knows that, but me and the Company.

"A hopeful thought," I pat her hand on my arm.

We turn with the path, coming face to face with a field of head-stones on the horizon.

"Is that a family cemetery?" I pull from Raven and go off the path.

"Yes, the ancestors that weren't killed or lost in the war are buried here. Calix and I used to play in it as kids. A bit morbid, I suppose." Her words catch up to me before she does. A breeze helps us up the small incline.

A fence surrounds the graves, falling apart and rotting from years of neglect. The gate swings open with barley a touch, scraping on the ground in a run-through path. Its squeal alerts the dead that we are entering.

Magnificent stones sprout from the ground—marble and lime-stone and granite. All as grand as those who lie beneath them, I am sure. Moss grows on the side and tops of a few, some crumble under the weight of age, and some are planted so close to each other they look more like one than two.

A garden of strange flowers.

"That is my four-times grandfather." Raven points to a stone that looks like a sword plunged into the grass. The one who started the war. I squat in front of it, reading the name and epitaph.

King Glavnok Omanduy Ushchiy Hendricks.

Loyal lover of justice. A strong fist with a warm heart.

A chill runs down my spine. Decomposed underground, and blood is still being shed on his behalf. Generations gone, and we haven't learned from the mistakes he made. I look up at Raven, the same look in her eye as the day we spoke in the gallery.

"No matter how much we evolve, one thing remains," I whisper, her own words repeated back to her. She nods, taking one last glance at the grave and slowly moving to the next. We go down the line, reading each name, a short history uttered of the ones Raven recognizes.

"This is my grandfather's."

We stop in front of a headstone in the form of a silhouette that reminds me of a cathedral. Even more than the grandfather that started all of this, this man was married to the grandmother who made the world burn to its very roots.

"All that is good and the Divine," I breathe. Raven nods.

We've never spoken the treasonous words, but I am sure we feel the same about the war. Raven doesn't have the throne to protect her words like Calix does. He is the future king, and thus, has fewer consequences for a liberal tongue. Where Calix's thoughts could be skewed as visionary when he reprimands the queen, Raven's could simply get her branded a traitor. I understand why she longs for the throne.

"How did he die?" I ask. She doesn't answer immediately, but drinks in the silence.

"No one is certain." The things she doesn't say come through more than the things she finally does. I wait, asking for more. Her eyes dart around, to behind us where the emptiness of the trail waits for our return.

"I am rather confident it was my grandmother. He didn't agree with her—methods. He thought we could reach a place of peace. He saw an end, but she wouldn't hear of it. I was too young to remember him, but hearing the whispers, knowing my grandmother—I am quite sure it was her." She whispers, even though we are far from the palace or anyone to overhear us.

"She was the queen, couldn't she just have him beheaded? Why the secrecy?"

"Politics. She didn't want to seem weak by murdering a husband she couldn't get to comply. Could you imagine the image that would send to Hedeon? A queen that can't convince her own spouse to be on her side? What hope would she have of controlling her people? Besides, his blood was the one to inherit the throne, not hers. It wasn't her call to make."

I nod, understanding in what little way I can. "That's terrifying."

"I've always taken after my grandfather, or so my mom tells me. I don't find myself alone in a room with my grandmother if I can help it." She laughs a little, as if she didn't just suggest her grandmother would have her killed too.

I follow Raven through the rest of the cemetery and back through the leaning gate. The sun has risen in the sky, bringing with it the lunch hour. We head back to the Zamak, our stomachs grumbling in conversation with one another's.

Such a nice day at the end of winter would cause the Zamak to be in an uproar of activity, but silence is like a layer of dust over everything, the moment we step inside. We rush silently to the Crown's apartments, not having to exchange anything other than a look to know we need to find someone quick.

In the Solar, Calix and his mother stand eerily close, the anger steaming from both of them almost visible. Someone has just shouted, but I can't tell which one. Calix and his mother share the same iron, and neither of them back down. The queen mother and Lev watch the fight silently from the side of the room, a small smile perched on the queen mother's lips.

"Mother." Naturally, Raven jumps in quickly, pushing herself between the two.

"I am your queen," their mother likes to remind them often, but she points the words over Raven's shoulder, to Calix.

"For how much longer, Mother?" Calix spits, allowing himself to be pushed back by Raven.

"Calix, watch how you speak." Raven hisses the words like venom, coming to her mother's aid. He rolls his eyes and turns abruptly.

"Sucking up will not gain you the throne, Rave." He throws the words over his shoulder, leaving right past me. I stare at my feet until he's out of the room. Raven sends a plea to me, her eyes begging for some kind of help. I nod as she turns back to her mother, trying to calm Milena's reddened face.

I move to follow Calix. He doesn't go far, through the court-yard, turning a hallway, and moves through double doors. I enter cautiously behind him, not sure if it is considered treasonous to follow him in.

He has a foyer to his bedroom. I'm not sure what I expected from a prince, but I always seem to underestimate the grandeur that comes with the title.

The room itself has one wall made of windows, thick curtains pulled and tied to the side. It is all rather messy for what I imagined his rooms to be. Not that I've imagined his rooms. His bed is unmade, clothes thrown around haphazardly. Books lie open on flat spaces, wherever they can find. Swords hang on the walls, six of them in total, each having a small cut out in the brick in order to display them.

"I don't want to talk about it." He throws the words. They grapple toward me and pin my feet to where I stand. We haven't spoken since he failed to kiss me, since I realized I might have actually wanted him to kiss me. However, I doubt that is why he doesn't want to speak to me now.

He grabs a carpet bag from the bottom drawer of a wardrobe and tosses it onto the bed. I stand awkwardly, unsure if I should speak or leave, or maybe just disappear into the floor altogether. My eyes dart across the room, taking it all in, hoping the walls will tell me what to say. The round desk in the corner to my right has papers littered on it, mathematic equations written in every blank space. I pick one up, but I am completely illiterate when it comes to the language of math.

"What are these?" I ask, hopelessly unable to understand them by myself. There are piles of these papers, different numbers, different solutions.

I glance at Calix when he doesn't answer. He's frozen on the other side of the room, a shirt dangling from his hand. His eyes burn the paper I hold. I set it back down carefully where I found it, realizing I must have stepped over a boundary in my curiosity.

"I'm sorry." I take a step toward the door to leave.

"No, it's fine." He stops me. "My mom just detests when I speak about my hobbies, so I am not used to having to explain. It's—" There he goes again, running through the field of words in his mind, searching for the right ones. "They're equations, data. I um—" He pauses again, transferring the shirt in his hand to the bag on the bed. I have never seen him so uncertain of himself. "I've been trying to figure out how to win the war with the least amount of deaths on both sides. Everything boils down to numbers, to statistics, so I thought maybe I could figure out where to strike and when, in order to save as many lives as we can. It's slow work, but I am making progress." He shrugs as if he hasn't just said the most beautiful words I have ever heard.

"You're trying to save both sides?" I repeat, making sure I heard him right.

"This isn't the soldiers' fight. It's hardly even the Crown's fight anymore. People who don't have to die, shouldn't. No matter which flag they wave."

I balk at myself, at how completely wrong about Calix I have stubbornly been.

He goes back to the dresser. Back and forth, back and forth. He piles the clothes on the bed, not into the bag.

"She is upset because I said I wouldn't fix the mess she has made, and now she's sending me to the warfront to do just that." He doesn't look at me.

"She's sending you to the warfront?" I stagger out. He starts folding and shoving the clothes into the bag, facing me now, across the bed. He looks up briefly, analyzing my reaction, and then back down to his hands.

"We've nearly run out of money, and only now does she realize what an imposition that is. But she won't call back the festivities for the Revel, and instead of allowing me to try and sort through the ledgers, she's sending me straight to the front line to get a firsthand account. A punishment for being right and telling her as much." He walks over to the chest and pulls out a drawer.

He stops suddenly, splaying his hands on the bureau as he takes a deep breath. He looks up at me through the reflection in the mirror on top of the vanity. His dark hair falls over his forehead, the curls almost reaching his eyes.

"Calix." I have no better words. His brow wavers, the muscles in his jaw feathering as he suppresses whatever it is he's feeling.

"I can't—" He cuts off his own words, turning around and rushing toward me.

He embraces me without hesitation. I stagger back at the force, but he holds me upright, his arms around my shoulders. I bury my head into his chest, my hands wrapped around his back. His heart races against my ear, the fear he won't show anyone, audible only to me.

"How long will you be gone?" Even if there were other people in the room, only he would be able to hear my words.

"She wouldn't say. Another part of the punishment."

I hug him tighter. Or he hugs me tighter. I'm not sure which. Either way, we press further into one another. I don't take the touch for granted. The lingering embrace means more than it ever could in Reine. I can't fathom what it means coming from him. I don't want him to let go.

How did we end up here?

"I'll see you when I get back, darling," he speaks softly, releasing me and throwing the last of his clothes into the bag. He grabs it off the bed and heads to the door. He stops only once, to nod at me, and give me a miserable excuse for a grin.

Then I am alone.

In Calix's room.

I scramble over to the desk, rummaging through the papers. I hate that this is where my mind immediately goes after such a sincere moment. But I have no time to question my allegiances.

Past the top layer of equations is orders to move troops, the next layer estimated reports of the treasury scrawled in terrible penmanship. It doesn't surprise me that the prince has such bad handwriting. A few papers are requests to send out ships to request coin from different allies across the sea, though they look unfinished. Either the ships didn't go out, or they returned empty-handed. And then, through the mess of paper, the one that will give reprieve to my people.

I hold it up, reading it over and over, memorizing how everything is stated so I won't forget a thing. Even if I was sure of when Calix would be back, I can't risk stealing the paper and being caught. I would be the first one to have fingers pointed at me. Calix left me in his rooms, knowingly. I don't stop to think of the trust that was so easily given. So easily betrayed.

I arrange the papers just how I found them, burying the treasure I found. I follow the way Calix left, heading back to the dining room to make sure everything has calmed and to check on Raven after hearing all the news I was privy to.

And then I will go back to my house. I have a pair of boots to set out.

20

T HE WALK THROUGH THE Krepost is cold. Just as plain as that. I stopped trying to make the sensation a beautiful metaphor some time ago. The nice day has turned rotten as the sun has set. It is cold, and miserable, and I am in a foul mood. Calix is leaving for the warfront, and I am a horrible person. I choose to believe it is the latter that makes me dreary company right now. The papers I've found might very well end this senseless war, and while I should be ecstatic, I have to wonder how far I will go for my kingdom, how far until I no longer recognize myself. It's not often I have such faithless thoughts, but the air is cold, and my ankle is beginning to throb from being on it all day.

Raven reacted well to Calix being sent off. Surprisingly, she didn't seem too fearful for her brother's safety, and I wonder if

Calix's aspersions of her relentless want of the throne might actually have some merit. Regardless, she still seemed a bit mad at her mother for the same things that angered Calix. To my knowledge, she would never say so to the queen, though. Raven never says anything to the queen's face in way of opposition.

I couldn't stand the silence of my house, so here I find myself, the most miserable walk there ever was. I round a bend, passing a tailor and a few other shops. A specter stands in front of the window to a bookstore that I have never seen open. Wrapped in pelts, standing still, not even letting the breeze move them. I approach with caution, and a face comes into view. I can barely make out blue eyes. A person truly lies underneath all that protection from the cold. She has a slim nose, blushed in frost and freckles, the only thing that really pokes out. She must be a beggar, or someone looking for shelter.

"Isn't it wonderful?" she whispers, a voice as light as the snowflakes starting to fall. I had thought we made it through the last of winter precipitation, but it seems I was mistaken.

"What is?"

Her eyes don't move from the window. I follow her glance as she lifts her finger, pressing it right up to the glass. A book by some author I have never heard of, written in the square language I am forced to always speak. I hate writing in Hedeon almost as much as I hate speaking it. It's always disheartening to read back my stories in the harsh language.

"I heard there are women authors here, but I hadn't believed it much. I thought it was just a fairytale, like dragons and people who can control the tides." She talks aloud, hardly caring about my presence beside her, as she has more important things occupying her. Her accent is smooth, unlike Hedeon or even Reine, it slurs the letters, pouring one word into the next.

I'm not sure how she got here, but she must be from across the sea if she speaks of Hedeon having women authors. I haven't heard of such things not being legal anywhere in Nadez. She can't peel her eyes from the book, and I can't blame her. Her ink-stained fingers, which barely poke out from her cloak, tell me all I need to know. What a sacred moment it must be for her. I look down to my glove-covered fingers, knowing the same sight lies beneath them.

"You must have travelled a far way." I take my gloves off and hand them to her.

"Oh, no!" She pushes my gloves back, but I persist. Her eyes lock onto my own fingers, understanding we are one and the same.

We share a knowing smile, and she takes the gloves with hesitation, pulling them on. Her eyes go back to the window.

"Back home, my words don't matter because I was born a woman," she whispers—to me or the book, is yet to be seen. "I am thought of as less than my male counterparts because of a few differences in anatomy. They hold strong to the ideology that I have nothing to say. Ironically, in the oppression, I think I find more words. Nevertheless, when I heard of the strange phenomenon in your kingdom, I had to come and see for myself." Though her accent is thick, she is eloquent in a way someone of higher education would be, especially for this clearly not being her first language.

"It's something I take for granted," I admit.

Behind the window, hundreds of authors' hearts sit, and from the titles I can see, an overwhelming amount have feminine names. I have felt oppression in many ways in my life, but my words have never been forbidden to come from my pen because the cosmos conspired to make me born a woman.

We are different but equal in Hedeon, in Reine. Back home, women train with the sword just as men do, but their maneuvers are different, playing up to their separate strengths. I have always thought writing the same. Though now, I may be questioning how far Hedeon is willing to allow this leniency to go. Will my play be banned when it is presented? Is there a limit placed on freedom, just because someone arbitrarily thinks they know better than the rest? Even if the queen doesn't see the commentary on Hedeon that I have written, she will, at the very least, see that I did not acquiesce to her original demands, and where will that land me?

The woman continues, "I have been writing since I learned to hold a pen. I was taught so I could write correspondence, but I stumbled across a notebook when I was seven and started writing stories. I hadn't realized it was wrong until I was fourteen, and one of my notebooks was stolen. I was relentlessly made fun of. It made me write even more—the anger had to be put somewhere. I have always dreamed of seeing a work of mine on a shelf. There is a kind of promise in seeing other women's names on the spine of a book, like I am closer than any of my ancestors have ever been. I write for all the women behind me, as if they're looking over my shoulder with each word. For them, my work will be bound. For them, I will say the things I mean. For them, I will prove we are worth listening to." The manifesto might as well be written beside her own stories, pasted right on the front cover. I have seldom heard such encouraging words.

"I think you could be very happy here," I admit, as much as I hate to do it. The thought of anyone happy in Hedeon makes me jealous that a life could be simpler than mine. "For all its faults, women are treated fairly equal here. If you keep writing, and if your written words are anywhere near as beautiful as your spoken ones, I am sure you will find someone to turn your dreams into reality in no time." I smile, though she still hasn't taken her eyes off the display.

Books suspend in the air, hung by strings. Books sit on the shelf, pressed to the glass. Books line the walls behind, arched to make hallways. It really is a beautiful sight.

With a deep sigh, she turns to me, piercing blue eyes crashing into me like waves. "I hope for a day when my country can be like your kingdom. A place where artistry is not banned, no matter the context or creator. It has been a pleasure talking with you." She bows her head, the hood made from fur shifting slightly. She walks off down the sidewalk, back the way I just came.

I didn't know how to tell her I'm not sure a place like that truly exists.

21

"**Y**OU HAVE GOT TO be kidding me," Tenny mutters more to herself than to me. I stretch my arms forward across the picnic table, eyes closed and lifted to the sun.

"And you don't know when he's coming back?" she asks. I shake my head. Tenny sits with one leg through the bench and one out, watching the boats pass through the canal. A river runs around the bottom of the Krepost, circling the whole thing. Less of Court comes down here, nobody of any propriety. It's a good place to meet Tenny.

That scarring night I sewed up Tenny, I brought her half-conscious state down here, to a safehouse the Network has. After the last week of recovering, and freshly dyed blonde hair, Tenny has taken up a new identity as a maid, thanks to my lie. She lives down here now, and works in the Zamak as needed.

Tenny hasn't told me what the outcome of her reckless night was, or why she is sure this new information I uncovered in Calix's room will fit nicely with what she found, but she told me not to worry, with a sort of glee in her voice.

I sigh. "The queen didn't give any kind of time frame. None of it feels right. Desperation hangs in the air of the Zamak. They're about to move the troops one way or another, no matter what Calix does there. Though, after looking at those papers, it seems against our favor—" I trail off, not being able to say the words. They have more troops than I could have imagined.

She breathes out, almost saying something but deciding against it.

Neither of us wears a cloak today, the weather of the past week has changed drastically. This is the first time she and I have been able to get away from our duties. The ball is in three days.

Three days, and we start the week of Revel.

Ten days until opening night.

Seven days since I've seen Calix.

"I will pass the word along to our people in Reine. If we can intercept the supply runs you uncovered, the Hedeon troops closer to Cotea might be forced to retreat even further. The information you found could be our saving grace," Tenny says.

I nod, finally opening my eyes. She stares with vehemence, her brow casting shadows over her eyes. Soldier through and through, despite her performance as a maid. I am not sure I have ever met anyone as strong as her. Her injuries still persist, though the black eye has gone down enough to look like lack of sleep, and the gash on her forehead is covered by newly cut bangs.

I look away, to the water, squinting, the sunlight glinting off the soft ripples from the breeze.

"Let's pretend we're people in Court. We can throw away our responsibilities and dive headfirst into the Revel. We can drink and sing and have no obligations to worry us." I spread my arms, swaying back and forth, as if I am dancing with a stranger.

"This is serious, Damira. People are dying while you play dress-up and dine with the Crown." Tenny's voice is full of resentment.

My gaze snaps back to her.

"You don't think I know that?"

"You're treating this like a joke."

"Every day, I am in those Zamak walls, praying to whatever Fait is listening that I am not betraying my people beyond penitence. I am working for the enemy, and it takes more and more restraint each day to not start screaming at the people who slaughtered my family. I am a ball of anger at all times. Just because I've had a lifetime to perfect hiding it, doesn't mean it's not there. So don't suggest that I am not taking this seriously, because I am putting myself and others in danger with this play, as a last effort to make a stand for what I believe in." I push away from the table, leaving her behind.

"Damira," she calls after me, and tries to make quick strides to get to my side. I glance at her, but don't slow down.

"I'm sorry. I didn't—I know you take this seriously. The Network appreciates all that you're doing. I didn't mean to suggest that you are just galivanting around without a care. The information you've given us will save what is left of our people. I am just as on edge as you are, and have a problem holding my tongue." Not many people wade around, but she still keeps her voice from carrying.

"Opening day is in a week. I can't have this distraction right now. Those papers can't be my burden. After opening night, I will do whatever you need—I will run, or I will hide, or I will set fire to the Krepost. But let me get through this week. Please."

"We can do that." She gives me a weary smile. I don't know how high up in the Network web Tenny is, but I know she holds some importance. Someone on the lower levels, like my aunt and uncle, wouldn't be trusted with this information.

"I meant to talk about this with you a few days ago, but the Network would like to offer you an official position with us." Tenny has been properly trained, lived as a spy in Reine, and was given a contract to work out here. She has other assets, other people who report to her, though she's never confirmed it to me. I might not be trained like she was, but I grew up in a double life. I catch onto things quickly. If she is the one offering me a position, it confirms that she holds some authority.

I am about to accept easily, when Tenny holds her hand up, halting the words on my tongue.

"Before you accept, I need you to know that the plan is to get you back to Reine quickly after the play is over." She fights the words on their way out, against her better judgment.

"And just leave the Company to the aftermath?"

She nods.

Can I leave them behind? Abandon them to deal with whatever the queen deems a worthy punishment? Though, perhaps with me gone, they can all plead innocence, lie, and say they were all just following my orders blindly.

"Take some time to think about it." I don't know why she extends me this grace, but it seems in these weeks she has started to understand me a bit more, at least enough to know how big of a choice this has become.

"I will."

"I'll see you in a week's time. Eyes and ears up." She nods, turning at the fork in the road. She heads for an alley, and I am to walk back up the steps of the mountain.

"Ears and eyes up," I mumble.

I can get through this week. Just get through this week, and then I can worry about the papers and getting my family safe and saving Reine. I have an overwhelming amount of things to do before then. Scratch all of that. I can get through these next ten minutes. Ten minutes is easy, shorter than a week. Yes, I can get through ten minutes.

I stop myself from slamming my head down on the piano. Calliope is not so constraint and does so for me. Deacon, who sits at the keys, stares at both of us with understanding. We are relearning the final scenes after the newest round of changes, and though it has been going well with the actors, the orchestra is struggling. Namely Deacon. Myka conducts at my side, but Deacon misses the run each time, stumbling over the wrong notes and then stopping altogether in a cry.

"Again," I mumble, ready to quit. If it wasn't for Deacon's stubbornness, I would have. But he insists he will figure it out, and will not let us change it again to accommodate his inadequacies. He cracks his knuckles, and I can almost feel the tingling in my own, knowing what it feels like to play until your fingers hurt.

We run through it again, Calliope reading through the lines, Myka conducting, and Deacon slamming his hands down in count. One wrong note comes out, and then he spirals. He can't manage to recover.

I do slam my head down this time.

"Okay, that's it. I'm calling it for today." I look back up and throw my hands, turning to walk somewhere, anywhere, else.

"How's it going over here?" I ask Pasha, bending down to grab a mug that is finished being painted.

"The clay we were using to mold isn't setting right, but we are going to send it to the kitchen to see if we can use their ovens. Hopefully, that will stiffen everything up correctly, and we will be on our way." Pasha smiles up at me. At least something is working.

The bell tower outside the theatre chimes, alerting us of the end of the workday. Everyone jumps up, putting whatever is in their hands into its appropriate place. A few of the actors stay, finishing the scene they are working through. I sit in one of the audience chairs, allowing myself to breathe. Rehearsals have been taxing on me. Physically and mentally.

I have to switch between parts of my brain with each new aspect of the crew I am interacting with. Music, acting, painting. I am running back and forth, as I am being asked questions between each department. Everything is finally falling into place, but I am still being pulled in every direction as rehearsals progress.

I listen to the chatter of the Arman while inspecting the golden bat fixed above us all. It really is an ugly thing to have picked as the champion animal of Hedeon. I'm sure they were only thinking of the intimidation of such a grotesque stance, with the snarl and spread wings, but why have need to intimidate your own people? After all, aren't those in Hedeon the only ones allowed in the Arman? Maybe it is just to further prove that the Crown watches everything, your pleasure, your work, your life. It's unsettling, whatever the answer.

Calliope and Anoki practice a scene from Act 1, their voices melodic together. They don't sing, but the cadences in which they deliver their lines sound like a song. They glide around each other, not touching, not this early in the play, but the tension and longing is reflected in their eyes. It's hard to believe they are barely more than colleagues in actuality.

"You both are beautiful," I smile up at them when they walk to me.

"Thank you for writing such beautiful parts," Calliope says.

"You know how all of this can be received. Are you two sure you want your faces to be the lead?" I ask—am always asking. Calliope sits beside me, wrapping her hand in mine.

"I haven't told you about my dad, have I?" she asks. Anoki doesn't speak, just watches in his usual silence. The most I've ever heard him speak is when he's in character. I shake my head, looking between the two.

"He died in the mines just outside of Dagrav. He was one of the guards working the prisoners. It was vile work, he always said as much. He hated his position, hated that he inherited it from a father he also hated. The funny thing is, with all the hate in his life, he was one of the most loving men I knew. One day, one of the prisoners started coughing up blood. My dad didn't know what was happening, but he rushed to the man and held him, calling for help. Help didn't come.

"The man, in between his choking, asked to die with the sun on his face. So, my dad half carried and half dragged the prisoner out. The man died in his arms, but at least he was in the sunlight. My dad was imprisoned for abandoning his post during a shift." Her words come with tearing eyes, staring deep into the memory. I don't urge her on. I just let her feel the emotions that are rising. She sucks on her teeth, eyes glued to the ground. She curls into herself. "He died in prison because the Crown forgot about him. He was supposed to have a trial, pay a fine, and go right back to his place in the mines. But they forgot. And he died. So, if I am going to do anything with my life, it is going to be making a statement of exactly what I think of those who rule this kingdom." Her despair turns to anger.

"We are all on your side," Anoki says, still standing above us.

"Thank you. Both of you." I reach out to hug Calliope, and she leans into my touch.

"We will see you tomorrow." She pulls back, nodding her head, and stands to go. She and Anoki exit softly through a backstage door.

The silence of the theatre is always the loudest the moment after everyone leaves.

I can't take my eyes from the stage. This seat, and all those around me, will be filled in a matter of days. I bring my knees up to rest my chin on them. Every single ticket has been sold, the queen working her magic. Not only were seats reserved for the most influential in Court, but the leftover seats were generously given away to peasants close enough to make the journey. All part of the propaganda. In order for the hope to spread, there must be people from all walks of life to go back home and spread it.

As director, I was offered a box seat, but I declined. I would rather be in the wings, available to anyone who should need me. And to calm the nerves that are already starting to bubble in my core. Being around the Company will help stabilize me, their surety bringing out mine.

Because I am sure.

Even if it's buried beneath many layers of doubt and fear, I am sure this is why I was brought here by The Faits, why I was made and molded the way I am. I am starting to see the multitudes in myself that Sumood spoke of nights ago. All this time, I have been holding onto this anger because of what Hedeon has done to my family. I thought this separated me from the Hedeonites, but after hearing so many of the Company's stories, I'm starting to believe it connects me to them more than anything. We all have skin in the game. Everyone who witnesses our play will have lost someone close to them because of the war. So how do we show them that ending this war is worth it? We must find hope that something better can come and outweigh the need for vengeance, for reparation.

I don't know what repercussions I will have. I have the chance to be long gone before the axe falls, but I am still not sure that is what I want. Even in my uncertainty, I am sure Milena will hold me at fault, never daring to lay a hand on the beloved Company. I am more than happy to take the fall for these people who need to tell this story as much as I do.

This has become so much bigger than me.

22

I THINK I'VE BEEN running from grief my whole life. I say *I think* because I can't remember the things I should be grieving very well. But I'm running anyway. I'm running and running and running, and then I run head into it at random times, like here in the billiard room of the Zamak after rehearsal with the rest of the Company, enjoying the benefits of Court.

Dilean laughs obnoxiously while obliterating Anoki in a game. Pasha lays against me, shoulder to shoulder, on the couch talking to Myka. Deacon laughs with Feliks, while they sit on barstools, leaning against the bar top.

It is all so beautiful, and it all stings fiercely.

These people are from Hedeon. Hedeon is all I know. Yet, there is always a line between us. Even if they don't know it's there, I do. I will always be from Reine, will always long to be back in my homeland. If this war never started, or even ended years ago, would I be in a different billiard room, in a different kingdom, with different people, laughing about the same things without the hesitancy I feel in my chest? Was there ever a life in which I could know the extent of myself, and others could know me as well? I wish for a life that wasn't packaged in secrets and shipped to Hedeon.

"Do you have your dress ready for the ball, Damira?" Pasha looks up at me as if I didn't just lose my capability to breathe.

"Raven made sure she spared no expense. I assume you have yours too? If not, I am told you'll have a terrible time trying to scrape one up this close to the Revel."

"I secured mine weeks ago. I have the final fitting tonight, actually. Myka's going to tag along if you want to come with." Pasha readjusts herself, sitting up from my shoulder so she can look at me properly.

Pasha and Myka have gotten close since starting rehearsals. They've worked together on three plays now, but this one has drawn them in as allies. It's been an honor to watch their friendship form, to be right beside them as our bonds strengthen. It's another thing that makes me grieve the life I could have had. Friendships that last years instead of knowing exactly when they have to end.

"I'd love to. I'll try and stop by if dinner doesn't go too long. If I don't reach you in time, just leave without me, and I will try to catch up."

"Perfect," Myka and Pasha say in unison, which causes a laugh from all three of us.

A ball flying from the pool table grabs our attention as it rolls to our feet. Dilean stares at Anoki with an open moth.

"You are trying to kill me!" Dilean shouts dramatically, trying to school the laugh in his voice.

"If I was trying to kill you, you wouldn't still be standing," Anoki assures him, also trying not to laugh.

I openly laugh at the both of them, and Myka and Pasha join in.

Dilean trudges over to us and bows deeply.

"My apologies, ladies, my counterpart has no manners." In the deep bow, he picks up the ball that is resting against the toe of my boot.

"You're just mad because you are losing." Myka raises an eyebrow at him.

"Well, that is utterly and completely true." Dilean winks and turns back to the table, replacing the ball and grabbing his cue stick and chalk.

"At least he's self-aware," Pasha shrugs, turning back to Myka and asking her about what they should do for dinner.

A grey uniform with a black strip down the side, walks in. He catches my attention, because unlike most guards that wander around the Zamak, I actually know this one's name. Kover. He approaches me with sure steps, and that's how I know he isn't coming to me as Kover from Cotea, but Kover of Hedeon.

"The queen mother has requested your presence," he speaks coolly, looking down his nose.

The whole of the room is silenced by the words, everyone having turned toward me. The smile Dilean wore moments ago ran from his face so fast it could be halfway to Reine by now.

"All that is good and the Divine," Pasha whispers under her breath, pushing back further into the couch.

"We won't count on you for tonight, but we'll be waiting to hear what she has to say." Myka leans over me, staring unwaveringly at Kover.

I pat her hand on my knee to assure her I will be okay, and then I get up to follow Kover out, the whole of the Company's eyes helping me stay upright.

We turn down the hallway, out of earshot of the billiard room. I look up at Kover, whose face is still frozen with duty, drilling a hole in the wall ahead of us with his stare.

"Do you know what this is about?" I waited to ask until we were alone in the hallway, and even at that, my voice is low.

"She only said that she wished to speak with you. Lev has his own errands to run today, so I was sent." His eyes check behind us, and then the hallway ahead that intersects with ours. "Truthfully, I put myself in the position to be sent, as I wanted to check in with you. How are you doing?"

"I am surviving. Trying to only focus on opening night."

"How's Tenny been? Any more news on the home front?" It surprises me to hear Tenny's name from him. I hadn't known the two knew each other, but it makes sense.

"You know the Network. I don't have much knowledge of her dealings. But she's healing well and seems optimistic for what it's worth. She wants me to leave with her after the play."

"Will you?"

"I've not decided yet. I don't belong here, but I am not sure how much Reine will feel like home after being gone for so long."

A maid turns into the hallway we walk down, silencing the conversation. We turn another corner, and large windows that look to the barren side of the mountain appear. Budding green trees and a valley beyond. A few people, courtiers and maids, stroll the hallway as we do, so we keep up the silence.

I take it as time to calm my breathing, forcing my face into a nonchalance I can hide behind when speaking to the queen mother.

We turn another hallway, down a small decline that leads to an unadorned door. We are in the heart of the Zamak now, no windows, so no natural sunlight to warm the chill that has settled on me.

"I will be here when you finish." Kover opens the door, which squeals on rusted hinges.

Heat only found in the middle of summer drenches me as I walk into a fire-lit room. A large altar is ablaze in the center of the room, a pyre of sacrifice. Just as it would be ridiculous to compare a regular house to the Zamak, a regular pyre of sacrifice would pale in comparison to this one. A few Mezdus linger around the walls, red uniforms even more sinister in the firelight. They don't even glance at me. In a square around the pyre, a row of pews are in almost new condition. Seems the royals don't often come to make sacrifices to the Divine. Or at least, the other royals.

The queen mother sits on the far side of the room, in the pew at the head of the pyre. Tapestries hang along the walls, stories depict interventions of the Divine. I try to focus on them instead of meeting the queen mother's eyes, but just as sure as true authority does not have to ask to be followed, she claws my attention to her.

"Come have a seat by me." She pats the wood beside her, her rings ticking the moments of my patience dwindling. I don't bother running through the list of things she could want me here for. There is no good in counting my sins against the Crown when they are so numerous. If this is death, I will have no way to fight against it. My stomach still churns, despite the outcomes I don't allow myself to think about.

She hardly left me any space between her and the pew arm, so when I sit, I am close enough to smell that her perfume is similar to the scent of decaying fruit.

"Your play is in a week's time, are you all prepared?" Her voice makes me want to cringe, to cover my ears from the screech.

"I would like to believe so, Moi Nachalnik." I stare into the fire in front of us, the heat doing nothing to help the nervous sweats I already have.

"I like to come in here and make sacrifices every so often. I don't believe in the Divine, but other people need things to believe in. Do you agree?"

"I do."

"Desperation might be the most dangerous plague in our land. That's why the Crown created the Divine, to give people an easy place to put their belief. As long as people put their future in the hands of the Divine—the Crown—our kingdom can run smoothly."

The queen mother stares into the fire as I do. She lets her words weigh on my shoulders. It is common knowledge that the religion of the Divine is a newer religion, but still, the admittance to complete fabrication of a deity doesn't sit right with me.

"You see, it's when people take their fate into their own hands that it poses a threat to our balance of life. Are you following my words, girl?" I'm no longer just suffocating by her perfume, but by her eyes that strangle me too.

"I'm not sure I am, Moi Nachalnik." If she is going to threaten me, I would prefer she is straight with what exactly I am being accused of. Faits know there are a myriad of things that I could be being implicated for.

"You have risen through stations in a matter of weeks. Almost unheard of, but if you give a rat a space large enough for its head, its whole body will follow. That usually will be fine, as long as the rat remembers it is still a rat." She pauses, but as if she thinks I am in need of further clarification, she continues. "And in case you intend to mishear me, let me make myself very clear. You have gotten close to my grandchildren in your stay here. My daughter insists on treating you as one of her own, despite your less than noble standing. Do not think there will be a place for you to return here after you finish touring with the Arman. I do not want you going out from the Zamak with any kind of delusions that you have the ability to take fate into your own hands. Do I make myself clear?"

"Yes, Moi Nachalnik." I save myself from exhaling deeply.

She is only worried about the purity of her bloodline. She has no suspicions of me outside of trying to settle down above my station. I will not die today. The play will still continue on as normal. The tension in my shoulders is relieved by this accusation. Out of all the accusations she could level against me, this is the least worrisome. However, it sends enough fear into my marrow, that the offer of joining the Network and returning to Reine seems like it may be the safest option for all parties.

Her threats are why I have to help save Reine, why I can't stay any longer. Once the play is out there, I must move on, must continue in my efforts. I have to trust The Faits that the Company will be okay.

"Leave me." She turns back to the fire, watching the rising flame.

I walk silently across the room, breathing deeply in the relief that washes over me, that cools me off, even with the heat of the flame at my back.

Kover is exactly where he said he'd be, outside the door, but he isn't alone. Raven paces back and forth, staring at the ground before she hears me close the door behind me.

"Oh, finally. I have been looking for you everywhere."

"What's wrong?"

The furrow in her brow, the tightness of her breath, reminds me how the longevity of my life is never as secure as one would want it to be.

"Calix is back."

23

Raven and I rush back through the Zamak. My heart pounds with every turn closer to him. Not because it's Calix, but for the information he holds. Definitely not because it's Calix.

Calix's room is dark, the curtains pulled over the grand windows. A lump lays face down on the bed, limbs spread out as if he walked in, flung himself there, and hasn't moved since.

"All that is good and the Divine." Raven doesn't bother to quiet her words at my side. Calix doesn't stir.

"Calix Glavnok Tsvesti Hendricks," she calls louder to him this time. He jolts out of sleep, turning his head back only enough to see us. His eyes glance over Raven and then slam into me. He sighs and drops his head back down, nose first into the gathered blankets.

"Go away," I think he says, but it is muffled.

"Tell us what happened. How'd you get back?" Raven presses, taking a step forward. I linger in the doorway, realizing I have no idea why Raven brought me with her for this. Calix doesn't move.

"Come on, Cal," she whines.

He pushes himself up, turning in a mechanical way to face us.

"I have not slept in days. I am chilled to my bone, and I think I audibly heard my brain sigh from exhaustion earlier today. Therefore, I will be sleeping for the foreseeable future. Is that alright with you, sister?" The lines of his face are straight, hinting at nothing other than the tiredness he spoke of.

"There are more important things than your sleep, Calix." I don't have to look at Raven to know she rolls her eyes. Calix grabs a pillow from the head of the bed and chucks it at her. She gasps, catching it in the air, right before it hits her face.

"Selfish brute."

She turns, shoving the pillow into my arms. "Maybe he will talk to you."

I am stuck between their two requests. Calix's eyes slide to me, but he doesn't protest for me to follow his twin out. He lets out another breath and falls onto his back, arms stretched out.

"She is just worried." I take a few steps in.

"I know, but I don't have the energy to play the part of prince right now."

"You could have been a brother." I place the pillow at the head of his bed again, with the rest of them. His eyes turn from the ceiling, his chin dipping slightly so he can see me.

"She didn't want a brother. She wanted a prince, darling." There is no room for question.

I won't pretend to know Raven even a third as well as Calix knows her, but I saw it in her eyes when she came to me. She wanted answers, wanted to see where the sword was going to fall. I don't know much about their relationship, except that it is strained now in a way it didn't use to be. Raven claims it's Calix's fault, but despite this, I am sure she's changed too in the years he was gone. Naivety never seems to survive childhood. That is one law that doesn't bow to anyone, not even the Crown.

"I'll let you sleep, then." I start for the door.

"Mira." He rushes up, grabbing my wrist so I can't continue. I glance back at him. His face falls, a tweak in his eyebrow before they soften, his eyes holding mine as he gulps for words, as a drowning person would for air.

"Will you—" His jaw clenches. He doesn't drop his eyes though.

"Will you stay with me?" he stammers. Gone is the Calix that is iron, and here is the silk side of the paradox. I don't know what he saw on the front lines, but the remnants of the blood he must have seen spilled is still stained in the reflection of his eyes.

In one movement, without words, I climb onto the bed, kicking off my boots. He shifts so we are both laying across it. I tuck my elbow under my head, face to face with Calix doing the same. His scent is all over the sheets. Cedar of Hedeon, and to my surprise, sandalwood. A sacred wood of Reine. Clean. Home.

Just this morning, he was in my Reine. I hadn't let myself think of all the consequences of Calix's departure. Hadn't even realized how close to my Cotea he was. I want to ask him about it—how the land was, how the time was, what he saw and who he talked with. But if his words hadn't told me he couldn't be a prince right now, the anguish etched on his face spoke for itself.

"Are you okay?" My quiet words travel the short space between us.

"I really just need to sleep," he whispers back.

I nod. His lashes flutter, heavy enough that it doesn't seem a deliberate choice when he finally surrenders to closing them. He really is iron and silk. His cheek bones sharp, but soft curls bend over his forehead, shining from bathing recently. The only light that peaks in is from the tops of the closed curtains, but the shadows find his face, highlighting the crevices of his eyes and the turn of his jaw. He looks different than the first night I met him. His looks change as I learn them. He is not just handsome because of his features, but more than that. I now know what I didn't when we first met—his heart matches the beauty of his face, amplifying his allure. It's painful to admit.

He shifts slightly, his hand sliding across the bed. I watch helplessly as, with his eyes still closed, he wraps his fingers in mine. I stare at them for a while, our hands as one. Two nations at war lay down their arms, at least in this room, by hands intertwined. Would we still be here if Calix knew the truth? If it were to be possible for us, could our people follow the same fate? My uncle's story continues to demand my attention. It is not our war to fight.

My eyes start to droop, and I don't bother forcing them open.

I roll over, my eyes slow to open. Darkness greets me. But through the dark, I can make out a desk. Not my rooms. I glance over my shoulder, Calix lays in the same place he fell asleep. I sit up, scrubbing my hands over my face, rubbing my eyes. Calix stirs behind me, and when I glance back, I think he grins, but it's hard to tell in the night.

"What time do you think it is?" His sleepy voice sends shivers through me.

"The middle of the night?"

He sits up, our shoulders overlapping. I make note. Of the action and my urge to stay as close to him as possible.

"We slept through dinner," he laughs.

"I'm surprised someone didn't come find us."

Though I am glad for it. I have no clue how I would explain this to Raven. Or anyone else. Even myself. I forgot all about going to Pasha's dress fitting, though meeting with the queen mother gave me a good excuse.

"They might not have even noticed our absence. With the Revel coming up, I am sure that is all my mom and Rave are focused on."

I drop my head into my hands.

"Don't remind me about the Revel. I have been so focused on the play that I haven't had time to learn the dances." I had been pushing off the anxieties, resolving to stick to the snack table and observe. Then Raven said I will be required to dance at least two songs, as is the polite gesture in being invited. I argued that no one will take notice of me, but she assured me it wouldn't go unseen.

I am sure Calix grins this time, his teeth visible through the dim moonlight sieving in.

He grabs my hand and pulls me off the bed, a second wind, and nowhere to be found the downturned man of earlier.

"Where are we going?" I try to keep my voice down, but a laugh explodes from me as Calix drags me out into the hallway. He holds a finger to his mouth as he pulls me along with the other hand. I stifle back a laugh this time, as I slip across the marble floor with my socked feet.

The Zamak has many parts, and the one we sneak through now is the same one I caught Calix and Milena arguing in. The part where people are hosted, the throne room, the grand dining room, the ballrooms. Court is close by too, but no whispers float to us. We might have found the only hour of night that chattering voices don't fill the halls.

Calix pushes open a door that reaches all the way up to the vaulted ceilings. It doesn't cry out as it opens, the hinges oiled and kept presentable for gossiping tongues. The room, if such a word can be used to describe such a magnificent space, stretches long in front of us. Oriel windows swell on both sides of the marble floor.

Moonlight dances in the place of people. Pastel colors paint the walls between the windows, gold lining everything.

Chandeliers of glass float in a row down the middle of the ceiling, little light fixtures dot the sides of the larger ones. Mirrors make up the ceiling, beyond the chandeliers. It reflects the grand staircase we stand on, as it melts onto the mosaic floor.

I glance back at Calix, who watches me take in the ballroom. He picks my hand back up and leads us down the stairs—our soft, socked-steps most likely the quietest this ballroom has ever heard. When we get to the middle of the floor, he brings his hand up and spins me. I try not to trip over my own feet. He pulls me in close, one hand placed firmly on my waist, and our intertwined hands out to the side. Except for the obligatory handshake, dancing is the only time Hedeonites get to touch without it being frowned upon. The best part of making rules is finding ways to break them, I suppose. A surety overtakes Calix, confidence he always feigns made true by these proper touches.

"Okay, place your foot where mine is," he instructs, looking down at our feet.

"Then I will step on it."

"I will move it, darling," he sighs, with a shake of his head and a roll of his eyes. That crooked grin, the reason I tease him.

He starts humming, a tune he has heard so many times in his life he's memorized it. He takes a step back, and I put my foot where his was, as I was told. I watch his feet as he pulls and pushes us around the floor. My foot moving to where his is, and he moving it at the last moment. We are waltzing.

Sort of.

Slowly.

"I am not good at this," I mumble, an ache in my neck from staring at our feet. More so than never having a reason to dance here, Hedeon's dances vary greatly from the few Reinen ones I partially remember seeing. It's frustrating having to assimilate to a culture when I am always on the outside looking in.

Calix's hand that rests on the small of my back moves up to my face. With a finger and thumb, he lifts my chin so that I am forced to look away from the ground and straight into his eyes.

"Hold my stare, relax your back. You are far too stiff. Don't think about it too much, just follow wherever I move us." His fingers stay after he finishes talking. I can hardly find a breath. His jaw feathers.

"Let's try that again," I manage to get out.

He puts his hand to my back again, pulling me tightly to him. Even if I were to stumble, the strength by which I am held to him assures me I will not fall. He starts to hum again, picking up the speed of the melody.

His eyes stay frozen to mine, and I am very aware of how alone we are. He spins me out and then back to him, in the sequence we just went through, but faster. I struggle to keep my eyes up, to loosen as Calix asked. With his hand on my back, and my hips pressed to him, I find it hard to be anything but stiff. I am turning into a Hedeonite. Nevertheless, I let him glide us across the room in steps that are customary.

I don't fall. I don't even stumble. Calix slows down after we twirl through the same steps multiple times. We start to sway, his humming falling away note by note, like petals plucked from a flower.

"You might not have my alluring grace, but I am sure you will not embarrass yourself beyond recovery at the Revel." He looks down at me with pride.

"We can't all be dancers of the ballet." How long ago he spoke those words to me. He laughs, a pure smile, and I am the one to cause it. I wish to put it there more often.

Silence connects us like a string. His hand grips my back without apology, our breath quickened from dancing. He doesn't pull away from me, not this time, not yet. But we were so close last time, and then he ran.

"Why didn't you kiss me?" I ask abruptly. So many things in my life are uncertain, this is one thing that doesn't need to be.

His eyes flicker, he almost looks away. Almost.

"I wanted to," he says, as if that makes things better.

"But?" I haven't pushed him on anything ever. I have been so careful, partially because I was scared, and partially because I know what these things mean to him. But I have to know this—if only, so when I leave, I will have no unanswered questions.

"But I couldn't."

I step back, but he steps with me, keeping his hand on my back.

"Just—" He sighs, needing to think. I look out over the ballroom around us. I shouldn't be here with him. And I certainly shouldn't be trying to convince him of something that would put me closer to being an enemy to my own kingdom.

Calix's hand untwines from mine, but instead of letting me go, his knuckles trace my cheek, my jaw line. With the softest touch, he pulls my face back to him. I have no choice but to meet his sure stare. His hand runs through my hair, resting on my neck, his thumb on my cheek.

"My mom has never been the same since my dad left. I didn't know how much that affected me until you—for many reasons—but the other day, when we almost kissed, I wanted to desperately, but—but all I could think of was the months my mom didn't talk to me because of how much it pained her. If I let you in, you could leave, and I don't want to turn into my mom."

I should be happy at the prospect of his vulnerability, but the truth only highlights the lies that encircle me. One way or another, I will have to leave. Even if, for some reason, Tenny can't secure my passage away after the show, I will be out on tour for at least half a year if the queen allows it, depending on how she receives my words. Or I'll be imprisoned. I'm gone, no matter the outcome.

I know, though, he will never be his mother. Maybe that's not my opinion to have, but that is the only reason I stay in his arms—because I am witless enough to believe that he is not like his lineage, and that maybe, perhaps, the future in his eyes, could be different.

Calix continues, tears starting to line his eyes. "But then—then I went to the warfront. I didn't see death firsthand, but I saw it lingering like a reaper, waiting, preying. I had the unfortunate luck of getting the last remaining tent, which just so happened to be by the healer's tent. Hour after hour, I lay awake listening to the lullaby of moans and screams from the casualties. I couldn't make sense of any of it. But somewhere, in the sleepless nights, I realized that you would have been able to make sense of it. You would have written or painted or orchestrated something that would have given some kind of insight as to why we are still fighting this useless war. I missed you. And life became too short to not do anything about it."

He doesn't give me time to respond, he leans in, so close, as close as last time, but just as I have been letting him close the gap between us, he is giving me the courtesy this time. He waits.

I wrap my arms around his neck, pushing to my toes. Softly, our lips meet, his breath catching. I almost pull away, his hands on my waist loosening, but then he regains his confidence, and his grip digs into my back, pressing his lips securely to mine. The hand that was on my neck, knots itself in my hair, my hands travel down his back.

With his lips on mine, everything seems easier. And that makes everything so much harder.

24

I CAN'T TELL IF the noise is coming from my head or the door. I had just closed my eyes and drifted, when the pounding started. Calix and I danced until the sun began to invade our perfect night. Unfortunately, the consequence of that is the pounding that is rattling off the walls of my mind.

The door to my room opens and someone walks in. It seems the pounding is indeed not only in my head.

"Damira," Raven's voice sings, sitting down on my bed. I squeeze my eyes harder.

"Why are you still asleep? The sun is up, and the ball is tonight," she squeals. I feel her move from the foot of my bed, and light suddenly floods the room. I roll over, pulling the blankets up over my head.

"Just a few more minutes," I mumble, but she peels the blankets back from my face.

"You look terrible."

"I'm not sure I like you in the morning."

I finally open my eyes and sit up. She is draped in a silk robe, her hair pinned up to hold her curls.

"Did you walk across the grounds looking like that?" I gape.

"Tunnels, my dear," she winks. "Now, why do you look so—like you were hit by a carriage?" She takes me in, and I am sure of what she sees. I could describe it without looking in a mirror. Tangled hair, dark circles beneath my eyes, disheveled pajamas.

I lean back against my pillows with a deep breath. I haven't even thought about how to tell Raven about me and Calix. I didn't want to believe there would ever be a me and Calix, the idea never moved far enough to get to the point to where I would have to tell Raven.

"I didn't get much sleep."

She purses her lips and squints her eyes, taking me in again with a more inquisitive glare. A smile slowly forms as she looks at me with a knowing stare that might as well trap me against the wall on the other side of the room.

"You were with Cal." Her grin rivals that of a sly criminal.

"I— We just—" I don't know how to explain myself. I smile a little, hoping she isn't irrevocably mad at me.

"You were! You two were up all night? Don't give me the gory details because, yuck, that's my brother, but what happened?" she exclaims, the complete opposite of anger.

"It wasn't like that. After you left his rooms yesterday, he asked me to stay, and we slept past dinner. We woke up in the middle of the night, and he offered to teach me to dance, because of your stupid Revel." I push her a little, but she just rolls her eyes.

"And?" She leans in, eyes widening.

"And—" I can't get the rest of the words out without a terrible smile overtaking me. She throws a pillow at me.

"You kissed!" She flings herself across the bed to hug me.

"I was so worried you would be mad." At least one of my worries has resolved itself. Now just to work through the ocean of other troubles.

"It is for purely selfish motives that I am not. I think you will be good for him. You are good for him. And though I haven't known you very long, I think he's good for you too." She points her nose into the air and grins.

I have no response but to smile from a deep place within.

"Now, get up! We are already late." She grabs my hand and pulls me from the bed. I trip over myself as she drags me back to the Zamak, through the aforementioned tunnels, the entrance at the back of a closet. Perhaps I should be concerned at the vulnerability of my home, but I leave it to think on later.

Raven has scheduled back-to-back pampering appointments. I go straight from being bathed, to hair, to eating lunch, to makeup, and finally, the most painful, being dressed. I have never worn a corset, and it brings me to wonder if everyone at court is so stuck-up because of the constant pain.

The agony is bearable when I am turned around and shown the magic the maids have been working on all day. I am beautiful. My hair is braided intricately, held in place by a gold headband dotted with emerald jewels. They stand in contrast against the elegant white dress. The sleeves billow and cinch at the wrist, a square neckline fitted to the corset beneath, an open back with a thick strap across the middle, and the signature full skirts of Hedeon.

The picture of elegance.

Raven comes out of the dressing room, fixing a stray hair across her forehead. She gasps the moment our eyes lock in the mirror.

"Stunning!" The compliment is so natural from her as she secures her earring, you'd think we've been doing this all our lives.

Raven wears a gown true to her name. Faux feathers, matching the iridescence of her hair, fall in rows down her skirt, the fitted bodice of her gown piped in an emerald green that matches the jewels in my own headband.

The picture of extravagance.

We are night and day in all ways of the term, but she still comes up behind me, wrapping her arms around my waist and resting her chin on my shoulder.

"Cal is going to think you breathtaking."

I roll my eyes. But I secretly hope he does. Or maybe I hope he doesn't, that will make the inevitable easier. I can't control the smile that falls from my face at the thought, but Raven turns and walks toward the vanity before she can catch it.

I hold my own stare for a breath longer. The next few days are going to be some of the hardest of my life, there is no doubt in my mind. But all I can do is get through the next ten minutes, and then the next, and the next.

Just ten minutes at a time.

I hear it in my mother's voice, these words that I've repeated to myself for as long as I can remember. I didn't even know I remembered what her voice sounded like, but it rings in my ears now. She used to tell me this, I think. Do whatever is right in the next ten minutes. And then the next. And the next. I was a little girl, crying because someone was mean to me. I had tried to punch him in retaliation, but my mom caught us. I was scared about something, and I think the boy was too. She sat us down and told us to just focus on doing the right thing in the next ten minutes, to not think about the scary thing.

I've been repeating those words ever since, but I never could remember where they came from. The sudden memory shallows my breathing.

A knock at the door alerts us it's time for the ball. I meet Raven's excited glance with one of nervousness. Ten minutes. Just get through the next ten minutes.

"Dramaturg Damira Letsov!" a man at the top of the staircase yells.

Thankfully, no one is paying much attention yet. No one knows my name like they will at the end of this week. A few ladies of

Court look up to me, I'm sure the same ones that like to gossip about my lack of proper title. I walk slowly down the staircase, intentionally feeling every step so I don't tumble down them. I try to keep my head up and not look at my feet, as Raven made sure to note. I spot a few faces from the Company who smile up at me, each draped in the height of fashion. Pearls and feathers and silks and jewels.

I head toward Pasha when I get to the bottom of the stairs. The dress she wears is lavender, flowers entangled in the tulle at the bottom and bodice, an airy cape is pinned onto the thin straps at her shoulder. The ponds of white on her skin are outlined in the same lavender shade. She wraps her arm around mine with a 'can you believe all of this' grin, turning us to the staircase to watch the others come down.

Name after name, people grace the stairs. Myka takes my other arm before long, and Kolyo and Deacon stand close behind us. After the crowd has filled the ballroom, a baton strikes the ground in an abrupt manner, making all those who weren't already watching turn to the stage.

"Prince Calix and Princess Cantrella."

It surprises me to hear Raven's true name come from the screaming man's mouth. As the prince and princess turn a corner, a collective gasp at their beauty resounds from the crowd.

Calix matches Raven in dark emerald tones. He wears a black cape, clasped with a collar at his neck, emerald filigree embroidered down the front. Golden chains attach to his jacket pockets and flash from under the cape with each step down the staircase. His eyes scan the room, falling on me, short enough to not draw atten-tion. Raven beams at his side, smiling in that intimidating way she has, like she holds a secret that could change the fate of the world, and she would tell you if you would only dare ask. They both wear matching crowns, sat back on the peak of their heads.

Milena is announced next. She floats down the steps with a certainty only achievable by someone with that much jurisdiction over people's feelings. Her gown is simple, lilac with hints of emer-ald to match her children. Her sleeves flow down past her hands in silk, wisping in the wind she creates as she moves. The same fabric layers her skirts, moving like waves in a sea. An emerald crown adorns her forehead. Raven had mentioned that only the reigning monarch wears their crown low on their forehead. Princesses' and princes' crowns are required to sit back on their head.

Milena stops when she gets to the last step, stretching her arms from her hips. "Thank you all for coming. I hope you enjoy these festivities my daughter and I have arranged for you. I know you are all itching to see what's behind the curtain, so without further ado, Happy Spring Revel!"

Everyone turns to the back of the ballroom where a large velvet curtain hangs.

I have hardly noticed the ballroom—the same one Calix and I danced in just last night. It is transformed with all the people in place of the moonlight. I was so focused on not tripping down the stairs that I didn't even take notice of the decorations. Bright florals of oranges and reds and pinks hang from every chandelier, snaking up between the windows in vines. They all snake toward the blood-red curtain.

Once everyone is turned around, the curtains swing apart, flashing open to reveal the night. Bright pyres burning, lanterns swinging back and forth from trees. Flowers seeping to the outside, vermillion and blush brightening up the dark. People walking on stilts and wrapped in vines with flowers holding hors d'oeuvre trays, weaving through the crowd that pushes through. Everyone rushes forward quickly. Pasha and I lose the grip on the rest of our friends, but we make it outside slowly, enjoying the sights.

In the distance, a village of striped red and white carnival tents are pitched, most of the children make a beeline to them. Flowered people hand out crowns of beads and vines, adorning every visitor. Pasha laughs in unison with me and pulls us forward to one of the bars freestanding among the crowd. It is draped in flowers, just as everything else, the bottles and glasses growing out of the counter like wildflowers. Most of the Company stands around getting drinks, and we join our group easily again. Myka and Dilean stand awfully close, Deacon is a few steps away talking to some man, and Kolyo has two glasses in his hand.

"Just ask her to dance," Myka rolls her eyes to Feliks who is standing with a sheepish look in his eye. "Tonight is the perfect opportunity to make an opening for yourself." Myka pushes Feliks on the shoulder. He doesn't look particularly convinced but nods his head anyway. Outside of him telling me what not to do with the lights in the theatre, Feliks keeps to himself most days.

"I'm not sure you're the one to be giving advice, Myk," Dilean pokes Myka in the side. She gives him a glare that would send me running.

Dilean puts his hands up in defense. "You didn't let me finish. Feliks, I do, however, think you should go and ask her to dance."

Feliks laughs a bit with the two and then takes a calming breath, nodding, and leaves our group to embark on his courageous quest.

In the distance, but before the tents, a stringed orchestra begins to play. A large parquet dance floor is set up before the musicians. Men and women drag each other to the large space. The music is full of jubilee, matching the colors of the night.

"Oh, there you are!"

I turn to see Raven barreling toward me, her arm reaching out.

"You have to come dance with me." She grabs my hand and pulls me toward the dance floor, ignoring the rest of the Company who bow respectfully in her presence.

"Yes, Moi Nachalnik."

She throws a pointed glance over her shoulder to me at my mocking.

She grabs both of my hands when we get to the dance floor and starts skipping, spinning us around, twisting our arms and twirling one another. I have never danced so freely as I do in this moment. The breeze giving me wind in my wings, creating a sort of airlessness as we twirl around the dance floor. Raven looks as carefree as I feel, the weight of revel-planning finally unbound from her shoulders.

Few times have I had the pleasure of becoming breathless from a physical activity that wasn't out of necessity. With the lanterns and flowers and singing, I can almost forget the war and the play and the betrayal. Those things are all lost in the crowd of people laughing. But just as I am on the edge of giving myself over to such fantasies, the song changes, slowing and weeding out those without partners to pull close. Raven and I yield to the proper couples, and we make our way off the dance floor, breathless and needing a drink.

Time passes quickly, the songs ushering us into the late hours of the night. I dance with a few men, as Raven demanded. Thanks to Calix's lessons, I keep up easily. I spend most of the evening at the side of the Company, making necklaces of flowers and playing games in the yard lit by the burning fires. After a while, Queen Milena takes her place in front of the band. Some would say she owned the room, but since the party is taking place outside, the same could be said that she owned the whole world. Seeing the extravagance of the party, I find it hard to argue against the thought. Even in our prime, Reine was never as prosperous as Hedeon. At least, not since long before the war.

Whispers always circulated of the way Reine was run before. Before the war, the battles, the massacres. No one knew when before was, just a long, long time ago. But apparently, if you go back far enough, it was magnificent. They say that is why the war started in the first place, because of jealousy. Wasn't that always how wars started? Because someone wanted to be the best, but there was always a better. The tale of the star-crossed king and queen being at the heart of the war has enough merit, the jealousy of unanswered love being the driving force. Jealousy left unkept turns to greed.

The noise finally dies down enough for Milena to speak. "I promise this is the last time I will interrupt the night. We all want you to freely enjoy without hinderance, however, I would be remiss if I didn't take this opportunity, being surrounded by all the people I love, to announce my son's engagement. Prince Calix is to wed Lady Orli of Maseton. If we could give them a round of applause and make sure the night is one for them to remember. To the prince and soon-to-be princess." Milena raises her purple-tinted glass and nods to where Calix and Lady Orli stand.

I didn't see her full face then, but the blue of her eyes is enough for me to recognize the young woman standing beside Calix. The writer from outside the bookstore.

Calix has always had a natural lean to his back, but now, under the eye of the crowd, he looks like a string has run through his spine, through his head, and is pulling up taut. Is it from the attention or the decree? I can't tell. My own posture, however, is from the decree. He just betrayed my own betrayal. I glance to Raven who has found my side, but she seems to be having her own crisis, nausea seeping up to lurch the color in her face.

Did Raven not know? Did Calix? The crowd erupts in applause, and for having to play a role I was damned to, I clap along with them. The excitement that bubbles through the air like in the glasses of champagne, does not intoxicate me. I should have seen this coming. I should have stayed far away from the prince in the first place. I can't even blame him, the tears that halt in my throat are all because of my own stupidity.

"I'll find you later," I shout to Raven over the applause of the crowd. She just nods with a blank stare at her family.

The crowd is thickening, pushing closer to the happy couple. I move against the flow, straightening my shoulders and making myself larger in order to fend off the whole Court. Despite wanting to find a dark cave to hide in, I refuse to shrink myself because of some game the prince was playing.

No cave seems to be in the distance, but the small incline on the outskirts of the party will have to do as refuge until I can get my breathing under control. Panic rises with each shoulder I pass. I need to get out of here.

The night air is crisp when it is not polluted with bodies. The moon lights the way to the top of the hill. It is not so far that the chatter of Court is inaudible, but far enough that I am not able to make out what specific congratulations are being offered. The nice white dress I wear will be ruined by sitting on the grass, but after the news tonight, that is the least of my worries. And so, I plop myself down right on the side of the hill, my ankle picking the most inopportune time to start aching. I try to ignore it as best I can, already too many things on my mind.

It all feels like a punch in my gut, that I was able to party with these people so easily, that the extravagance of the night isn't what made me nauseous, but the engagement of the prince of my enemy is what finally made me leave. How could I possibly face my people again?

The play is in four days. It will be atonement for all the sins I've committed here. At least, that is what I tell myself.

Music starts back up, the stringed instruments resuming the jolly songs from before the news. People sway to the melody, little kids scream, and the sound is so uniquely human it almost hurts.

A shadow breaks from the crowd. This late into the night, most people are drunk and falling over each other, too involved with who they are spinning around to notice the silhouette leaving the gathering. I straighten, the man coming toward me. There is nowhere to run, and yet, I get up and turn to the forest at my back, wincing with each step, the pain a reminder as to why I will never belong here. I crest the hill when Calix calls my name.

"Damira, please!" His voice is loud enough to reach me.

Being on the other side of the knoll hides us from the rest of the party. If we are going to have it out right now, it might as well be here. I stop in the tree line, turning and waiting for him to tumble down the backside of the incline.

"Thank you," he pants when he reaches me, out of breath from the pursuit.

I almost curse under my breath. He is even more stunning up close tonight. His jewels taking the moonlight and claiming it as their own. The finery of his shirt on display as he's discarded his previously worn cape. It's just not fair.

"How long has she been planning that?" I ask before Calix has a chance to defend himself.

"Since she sent me away, I believe. Two or three weeks ago." He answers directly, meeting my eyes, waiting for the next question.

"Did you know?"

I didn't know my heart had more room to plummet, but it finds the space as he nods his head.

"She told me almost the moment I got back. I was so delirious from lack of sleep that I didn't process it fully. It's her master plan to save the soldiers out south and to finally end this damned war. Lady Orli has very wealthy parents, and even that is an understatement. I was going to tell you, darling, I promise— I just—"

I flinch when my endearment comes out so familiarly. It feels more intimate now than it did when he used it to tease me, a layer of myself given that I can't reclaim.

Calix recoils at the contactless hit.

"You what, Calix? You are a prince, and I am nothing, serving your queen faithfully. What was the best outcome here?" I fold my arms close to my chest, the chill of the night finally becoming too much.

Calix starts pacing, the trees all but moving out of his way in further proof that we are from different worlds. He lives in a place where even nature bows to his authority, and I am not even in charge of what I eat for dinner tomorrow.

He turns back to me, down the hill just slightly, enough to where I look down to him. "You drive me insane, Mira. Do you know that?" He throws his hands up, exasperated, as if I did anything, as if I was the one with a betrothed.

"Then leave, Calix! You are engaged. Wipe your hands of me and get back to your engagement party." I hold my high ground, the wind picking up with our quickening emotions. I have to run my hands through my now unbound hair as it gets tossed in a current.

"You scramble my words. I am a mask of perfect poise around everyone else, but when I am around you, I have to fight for every word. I don't know what happens, but all of the reasoning and sense beaten into me since childhood flees in the intimidation of your unapologetic pursuit to be so loudly yourself. It makes me want to abandon the tales my mother has spent years crafting, because I want to be someone worthy of your authenticity."

I deflate, all my resentment going out with the wind to uncover what I truly feel. Sometimes grief is just parading around as anger.

"You hardly know me, Calix," I plead, not wanting to hear these beautiful words when I know just how deceived he is.

He takes a step toward me but stops abruptly, looking up to the sky and holding out a hand. I look up too, a rain drop hitting my cheek. Good, it will conceal the tears that I can't stop from falling. Our eyes meet again, disregarding the coming storm, and he continues.

"I know enough. I know that anytime someone challenges the things you love, you stand your ground with iron feet. I know that you have cared for the Arman in ways they could never begin to thank you for. You have loved Raven and Anya and Alek, even though I know firsthand your feelings for our policies. I might not know your burdensome past, what with your parents and everything, but I know enough about you that I want to be a part of your future."

He doesn't press closer to me. The rain has picked up between us, but not enough to make us run for cover yet. We have to have this out.

"I leave in a week to go on tour with the Company. Even if I manage to find my way back to the Krepost, it is not like we, like this, could ever work out. You have to marry someone of standing, and I am from the Hovel. Don't you see that we were playing a game from the very start? We knew it was set to fail, yet we expected a different ending. You can't change who you are, and I can't change who I am. This was inevitable." Maybe this is for the best. I knew we had an expiration date, better that he gets a gentle girl like Lady Orli out of it, so he doesn't have to bear my betrayal alone.

Calix reaches out, but I step back before his hand touches me. I'd be unable to stop at just one touch.

He runs a hand through his now-wet hair, moving it from his eyes. "This wasn't inevitable, but we are. We are inevitable, Mira. From the moment I met you, I knew all else was over. You can run, and I can be engaged, but that isn't going to stop this. I will find a way out of this marriage, a way to help Hedeon pull back our war efforts without auctioning off my hand to the highest bidder. It was yours from that very first moment, and it is yours still. I will not let this be our ending. We deserve a grand ending, darling."

If only he knew what he was asking. I want to believe his procla-mation, but there are so many more reasons that stand in the way than Calix can fathom. The silence rides in on the hurrying raindrops between us. A few screams jump over the knoll behind us, the partygoers running to shelter. I wipe my eyes, truly unsure if it is the rain or tears that block my vision.

"You should have told me." I'm not sure how to more address all the things he said without unraveling my lies like a spool of yarn.

"I should have," Calix nods.

"You are engaged."

"I am."

"That is where we stand."

"I'm sorry," he whispers.

Calix can't hold me now, won't ever be able to hold me again, but he doesn't know that. And so, he stares with hopeful eyes. But I know how dangerous hope is. It's why Milena wanted me to write of it, why I am in Hedeon, why Reine is still fighting a war that has no foreseeable victory. Hope is not a delicate thing that blooms like a bud in the spring. Hope is the weed that gets trampled over and over but won't seem to die, even in the harshest conditions, even when dying would definitely be easier. It makes fools out of even the smartest of men. It makes them do reckless things because, in their eyes, there is a someday.

"Me too."

25

THE STAIRWELL IS AS friendly a space as any in the Zamak. That's to say it's not friendly at all, but I had needed a place to rest my ankle before continuing across the grounds. Two nights into the Revel, it is customary to have the Christenings of the Parks. All around Hedeon, the parks and gardens are christened for the year by Mezdus. The Zamak is the first grounds to receive the blessing, and then the rest of the day is comprised of picnics and games and reading.

It should have been a lovely day, but now I find myself crying in a stairwell.

The sun went down hours ago, the party still roaring outside the stained-glass window I sit beneath. A few people walk back and forth in the foyer I lurk in, but everyone is far too concerned with their own pities to take notice of mine.

My ankle throbs, and I try to rub it through my boot. I know it will offer slight reprieve if I take the boot off, but I can't do that until I get home. I can't walk home because of the pain in my ankle. It is a cruel cycle of unmerciful suffering, and the frustration alone is enough to support these tears in my eyes.

But the tears aren't only for the pain. At least, not my ankle pain. Calix and Orli have to present a unified front, I understand that, but it doesn't help the knife that was pierced further into my stomach each time I witnessed Calix smiling at Orli today. He warned me early on that he is a mask of his mother's making, but he plays the part too well for even me to not believe.

Maybe Calix was right, I cry too easily.

I am being torn in too many directions, my heart wanting too many different things. I want to focus on the play, focus on being the best playwright I can, focus on helping my people, but all I can see is Calix laughing with Lady Orli.

"By the Divine," Pasha appears around the corner, a drink in her hand and a quickly disappearing smile on her face.

"What's wrong?" She rushes to me quickly, easily throwing her arm around my shoulder.

"My bad ankle, it's giving me problems again." I wipe the tears from my cheeks and give her a smile, brushing off the burden so she doesn't try to carry it.

"Are you sure that's all that's giving you problems?" She lays her cheek against my shoulder so I can't see her pitying face.

"Yes."

"Damira."

"Pasha."

She sits up so she can look at me straight on. I wipe more tears as they come.

"You think we haven't noticed you and the prince? He might sleep during our rehearsals, but Court talks, and they've seen you two together enough that it's reached our ears."

I hadn't thought of me not mentioning my closeness with Calix as a lie to the Company, but the way Pasha accuses me, it sounds like another betrayal.

"I didn't know what I was doing. It has all been an awful mistake."

She leans back into my shoulder with a deep exhale.

"You've been miserable company since the ball, I had figured as much," she laughs. And I exhale with the relief that I didn't sever anything between us.

"I hadn't known he was to be engaged." I stare at the same spot on the floor, tracing the cracks in the stone.

"I'm not surprised. The Crown likes to find ways to remind us that they don't owe us anything."

Right as I'm on the verge of defending Calix and Raven, the rest of the Company rounds the corner in an uproar.

"Oh, Dramaturg—" Dilean is the first to spot me. He shoulders a slouching Myka, Kolyo supporting her other shoulder. Blood drips from her forehead.

"By the Divine," Pasha mumbles as we both stand and hurry to them.

"What happened?" I go straight to Myka, regardless of how Dilean tries to shield me away.

"It is not as bad as it looks, merely a flesh wound," he assures me.

"Myka?" I ask her directly.

Her head bobs a little, but she grins with a small laugh. "Yes, Dramaturg, a flesh wound."

"What happened? I left you for all of five minutes," Pasha asks, scanning the group behind the trio.

The rest of the Company suppresses smiles, none wanting to be the first to rat someone out.

"Kolyo, what happened?" Out of the lot of them, he is the one that I would expect to break first.

To my surprise, he tries to suppress a smile too, but he gives in before long, if only to get Myka to a healer more quickly.

"Dilean here bet Myka that she couldn't flip off the stone ledge."

"And I proved him wrong," Myka straightens, despite the gouge in her forehead.

"With minimal maiming," Dilean agrees, nodding his head with a content smirk.

"You hit your head doing a flip off a wall?" I echo the story.

"Yes, but I did complete the flip, so I won the bet. Don't forget that part."

"The play is three days away!"

"Which is why we need to get her to a healer." Kolyo motions to the path they were trying to follow.

"By all means." I step out of their way, allowing the trio to pass. Pasha and I follow in with the rest of the Company.

The lists start running through my mind, all the ways I would need to change the show should one of the Company further hurt themselves. Our backup plans have backup plans, but I still run through all the possible ways something could go wrong.

As we turn the final corner to the healer, a hand rests on my arm. I look over to Deacon, who is beside me as we all shuffle.

"We have put on many plays in the past, and this one is no different. Opening night will be all it needs to be, Moi Dramaturg," he promises as we enter the healer's room.

My ankle screams, and though this would be the best place in the Zamak to pass out, I fight it with all I have. Myka sits on one of the tables the healer cleans off for her, and I lean against a counter at the back of the room. The rest of the Company, besides Dilean and Pasha, wait outside in the hall.

"Please tell me she can conduct on opening night," I ask the healer before she's had a proper amount of time to examine Myka. Dilean doesn't leave her side, but Pasha comes to stand out of the way with me.

The healer doesn't answer me, just gets to work. I glance at Pasha by my side, and she grabs my hand. I lean on the counter with all the weight I can, trying to appease my angering ankle.

After much longer than is good for my sanity, the healer turns to me.

"She will be fine. The scrape barely needed a stitch, so she should heal alright as long as she takes it easy over the next few days."

"Oh, praise the Divine." I almost slip, almost thank The Faits aloud, but I catch myself.

"You two are no longer allowed to hang out over the next few days," Pasha crosses her arms with her decree.

"I second that."

"I really am fine. I am sorry to have scared you though, Dramaturg." Myka reaches out for me, and I take her hand, coming beside Dilean.

"Please keep both of your feet solidly on the ground until opening night," I plead with her.

"Promise." She places a kiss on the back of my hand.

"It has been a long week for all of us," Pasha says, but throws the meaning at me, "and it is only going to get longer. I think we should all be getting to bed."

The healer speaks up from a corner where she is cleaning up the mess she made. "You are free to leave, but the composer here would benefit from a little rest before embarking home."

"I'll stay with her." Dilean doesn't even let a breath pass before volunteering.

"I'll walk Damira home." Pasha gives me her shoulder to lean on.

With the help of Pasha's strength, we dismiss the rest of the Company and find our way across the Zamak grounds. The lights to my house are already lit by Katiya, just waiting for me to come in.

"Would you like to come in for tea?" I ask Pasha as we're halfway up the steps.

"Tea sounds exactly like what we need." She isn't an actor supporting her playwright in this moment, but a friend comforting a friend.

I'm not sure specifically what I did to earn her fierce loyalty—or any of the Company's, really—but I will spend the rest of my life trying to be worthy of it.

The pitched tent casts reds and yellows on the faces of everyone who stands beneath it, making those in attendance at the next-to-last Revel-week activity look horridly ill. Or maybe everyone is just that worn out from the week of celebrating.

A full dress rehearsal is planned for tomorrow, and then rest for the remainder of the evening because the next day is opening night. If I were to focus on it too much, I would blend in with the ill-looking revelers.

I've been avoiding the Crown altogether. The only one who has noticed and audibly expressed it has been Raven, who only told me she understands why I haven't been around before dropping the subject altogether.

Pasha keeps her arm in mine as we weave through the crowd, looking in the stands for a place to sit. Besides Pasha, I haven't told the rest of the Company about what happened between Calix and me, but they all know, and they all keep protective arms around me when we've had to be in Court.

I am just starting to wonder if everyone looks like they are about to pass out, not from the fatigue of the Revel, but because of the horrible circulation of air in the tent, when the Crown wanders in through the opening. Calix's arm is wrapped in Lady Orli's, who laughs at something Raven says at their side. The three follow Milena, shaking hands and holding short conversations with their subjects as they pass through on the way to their seats. Calix's eyes roam casually as Orli talks to a man in an oversized hat. Sweat beads from his forehead, and I have to applaud Orli for not stepping back when the man easily invades her personal space.

My efforts to avert his eyes fall short as Calix spots me. We hold one another's stare, the crowd moving between us, unaware of the constraint coursing back and forth like electricity. I turn back around quickly, letting Pasha move me forward. The sweaty people pushing around me, and the humidity of the tent, suddenly become too much. I turn to Pasha, as we both spot Nikita and Kolyo.

"You go ahead to the stands, I need some air. I will meet back up with you all before the circus starts," I smile, trying to hide the panic rising inside of me. She studies me for a moment.

"If you need me, I am here," she says with a sad smile and lets me fight back through the crowd to the outside.

I push past the last wall of people, the cool air caressing my warmed cheeks. There are just as many people out here as there are in the tent, but they are spread out, enjoying the carnival set up around the grounds. I find a quiet place to the side of the circus tent, behind a stall that is running a card game for kids to try and win a prize. Squeals of the children overlap the chatter of adults, and music that comes from a band is somewhere in the mix.

It's not just Calix that has set me on edge during the Revel, but more so, what it means that I was so hurt by him. I am seeing just how far behind enemy lines I truly am, how I am losing myself in the midst of it. Wanting Calix to choose me means I have started neglecting my mission here. I just never expected these people, the Crown, Court, to be so similar to me, to Reine.

It's terrifying to look a monster in its face and realize it is nothing more than a mirror.

"I'm told you are the woman they commissioned to write the play that will wrap up our spring celebration?"

I turn to Lady Orli standing behind me, the light breeze picking up her blonde hair and waltzing with it. I bow my head slightly, acknowledging her title and future title over mine. She wears a beautiful blue gown that matches the sky, wisps of white fabric like clouds tied at her shoulders and waist. She doesn't need an extravagant dress to be beautiful, she simply is. My own dress of light green pales in comparison.

"Damira," I extend my hand to hers. She shakes it with a gentle touch.

"It's nice to *officially* meet you." She gives me that same knowing smile as she did when she saw my similarly ink-stained fingers. Neither of us further acknowledges that night. She is an artist, a writer—we understand each other beyond pleasantries.

"Likewise."

I have no reason to hate her. I don't know what she stands for, and I am quite sure she has as little say in her new betrothal as Calix does. She has a kind way about her, like one of those people who have things just work out for them, no matter the circumstance. If anyone is to have such a gift, I am glad it is the one to whom Calix is now linked. Maybe some of her good luck will rub off on him.

"I was looking for solace away from the crowd for a breath, but I am glad to have run into you. You have gotten close to the Crown since you have been here. You dine with them nightly?" she asks with a tilt of her head.

"Indeed, I have become quite close to the twin royals in my short months here."

I have been spotted publicly with both Calix and Raven, it would be foolish to hide such information that she already seems to know. Though, telling the truth makes me feel as if I'm doing something wrong. I am always caught between being a bad liar and it being second nature to hide the truth. Calix is a paradox, being too many things at once, but I am an absolute zero on a thermometer, nothingness, falling just below anything. Obsolete because of my contradictions.

"I was hesitant to come here, upon my father's wishes. It sounds as if you can tell me honestly, though—what have I been thrown into?"

I laugh a bit, knowing her nervousness well. I wore it close to my chest like a familiar scarf just months ago. "I might not agree with everything they stand for, but they are good. At least, Calix and

Raven are trustworthy. You will live a full life here," I assure her. I wish my words were a lie.

"I hope I am not overstepping a boundary with this question, but I've noticed you and Prince Calix always seem to find each other in a room." Observant eyes, she might actually do well at Court.

"I'm not sure I understand your question, Lady." I have learned a thing or two of Court as well. Always clarify what one means in order to give the least amount of information away.

"Will it be a threat to my marriage?" I don't bother denying her claims. She isn't looking at me like I am some kind of competition, but more like a person trying to learn a new language. She's trying to get an understanding of a life she was pushed into, just as I was.

"No, I assure you. We are nothing." There has been too much truth today, it makes my skin itch.

She adjusts her dress, flattening a layer that has been tossed by the wind. "There are some people we will always be aware of when they walk into a room. Even if you are no more than strangers at that point in time, you can never go back to nothingness. My father is an astronomer, he talks often about the stars and things much above my understanding. However, from what I gather, you cannot reduce a thing that existed into oblivion. It is impossible to completely erase mass. You can rearrange it, but to take something that once was and diminish it to obscurity is impossible. Love never truly disappears, it only changes forms."

I take in her words, what they mean, especially coming from the woman betrothed to the man she infers.

In my silence, she adds her driving point again. "You will always find him in a crowded room. You cannot erase that." She means to be comforting, that just because our circumstances prevent us from being together, we can never erase what we once were. But I don't find the succor she tries to offer. It feels like a life sentence instead. I am sentenced to live a life without reprieve from his memory.

I can leave Hedeon behind, but I can never erase it.

Music erupts behind the curtain, drums and brass instruments screaming an inviting tune.

"We'd better get back, Lady. Thank you for your words, I appreciate your kindness."

"I am glad to have a friend within the Zamak walls." I believe she truly means it.

We walk back into the tent, separating when we reach a fork to our seats. I settle in between Pasha and Deacon, just in time for the band to finish their opening number. Deacon takes my hand in his, giving me a reassuring smile. I glance around, taking note of all the people who are here. Across the dirt pit, the Crown sits, Lady Orli just finding her seat beside Calix. Raven and Milena laugh to each other, pointing at the jesters that are exiting from behind a small curtain.

My eyes trace past Calix, but at the same time, he is scanning the crowd. Our eyes meet accidentally across the chaos, landing for only a breath. We will always find each other in a crowded room.

26

"THE FLOWER PICKING WAS my favorite!" Anya shouts in front of me.

"No! The carnival was the best, the fortune teller told me I would marry someone rich with luscious hair," Alek protests, taking a piece of my hair and spinning it around itself. The two miniature royals sit close to me, playing with my hair and poking the lines of my face. I lay on the floor in front of the couch where Calix reclines, suspiciously close. Raven and Milena rest in the armchairs.

Milena made sure to insist my presence at dinner tonight. The last before the play. Before my world changes once again. I'm not sure if it was Calix's or Milena's doing, but Orli didn't join us for the meal. Everyone chatted as we ate, except Calix and me.

"I think seeing Damira all dressed up was actually my favorite. She looked like a princess, like one of us!" Anya corrects herself, shooting her hand into the air, making sure all of the attention is on her.

"She looked very beautiful," Milena agrees. Raven nods at her side, and I have to force myself not to glance at Calix.

The fire warms my back, and though I am glad to be rid of this whole experience in the Zamak, I might actually miss moments like these. Moments where I am allowed to be soft. It's difficult to remember who I was before all the tragedy, but I think that if I grew up in a different life, I would be a softer person, a daydreamer. I believe I am these things at my core, and they peek out in different ways, but they hide behind a shield of anger. I think of that statue once again, the one I saw all those years ago, the woman using her soft body to protect the city behind her.

She didn't take up a sword, she defended those she loved with all she had. Herself.

I'm not sure who myself is, but I want to find her. I want to tear off the anger like scales and reveal who I am without any armor. Someone who cries and loves with no fear, and dreams and laughs loudly, and loses herself in the enjoyment of flowers.

The door swings open, the queen mother and Lev enter so quickly I barely register to sit up. Steam might as well come from the hot heads of the pair.

"We know it was you!" The queen mother relies on her cane as she walks in, Lev on her heals.

She points right at me.

I sit up on my elbows, Alek and Anya spinning around on their knees.

"You have infiltrated us with your lies. You think you can just come in here and play us for fools. How dare you!" The queen mother screams at me. I stand, Calix jumping up just as quickly. He stands in front of me, but I can't tell if it is because of where we were sitting or if it is out of protection.

"Mother, what is going on?" Milena demands, standing as well.

"She is friends with the spy we caught," Lev accuses, pointing straight through Calix and to me. It takes everything to coax the dread from my face. I truly am a horrible spy.

"Who?" I ask quietly, knowing it has to be Tenny.

"A maid. She was caught lurking in the treasury. The same maid that my spies have seen you with down at the base of the Krepost, and the one that Katiya found bleeding in your kitchen a few weeks ago." The accusation from Lev hangs in the air.

Everyone slowly turns to me.

"Alek and Anya, out. Now!" the queen demands. The two scurry away without contest.

"I didn't know being friends with a maid was call for treason," I laugh nervously, keeping my eyes down and pleading innocence. The shock is real though. Katiya sold me out. I should have suspected as much, but I didn't want to believe it.

"It's not, don't be contrite." Raven moves to my side, taking my hand. "Lev, what other evidence do you have? Because, if this is all, you are making wide claims." The ice in her voice like that of a future queen.

"Why was she bleeding in the kitchen?"

My eyes flicker around the room, to each face. I have exactly one way to get out of this, so I need to be careful with these next words.

"She came to me beaten and bleeding and said it was at the hand of her employer. I didn't have the heart to make her repeat a story of such trauma, so I offered to clean her up. She was terrified and needed help."

"How do you know her in the first place?" The thought of being friends with a maid so beneath the queen mother, the only right answer must be treason.

"We knew each other as children and ran into one another while I have been here. We meet at the bottom of the Krepost because that is where she stays. She talked about her maid work, and I shared about my play. I assure you, I have no knowledge of her being a spy." Most of my dishonesty is generally by omission, I just carefully leave out the entirety of the truth. But this is a flat-out lie, and I pray to The Faits they don't see through it.

Lev glances to the queen mother, no doubt having already questioned Tenny. He nods once, telling her my story lines up.

"I stand by my accusations." The queen mother keeps her chin up, eyes angled down only to Milena.

"Unless you are calling a formal hearing on the matter, then I think you'd better leave, Grandmother." Calix meets her stare.

She huffs, waiting for the queen to say something more, but Milena silently backs Calix. I want to hug him and yell at him at the same time. Choosing me over his family, even if it is the ruler of nightmares, is going to scar him one day when he realizes he's defended the enemy.

"I will come back with my proof. You all are disgraces, standing behind a peasant girl rather than your own blood. How did we end up here? Our ancestors would be appalled." It would be a yell, if she had it in her, but instead she points her cane with a jut and leaves the room. Lev follows her silently.

I exhale audibly, the tension leaching from the room. Calix turns to face me.

"Damira—"

"I am so sorry to have been the center of all of that discomfort. I think I will take my leave for the night." I smile softly to each of them.

"I apologize for my mother, Damira. I hope you take no personal offense to her and Lev's whims. They must busy themselves somehow. I am just sorry you are the fixation this time." Milena nods her head to me.

"Thank you, Moi Nachalnik. I am just shocked by the news of my friend. Have a goodnight, everyone."

I see myself out and back to my house, Lev not escorting me tonight.

Katiya is just heading to bed when I arrive. I can't find anything to say to her, so I just see myself to bed. I had already lingered after dinner, and then all of that with the queen mother. It is much later than I should be awake, especially with opening night tomorrow.

But all I can think about is Tenny.

My hands buzz with creating. Sometimes I can't understand my own feelings until I write them down. The world doesn't make sense to me until I put pen to paper. I sit down at my desk and pick up my journal. The world comes alive at the tip of a pen. Words explode, always as free-flowing as the ink. No tongue to gatekeep, to taste the words before deciding whether or not to spit them out. Thoughts and emotions pour out onto the page like blood from an open wound.

I haven't shared with Tenny my decision to join the Network. If she's caught, my passage won't be secure. I will be forced to stay, unable to escape after the play. I will have to go through with the tour if the queen doesn't have me imprisoned, and continue playing this role I was cast into without an audition.

That is the next thing I must focus on. Not the fact that Tenny is in a cell, that she could be forgotten about like Calliope's dad. Because as long as I am here, she won't be forgotten. I will get her out. Somehow. The Network is extensive, woven through the fabric of Hedeon. Surely there must be a way to use it to help Tenny. There have to be protocols, backup plans. Tenny is higher up in the Network, I know she is. They wouldn't just leave her to rot. They can't.

As much as I try to keep my mind away from it, I am met with the reality that this is all my fault. If I hadn't insisted on staying out of the Network dealings until the play, if I hadn't made Tenny think this is all frivolous to me, if I hadn't been so focused on Calix and his betrothal, I could have been helping Tenny. I could have been eyes where she needed them, could have saved her from ending up in a cell.

A creak comes from behind me, and I twist to my door, dropping the pen as if it were on fire. The door opens slowly, and I stand to meet the intruder, only armed with the pen I pick back up for defense, certain the queen mother has sent someone to finish the job. Maybe it's Lev, finally holding true to his words that he would be my end. Thoughts race past my eyes in terror, all of the people who would want me dead if they found out any of my secrets.

Calix's head emerges from the crack in the door, with only candlelight in the room illuminating his eyes. I exhale, setting the pen on the desk behind me. If Calix was here to end me, I would just have to lie down and let him. I am plagued by an inability to fight against him. He smiles softly, meeting my eyes and deciding it is okay to come in. The door pushes further as he enters.

I don't think, and clearly, he doesn't either. His arms find me, and I am wrapped in his embrace inside the span of a breath. He is engaged. We are friends. Friends hug. The reasoning is sound when his arms are so secure around me, holding the thought firmly in my head.

"Are you okay?" He finds words better than I do.

I give no answer to the loaded question. I haven't been okay since my last step in Reine. For all the things I don't remember, I remember when my foot left the soil of home for the last time. It haunts me, the vow I made, even at so young an age. I would be back. I would not rest until I ran, walked, stumbled, crawled, back. I have been fraying at the edges ever since, losing strings of myself, a trail somewhere in the tangle, leading me back to who I am, to Reine.

I just look up at him.

"Do you want to speak with her?" he whispers, scared of the bed and chairs and walls listening. My eyes grow, the possibility hadn't even entered my mind. I could see Tenny.

"You would let me?" The shock not something I have to fabricate.

"You looked beside yourself when you were explaining to my grandmother. She was your friend. Even if she is a traitor, your friendship was still real. At least for you it looks to be." His voice whirls with the night, two of the same darknesses chasing each other like playful foxes.

"I would like to see her, just once," I conclude, after looking in his eyes and weighing the option.

"Follow me." He turns, intending to grab my hand, but then stops, remembering himself. I follow him into the hallway that is coated in night just as my room. Maybe even a few extra layers. Calix takes certain steps. I have to squint to follow him.

He pauses so abruptly I almost smack straight into his back. He pushes the wall in a few places before a click bounces off the empty hallway and a portion of the wall opens in on itself. The darkness gives way to two torches hovering just below Raven's smiling face.

"Seems we had the same idea," Calix explains Raven, grabbing a torch from her.

"He bumped into me in the tunnels. I would like it noted that I was ahead of him, therefore it was my idea first." Raven turns to lead us through the shadows.

"We wanted to make sure you were okay," Raven softly adds.

Calix lets me follow after Raven, pulling the door shut behind us. I wonder how many more tunnels are carved into the walls of my house.

"Take a left up here, Rave. That should lead down to the dungeon," Calix throws his words over my shoulder to his sister.

"You don't think I know that? I have been exploring these tunnels just as long as you, Cal," Raven mutters, the impatience with her brother ever on display, something I will miss.

Our silence is as quiet as the dark, only punctured by the two small flames. We continue that way until we hit a set of stairs. I welcome the sight, pained by walking, and hope it is a good sign that we have almost arrived.

"Down the stairs, two rights, then pull the lever," Calix nods toward the steps, handing me his torch.

"We will wait here for you," Raven nods with sympathy in her eyes.

I don't know how to repay them for the help they don't know they are giving me.

The stairs are steep and slanted forward, making it incredibly easy to slip. I walk slowly, one misstep and I will slide down the remaining steps. Two rights. The light comes with the first turn, lanterns and torches held to the wall by iron bolts. The stone cracks below it, like someone has pulled on them, trying to get the fire to release from its holds. Streams run down the sides of the hallway, descending lower into the heart of the Zamak. I follow the water.

One more right. The cells come into view. A sinking feeling in my stomach comes with it. Ten oddly shaped cells are built on square islands. Water, a pond—an ocean surrounds the cells. Most people, peasants especially, can't swim. Never finding enough time off to get close to a body of water. It is an extra coat of control, of containment.

A large lever hangs from the wall to the right of the passageway opening. I tug it, as per Calix's instruction. The ground shivers, rock scraping against rock. A pathway emerges from the water, steppingstones to the cages.

I follow the path that leads to the clump of cells. As I get closer, I can make out Tenny's silhouette in the furthest cage to the right. I break off the main path, to the trail that leads straight to her personal prison.

The cell has one curved wall made of stone and three walls of iron bars. She huddles where the solid wall and bars meet, her back pressed up to the metal. Her head is tucked into her knees, and she is deathly still.

"Tenny," I whisper as I get closer.

The others in the cells haven't taken notice of me, and I would like to keep it that way. Though, they all seem deteriorating enough that I could overpower them with one brisk blow, even with my ineptness at fighting. Something tells me these prisons are reserved for those who commit serious crimes against the Crown, their treason an unforgettable kind. I assume they are playthings for the queen mother.

"Tenny," I whisper again as I jump the last stone to her island. She turns around, either at my voice or the sound I make hitting the loose gravel.

"Damira," she perks up, unfolding herself from the contorted way she was sitting.

"I thought you were the guards." She straightens her back and looks more like the wildfire I know. She stands, gripping the bars and looking like, if she pulled hard enough, her steel would be no match for the iron.

"What are you doing here?" Her eyes dart back and forth, left and right, more alert than usual. For good reason.

"Calix and Raven brought me. They thought I might want to talk to the friend that betrayed me," I tell her, eyebrow lifted.

"It was an accident. I told you I would keep you out of it, and I was trying, but we needed one more thing from the treasury, and I thought I could sneak in and out without being noticed," she explains. "Turns out I couldn't." She gives me a toothy smile, her calmness reassuring.

"So, you have a plan, then? To get us out of this?" I keep my voice down. She nods, smiling with her eyes.

"I want to join the Network," I rush out before something else can get in the way of me uttering these words.

"I know."

"You do?"

"I know you better than you seem to think. I already took care of everything that we'll need to get us both out after the play."

"Anything I need to do?" The relief floods through me so quickly I almost need to sit down. We have a plan. Tenny will be okay. We will still get out.

"Nope. I told you, I will keep you out of this. Continue with our plan for after the play, nothing has changed. I can still get you out of the Zamak. Think of this as nothing more than a little hiccup."

"You are in a cell."

"Fine, it's a belch. Whatever. Nothing has changed. I will be out of here soon enough, and so will you."

I nod, glancing back to the passageway. I need to keep this brief.

"What do I tell Calix and Raven?"

"That we talked, and I apologized for lying to you. Nothing more needs to be said, it doesn't seem like they suspect you," she shrugs.

After all of the lying I have been forced into, you would think it would come naturally by now, but it does not.

"See you on the other side," she nods, and I return the gesture.

"Eyes and ears up."

"Ears and eyes up."

I jump back through the path, making it to the passageway, only stopping to push the lever back in place like I was never here. Raven and Calix wait at the stairs where I left them. Raven sitting on the top step, and Calix leaning against the wall with crossed arms. They don't seem to have been talking, the strain still between them. If they spoke, I am sure they would see they are much more alike than they think. Their lack of communication will surely spite them both eventually.

"How'd it go?" Raven stands when she spots me.

"She apologized, said she hadn't meant to bring me into the middle of this." I add a dumbfounded look and a question in my voice.

"Let's get some rest." Calix lets that be that.

"Cal, I think you can see Damira back to her room. I am utterly exhausted and want nothing more than to jump into bed," Raven sighs, taking off ahead of us and turning the opposite way we came, leaving no room for opposition. Though she is in a quarrel with her brother, she is still trying to do what's best for him, and in her eyes, that seems to be me.

"Guess it's just me and you." Calix gestures his hand out, letting me take the lead again. I wish the thought of him and me together didn't set tongues of flames off in my stomach.

He calls out directions when I hesitate at which path to take, but we find the door easily. My hallway is still dark, still quiet, still protecting us from the exposure of light. Everything comes out in the light. There is nowhere to hide in the day, not like how you can leave secrets in the night.

Calix walks me all the way back to my room, though we both know there is no reason for him to do it. We are secured behind my door before I speak.

"Thank you." I dip my head, putting a fair amount of space between us.

"Mira—" My name on his lips melts through me like warm honey sticking to every exposed part of my body.

"Cal—" the nickname slips off my tongue. It is all I can offer him. I can't touch him, can't explain why I will be leaving, can't promise myself to him in the way I so deeply wish I could.

So, this has to be enough.

"I will see you tomorrow." The first hint of tiredness comes through his words.

"Tomorrow," I agree.

He leaves without saying anything else. I sit on my bed, staring at the closed door he leaves in his wake.

27

I DON'T RECOGNIZE THE girl staring back at me, though that's become a common occurrence. The dress I helped Port design for the night is blue—cobalt, the tailor whispered to himself. It sparkles like the night sky. Raven had left the room when I gave the instructions to the tailor. It was risky, and it could be suspicious after the contents of the play are revealed, but I will be long gone by the time anyone is onto me.

In true Reine fashion, the dress is fitted, long, and slim. I have never dared wear anything that points to my kingdom, but the vague memories of women from home always wearing such exquisitely simple dresses like this one connect me in some way to my ancestors. It gives me confidence to overpower the fear that lies so close to the surface.

We still have hours until the theatre doors open, but I had to get ready early so I can see to everyone else's needs and make sure everything is put in place. The halls are quiet today, everyone holding their breath in anticipation for tonight. I come up the back stairwell, into the foyer of the Arman. The walls are bare. I had all the extravagance of the room stripped. Mirrors covered, paintings removed. If it wasn't a permanent fixture, it is residing somewhere else for now.

In the place of extravagance, my portraits stand. Faces of those who raised me. Faces of those who live on the streets of the Hovel. Each face in perpetual pleading. I hadn't meant to paint them with such desperation, but when I remembered their faces, I realized I've never known them to wear a different expression.

Eight paintings in total.

Eight faces victimized by the Crown.

The tone will be set the minute the audience walks into the foyer. The strangeness of the night glaring in everyone's faces. It is all or nothing now. I stall in front of Safler's portrait. I hope I did right by her. If she were to ever know what I am doing here, I hope she would be proud.

I glance back one last time as I exit the foyer, the emptiness, the sacredness of quiet. I leave them behind once more, making my way down the hall. Backstage is alight with light, a buzz of energy so electric it could power the theatre itself. Laughing and talking float through the tunnels and rooms, all the doors flung open so the Company can stumble back and forth to help one another dress.

Someone whistles, and when I turn, Dilean winks, leaning out of a doorway. His military jacket is halfway buttoned, his undershirt sticking out, contrasting the vintage embellishments.

"Looking good, Moi Dramaturg," he calls.

Nikita and Kolyo stick their heads out of the rooms that line the long hallway, agreeing with Dilean with giant smiles. It coaxes a laugh from my tightly wound core.

"Trying to impress us?" Myka calls as I continue.

"How's your head?" The bandage has been painted over with makeup so it's barely visible.

"Still attached to my neck," she smirks, turning back into her room.

I roll my eyes but am thankful she is in good spirits. A few more whistles and shouts from the Company follow me before I find the room I am in pursuit of.

Deacon sits in front of a vanity of mirrors, looking himself dead in the eye.

"You're going to do great," I lean on the doorframe with crossed arms. Deacon looks up to me and sighs heavily.

"I know. I think I know, at least. I always get terrible nerves before a performance. But I am sitting here, and I should be more nervous than I ever have been because this is more important than anything I've ever done, and—" He loses his words, chewing on them for a moment. I wait, knowing I need to give Deacon a few extra beats of silence to construct his thoughts.

"I am not nervous. I am so confident in the music I can feel it in my bone marrow. My whole life, I have been preparing for this performance, even if I didn't know it." He speaks with assurance. "Thank you." He stops abruptly, turning around fully to me. "Thank you for giving me a voice and for letting me have a chance to put my heart into this. They might have never heard me before, but they will hear me tonight." In the gratitude, there is a vow.

"I will see you out there." I bow my head, delaying the final words that are inevitable. I stay a moment longer, watching him finally pull a comb through his hair, not that it looks to be doing anything.

The rest of the Company condenses into two dressing rooms, patting on makeup and sewing up last-minute costume malfunctions. I watch on in silence. The Arman has been working together for many shows. They have a rhythm when they practice, but when they work together in full action, in their element, it is mesmerizing.

Calliope and Anoki sit in front of mirrors, speaking quietly, almost in full costume. Calliope in an extravagant dress and headpiece, Anoki in a long jacket with fake jewels around his neck. Their attention pulls from each other to me as I approach them.

"You two look—" I can't finish my sentence, there are no words to describe the things I feel. The idea in my mind has come to life and sits in front of me. No one has created language to describe such an occurrence. Calliope and Anoki let me stare, tears threatening, but I hold them back. Not yet.

"I could never thank you two enough." I want to say so much more but lack the ability to do so. It has been hard to keep my secret from Cal and Raven, but it has been near impossible to not confide in these friends. These people who are putting so much on the line for my silly little story.

As if Calliope knows my thoughts, she stands and hugs me, whispering in my ear, "*Thank you*, Moi Dramaturg, for speaking your heart, even when it is dangerous, even when it is easier not to do so. You have changed us." Calliope pulls back, taking me by the shoulders.

"We both mean that." She looks back to Anoki who offers a little nod.

"I will see you in ten," is all I can choke out.

"You look alluring, by the way," Calliope winks as I turn to walk back through the dressing room and down the buzzing hall.

I am the first to arrive. The stage is empty, the theatre quiet, the bat peering over us all. The doors will open soon, and the room will be packed, completely sold out. The stage is assembled with the set, the crew took my vision and surpassed it. I wish I could sit in this moment forever, in the silence. In the protection.

Few by few, the Company starts coming in, invading the silence with their symphony of voices. They hug and lean on each other—Pasha's arm is around my waist, so I seamlessly blend in with the others. Before long, we are all assembled in a circle, every eye looking at me.

The heaviness has been sewn into the air, but it isn't the only string connecting us. Through the impossible task that we are about to undergo, the excitement of sharing our creation with the world is wound just tight enough for us to hold onto. That is the thread I cling to now, desperate that if I keep it within my grasp, then perhaps the string that holds the sword above my neck won't be loosened.

"Well, happy opening night, everyone," I laugh. All at once, they erupt in claps and hollers. Dilean chants senseless words. Kolyo whistles with fingers between his teeth. Ira looks like she might puke.

I have run through this moment again and again in my head every night before falling asleep. I should have the words down—should have taken a moment to write something, but every time I tried to perfect the things I wanted to say—well, fear is a stifling thing. So that is where I begin.

"Two months ago, I was terrified when I was summoned to the Zamak by the queen. I had no clue what I was to write, what this play should be. But here we are. This play would not be what it is without every one of you. You have brought the world in my head to life, and I could never repay you for being willing to tell this story."

I try not to stumble over my words. I'm not sure if I make any sense, if they can feel the gratitude I am unable to convey. Pasha takes my hand, and Deacon at my other side presses in even closer. Perhaps we are all the same in this—our words could not do the justice that leaning into one another's strength can. I take a shaky breath, having to continue with the words I don't know how to say.

"Before we go on, though, I want to make sure everyone is still certain in their position here tonight. This is your last chance to walk away. We are all aware of how this story could be construed.

There could be consequences that will change your life if the queen is disappointed. If you do not want that, I understand, and you can walk away right here, right now. We will manage, I will take the fall, but this is the last chance before there is no turning back."

I pause, making sure to lock eyes with everyone in the circle around me. Deacon and Pasha and Myka and Calliope and Anoki. Kolyo, Dilean, Ira. Pasha picks up my hand as I can't control the tears rising in my eyes. But it doesn't stop with me, on my other side, Deacon picks up my hand and Ira's next to him. All around the circle, one by one, everyone holds the hand of their friend beside them.

"I could never thank you all enough. Whatever end, it has been an honor," I choke out, having to be okay with these being my final words to the whole of them.

Everyone shares silent glances, but then Ira nudges Deacon, and he speaks up.

"We have a present for you." Deacon drops my hand and Ira's hand, scurrying off to the side stage and returning with a small, wooden box. I take it with shaking hands, standing only with the strength of these people beside me. The Company collectively holds their breath as I open the box. I can't even pretend to stop the tears that streak my cheeks as my eyes land on the most beautiful thing I have ever seen.

Attached to a chain, the Company somehow commissioned a flat pendant made into a replica of a woman guarding a city behind her with all that she is, a sword pointed at her finger. The statue that I saw all those years ago, perfectly depicted on this necklace.

I pull as many of my friends as I can fit within my arms into a hug.

The clock tower cries out from outside the Arman. It is time to open the doors.

We stay as one for a breath longer, holding each other tightly in the face of the unknown that awaits us.

Pasha and I are the last to release from the hug. Kolyo grabs the necklace from me and secures it around my neck. The intimate gesture causes more tears to rise and fall. They have all been so kind to me, and I could be sentencing them to life in exile for this play.

"I will make it worth it," I promise again to Kolyo. To them all.

He pats me on the shoulder and fades back into the group. We all linger on the stage, the final calm before we change our lives forever. The stage makeup the Company is coated in hides most of the splotchiness on their faces from crying, except for Deacon, who will surely have to go and redo most of his face.

"See you all on the other side," I lie.

Everyone takes their turn hugging me individually and then exiting to take their places. After Myka leaves last, I walk down the stage stairs and stop in the middle of the chairs. The golden bat lurks atop the stage, watching over the sets that we have put our all into creating. I thought my whole life was leading up to me going back to Reine, but perhaps everything has been leading to this moment, to this stage.

I send up a quick prayer to The Faits that tonight will not end in utter defeat, before turning and leaving the empty theatre for the last time.

The hallways wait in silence to hear the verdict of my future before passing judgment. For now, I am still allowed to walk through them unobstructed, but in the calm, I can't help but wonder for how much longer.

The grand doors open slowly, the heaviness adding to the dramatics. I walk down the grand staircase as the first few people enter, and then the flood follows, a crowd surging through the theatre.

Court has arrived.

I stand at the edge of the stairs, watching everyone's faces fall when their eyes land upon the portraits. Confused mutters and questions puncture the easy air they brought in with them. I watch as Court works through the confusion.

"Your dress—" Anna exclaims as she walks up to me, eyes tracing me from head to toe.

"Progressive in fashion, as always," she winks with an approving nod. I sigh a little.

"Good to see you, Anna," I shake her hand in greeting. If she only knew.

"We are excited to see what you cooked up here, Dramaturg." She glances back at the portraits in a circle around the room. She nods to me with one last small smile and walks to a group of ladies chattering like birds.

The foyer empties quickly, everyone either excited to see the play, or just wanting to get out of the odd air of the hall. Everyone is here, from all of Court to peasants who have barely the funds to scrape an outfit together. The queen has talked the show up for weeks, if only she knew what she was promoting.

A man walks by me, alone and obviously one of those here on the Crown's coin. His hat has a hole in the side, but the rest of his garments are much more presentable. He glances at each painting thoughtfully, not grimacing as I watched many do. Most of the crowd has made their way up the staircase, but he observes, taking off his hat in what I can only assume is respect.

"I know her. It's been years since I've seen her, but I know her," the man whispers to me when I approach him. I stand at his side, gazing upon Safler. Of course, it's Safler.

"She used to be friends with my mother. I forget her name, but she would come over to my house growing up. Not often, but enough that I still think of her from time to time." His accent is thick, of the rural areas around the Hovel. I don't name Safler to him. I don't sense that he wants me to say anything at all. He just needs me to listen.

"She's about twenty years older in this painting than when I knew her, but even then, she looked like she was deteriorating. And yet she was always so full of life. I suppose you can't have one without the other, but the contrast never failed to surprise me. My mother passed last year, but it's good to see her friend still has some havoc left to wreak," he laughs to himself a bit and then bows slightly, walking past me and up to the theatre with the others.

After a few moments of pondering the stranger's words, I follow the last stragglers up the staircase that sweeps through the foyer.

"Damira." The voice of iron calls from behind me, stilling my entire being. The way his voice molds to something in me will always set me on edge. He shouldn't have that much power over me.

I look over my shoulder, halfway up the staircase.

Cal waits at the bottom, looking up to me. He wears a grey uniform, a gold embroidered bat across his chest. Pins are attached above the wing of the bat, ropes woven on his shoulder. He looks all the prince that he truly is. His hair is tame for the first time since I've known him, combed back and styled. It makes his green eyes shine even brighter.

"You—" he breathes, walking up a few steps. "You are incomparable."

I drop the hem of my dress, turning more to face him.

"You're late," I say, a lack of sufficient words for the second time tonight.

"I was caught up in some things. Mother should be here, though. I believe she went the back way as to not draw attention. Rave is with her in the box, waiting for me." He walks up a few more stairs, slowly, as he talks.

"And your fiancé?"

"Back home for a few weeks. Something came up, but she sends her condolences for not being able to make it." He nods, reaching the step below mine and not giving me anything more. Probably best. I will be gone tonight, and then I will be a distant memory to him. Lies always taste better when they're rooted in truth.

"I hope you enjoy the show," I nod in return and turn to leave.

"Mira," Calix grabs my wrist. I let him.

"Cal," I warn, turning back to meet his eyes. He doesn't need the warning, though. He knows.

"I hope it is all you wish it to be, darling," he says in defeat.

I try to smile, but I can't form one. Not when I'm looking at Cal and knowing it might be the last time. I have so many things I wish I could say to him. So many lies I wish to bring truth to. Instead, I turn and walk up the stairs. His eyes are on me, but he doesn't call out again. And while everything in me wishes he would, I am glad he doesn't.

Tomorrow morning, I will be out of here. Tomorrow morning, I won't have to grapple with the delight and dread that comes with the sight of Prince Calix.

Tomorrow morning.

A mantra. A melody. With each step it sings, with each pulse it beats out.

Tomorrow morning.

Milena stands in the hallway outside her box, Raven at her side, arms linked. She has never looked matronly to my eye, has only ever been the queen she claims to be. Tonight is no different. Dressed in fine jewels and cool shades, she is regal, first and foremost. Her silver hair is bound up, the dress clouding around her a deep, deep emerald. Raven's dress silhouette matches Milena's, but the color is gold with a much more sheer fabric. I can't sneak past the royal pair on my way to the wings. Raven sees me first, gasping and rushing to me.

"You are a visionary. The best Dramaturg of our time, I already know it," she squeals, leading us back to Milena.

"Damira," Milena nods to me.

I bow. "Moi Nachalnik."

"Are you excited for the first voyage of your show?" she speaks softly, the others who pass around us almost breaking their necks to get a glance at the spectacle.

"Nervous would be a better word," I admit, trying not to wrinkle the paper someone handed me at some point. I don't know how it got into my hands, but here it is now. The chaos of the night has narrowed my perception.

"After having gotten to know you, I hardly believe the show will fall short of our expectations. You will shine, Dramaturg."

"Thank you, Moi Nachalnik. I must be getting backstage." I bow to both of them, Raven beaming and Milena dismissing me with a brief nod.

I take the backstairs down to the stage. The theatre is an entity of its own. Chatter from the audience, a swarm of actors behind the curtains, the anticipation tangible.

"Everyone ready?" Kolyo shouts to the others.

"Places!" Pasha yells.

It sets the controlled chaos into motion. The orchestra runs down the stairs, the actors take their places on the stage, Deacon sits at the piano.

I can't see the golden bat from here, but I know it watches over all of us as the Arman Company takes a collective breath.

Let the play begin.

28

S OME STORIES ARE SO old, so sacred, that few people have the privilege of repeating them.

This is one of those.

Ira comes onto the stage first, sweeping a grand staircase that climbs to nowhere. An optical illusion made real by the incredible geniuses that are Pasha and Kolyo. Calliope floats down the stairs, her makeup making her look young, her dress further emphasizing the teenager she is trying to portray. She passes Ira without even a look, her nose in the air, even with the youthful smirk. When Calliope passes Ira, Ira makes a face at her back, sending an apprehensive laugh through the crowd.

When Calliope reaches the bottom of the stage, people swarm her, courtiers dressed in high elegance. Ira comes off stage, exiting in the wings where I stand. She quickly changes her outfit, slipping on a bright colored wig to match the others that now hold Calliope in conversation.

The orchestra swells below the stage as Calliope converses in incoherent chatter. I can't see Myka swinging her hands as the instruments build, but I've seen her do it enough times in practice that I know exactly what sweeping moves she makes with each melody.

Pasha is across from me in the wings, barely visible in the dark. She claps two pieces of wood together to signify a staff demanding attention. Anoki enters down the stairs. He is dressed regally, pins and a wing-spread bat on his chest. The chatter quiets from the background actors, the orchestra finding their first moment of silence. Anoki descends the stairs.

"Prince Glavnok Omanduy Ushchiy Hendricks," an announcer from the wings yells, causing not only the actors on stage to gasp at their prince, but also those in the crowd who finally realize what is happening.

This is the genesis of the war. A story so sacred it is only repeated to those with the highest of honors in Hedeon, and thus forgotten by the common folk. Every common folk except for me, because I didn't grow up in Hedeon, and this story has survived the pockets of memory loss from my childhood.

"I know just about every eligible woman in Hedeon, and yet, your face escapes me." Anoki comes up behind Calliope with a grin I've seen worn many times on a different prince. No matter how many times I've watched Anoki in rehearsal, I am always startled when he puts on the mask of his character. The cadence of his voice fastens, the way he holds himself straightens. He isn't silent and unbothered, he is commotion and feeling.

Calliope turns, and with a confidence that truly belongs to a royal, she speaks. "I don't believe we've had the pleasure of meeting yet. I am Princess Estée Amandine of Reine."

The remainder of the first act continues smoothly. Calliope and Anoki's characters keep in touch from across the Aadria River, writing letters and becoming close confidants with one another, even though their meetings are few and far between. I watch from my same place—a chair having been brought up for me—holding back tears for the entirety of it. Calliope and Anoki swing around each other in a dance without a song. The words are bitter as they speak of their people with disdain, but their delivery is as light as a spring breeze.

Deacon comes in with his first song—behind the dialogue—but slowly, it grows. Filling the gaps of emotion in their longing looks, Calliope and Anoki share from their sides of the stage, showing the distance between their kingdoms. Their characters love each other, they just don't fully know it yet.

"Damira!" Pasha whispers loudly behind me. I turn quickly to see her holding together a tear in her dress. I grab a sewing kit from an emergency stash by the stage and get to work. Ira's voice carries over us, her lines delivered with the punch we had hoped, the audience laughing and then getting quiet as the reality of the joke sets in. I want to cry out, to clap in achievement.

We are doing this.

I finish Pasha's dress, and she hugs me before scurrying back behind a few curtains so she can enter through down stage. She hits her cue perfectly, the one we have run time after time. Anoki fights with Calliope, arguing at a ball when Glavnok gets jealous of Estée talking to another man. Myka comes in with the strings, bringing in the changing of the set. The audience claps with the turnover. The piano swells, the orchestra building on top of itself. I peek out the side of the curtains, the audience's faces lit up by the stage lights.

It's been a long time since I've seen this many people gathered. All for me. All because of me. The first act is ending, and the second comes in with force. There is no going back after the second act. Rows and rows of seats packed with faces expecting to see the next biggest thing in Hedeon.

The theatre boxes are gold filigree mixed with red velvet and pastel paint. Also filled with people. My eyes run over them until they land on the one I was dreading to look at. The royal box. In the front row, the queen mother and the youngest royals. Behind them, Raven, Cal, and Milena. All watch with intrigued eyes, far from disinterested. Even the queen mother seems enthralled amidst her suspicion. It's hard to make out from here, but Calix's eyes roam over every person, every piece of the set. He even stalls on Deacon's fingers tickling the keys in a lighter moment. It only gets darker from here. I have to wonder if anyone realizes what is going on yet. No one's face gives a hint.

I return the curtain to its place, turning back to the other world. Backstage is havoc, people running and whispering and sucking down water when they get a moment offstage. Quick changes and touch-ups to their makeup.

I far more belong back here than I ever did out there.

I help with a few changes of costume, pulling on wigs and taking off shoes. We have it down to a science, so quickly that no one trips or gets more than a moment of breath before they are needed back in their place on stage. I watch the tech crew on the other side of the wings, all narrowed in on a world I still know little about.

The light changes, the music shifts, and Act 2 begins.

I hold my breath as the actors move in darkness, setting their spots and faces.

Anoki and Calliope, Glavnok and Estée, embrace center stage, their clothes more mature, their makeup showing that years have passed. They are middle-aged now, alone in the center spotlight.

"Leave her, forget about her. Please, Nok. Please," Calliope begs.

Anoki, with such pain in his eyes I would think he truly loved Calliope, takes a step back. Dropping their hands between them.

"I can't end this engagement, Estée. Hedeon needs this." Anoki shakes his head, taking another step back. The crowd collectively sighs as he crosses the room, leaving Calliope in tears as he chooses his kingdom over the woman he loves.

The second act bleeds into the third with no intermission.

Glavnok comes back to Estée after trying to live with his be-trothed for a number of months, but when they meet again, Estée too has become engaged. The roles are reversed this time. Glavnok begs Estée to flee to Hedeon with him, where they can be wed, and this game they've been playing will no longer hinder the love between them.

It's Estée's turn to drop the hands between them. For Reine to prosper, she needs to go through with her engagement. Not only that, but Estée has started to slowly fall for her newly betrothed. Dilean plays the part of fiancé to Calliope well, trying to convince her to love him by showing up for her, by bringing her flowers, and being what Glavnok didn't know how to be—kind.

Estée cuts ties with Glavnok, but he won't go so easily. He will fight for her. And he does.

From the parts of the story I have been able to gather from Hedeonites, this is where the retelling forks. I had been taught in Reine that Glavnok burned Reine in his rage, taking the rejection as well as a toddler takes to being told no. Hedeonites have been told that Estée was so cold, she couldn't be satisfied with just taking Glavnok's heart from him, but she was greedy for his kingdom and stole his land.

I don't retell either version.

The fourth act opens at the start of the war. Estée is in tears in her new husband's arms as her Reine suffers from being cut off from Hedeon's goods. Glavnok is alone and plotting to keep his Hedeon intact while his citizens die from not having Reine's grains. The war hasn't drawn blood yet, but it already sees people suffering. The reality is magnified by the orphan, Ira, frozen in the streets. The despair borrowed from the paintings in the foyer and displayed here on stage.

I am holding my breath as Deacon's big piece is coming. No one in the audience has made a noise for quite some time. I can't bring myself to peek back out from the curtain. I am not sure I want to see what waits for me.

Anoki, Calliope, and Dilean are alone on stage, facing each other. They freeze in place as the spotlight moves from their angered words and heavy breathing after a fight, to Deacon at the piano. The three quietly leave the stage, so Deacon is alone. With a breath, his fingers finish the transition melody. He lets the silence linger as he stares at the keys. I am not sure anyone in the audience is even breathing. I didn't know such silence could be achievable in such a large crowd.

Deacon takes a deep breath, the silence yielding to it. He brings his hands down, they land exactly where they need to hit. His fingers trace the notes he has been practicing for close to two months. Played over and over again, but he hasn't lost any emotion. If anything, the repetition only added to the feeling oozing from the notes. With every repeat in the times he practiced, he unlocked a new layer, a new understanding of his emotions, allowing them to break through. He's turned every note upside down and right again, knowing the music in a way no one else could. This is how he makes the audience feel every beat, every breath, every moment.

He demands attention like the tragedy we are.

The music builds and then falls, he passes right through the runs he was having trouble with, giving no sign of relief. He is one with the song, there is no way he could mess it up. I bleed onto paper when I write, he bleeds onto the piano when he plays.

Abruptly, the piece ends, he stands, hovering over the keys and panting. A beat passes and no one claps for him, another beat, and I think we might be stopped before we can even finish the last scene. But then the crowd erupts in deafening applause. Instead of smiling or bowing, Deacon regains his bench, sits and continues on with the underlying melody of the show, calling for the actors' last words.

In the final scene, almost everyone is on stage in their battle gear, hiding in the shadows. The music starts to fade, the words whispering into nothingness. Dilean dies in Calliope's arms. This is a part of the story that I am sure is true but hasn't been echoed in Hedeon in all my research. Glavnok was aiming for Estée, but her betrothed was the one greeted with death when he jumped in her defense. Calliope weeps over him. She is a good actor, an amazing one, but those tears are real, and everyone knows it. She screams and yells and displays the emotion she's had to keep hidden for years. It might be Dilean in her lap, but I wonder if she sees her father, her brother, the rest of the kingdom who finds themselves in the same position.

Fighting a war that never had anything to do with them.

"We didn't have to end like this," Glavnok—Anoki—roars.

"No, we didn't have to end like this. And we don't have to continue on like this either." Estée—Calliope—bears the ice that can no longer only be claimed by Hedeon.

The spotlight expands to the background actors, the soldiers on the battlefield. But as the light illuminates them, each side doesn't wear the antique uniforms they have been wearing throughout the play. Reine wears uniforms familiar to my childhood, and the Hedeon side now wear the modern grey uniforms with a black stripe down the side.

The lights cut off. Silence. People mutter, whisperings of uncertainty. One sure clap cuts through the hesitation, a few claps follow. A sad excuse for an applause.

The lights turn back on, and the whole of the cast and crew come out, hand in hand. No one smiles, they are stone-faced as they stare at the crowd. They all turn to me, beckoning for me to make my debut in the spotlight.

I walk out in the silence, the audible gaping in the air. This dress, this play, is all I could do for my kingdom. In a place where I have no power, this was my contribution. I am not going to let the fear of consequences belittle my moment.

I stand before a line of my closest friends. I take a step back as they break for me, and I align myself with them. My chin is up as I look out into the audience, meeting as many people's eyes as I can. They all have horror on their faces—surprise and dread. Slowly, I raise my chin higher, my eyes going directly to the box I found earlier.

The queen writhes. Calix is unreadable, and Raven has a look of surprise she isn't able to conform. For the first time, I see the resemblance between the queen mother and the queen. I lock eyes with Milena, finally, unwavering. If I am going to stick my neck out, I might as well get the whole thing chopped off.

I raise my hands slowly, to the side, fully extended.

But I don't bow.

I will never bow to her or to Hedeon. They might not know my true allegiance, but it is enough for them to know I do not support anything the Crown stands for. The rest of the Arman stands just as tall as I do, throwing condemnation with their glares.

The curtain falls, and I am left breathless.

29

S OMEWHERE IN THE DEPTHS of the Hovel, someone whispers. A whisper that sparks with admission. Somewhere in the depths of the Hovel, someone murmurs. A murmur that flickers with continuation. Somewhere in the depths of the Hovel, someone talks. A talk that catches with perseverance. Somewhere in the depths of the Hovel, someone shouts. A shout that burns with outrage.

After the Hovel, Elbrus lights.

Then Damiter.

Then Dagrav.

All through Hedeon, fire sprawls, burning everything in its path. Burning the corruption that has spread like a disease. Burning the places claimed under the Crown's authority. Burning the mines and the aqueducts and the factories. Purging the things that once were and never will be again.

Shouting begins in the streets and can be heard all the way up to the Krepost. Shouts as they push back the soldiers, shouts as they make their way to be heard, shouts as they are shot dead.

Blood. Red. Crimson. Scarlet. Leaking through the streets.

The first shot was accidental, but the second wasn't, and the third was earned. That's what the soldiers claimed.

No more death, no more war, no more starvation. That is all the people want. How can that be too much to ask?

The Zamak sits on its hill, clad in iron and crystals and jewels that were bought at a steep price. But when the people want to survive, the palace suddenly doesn't have enough.

It's just a riot. Just a temporary fixation. Give them food, give them water, and they will be fine. No need to worry, no need to fret, this won't turn into anything but a momentary nuisance. The queen's advisors lie through their teeth.

Food and water are things people need when they want to survive. And who would want to survive in a world as cruel as this one? Hope is a dangerous thing when people have no need for preservation.

A child screams somewhere in the Hovel, scared by the soldiers who are marching through, scared of the gun shots that echo off the alley ways, scared of the boots that shake the ground.

A mother pulls a child into her arms somewhere in the Hovel. The soldiers are frantic, the Crown unstable. No one knows what is going on, no one knows who the enemy is. All they know is the soldiers don't want anyone outside of their houses right now. But where does one go when they don't even have shelter?

The mother backs up, inching away from the shadows that pass. She steps on a vase, one already broken, crumbling even more with the weight of her foot. A soldier turns the corner. The mother stares down the barrel of the gun.

"Put your hands up," he yells from a distance, shaking—but the woman is at too far of a distance to tell.

The mother doesn't move, doesn't dare throw her hands to the air, not with her child in her arms.

"Put your hands where I can see them!" he yells again. His finger is on the trigger. He was never trained to only keep it there when you actually plan to shoot.

The baby whimpers. The soldier does too. The mother stands as still as possible.

"I—" The mother opens her mouth to speak, to explain, to plead.

The gun sounds.

Scaring the soldier and the baby.

The mother never had time to be scared. The bullet finds her right between the eyes, and she crumbles to the ground.

The soldier runs. The baby screams.

The mother is dead.

All because of a play.

30

AT LEAST I'M NOT in the dungeon. A cell might be a cell all the same, but at least sunlight hits me here. The window is too high up for me to see anything out of it, and it is too thin to climb out. Every once in a while, a breeze wanders through, having the freedom I might never have again.

No one came to find me after the play. I certainly didn't seek anyone out. I fell asleep in my midnight dress, hardly able to keep my eyes open when I got back to my room. The Company and I had a small gathering after the final bow. It was solemn, the consequences hanging over our heads, dropping closer with every breath. But despite the oncoming storm, we were proud.

Four people died that night. The Krepost was caught on fire. I still don't know how it happened or who started it. The consensus was clear, though. It was because of my play. I woke up during the night to soldiers bursting through my door and dragging me here. It's been a week, and no one has bothered to talk to me. I don't know what has become of the city or the people. I hear screams every once in a while, carrying up the Zamak and through my window, finding the person who is truly responsible.

My cell is three solid walls and bars locking me in. It doesn't look out to anything but a wall. They blindfolded me when they threw me in here. I have no clue where I am, and maybe if I listened better to Uncle Sumood's talks about the position of the sun, I could orient myself. But I am unable to read any of the clues it gives away.

Shuffles come from the left of the hallway. Someone is coming down the stairs. I don't perk up, not right away. I've had a few visitors, mainly to feed me or to ask obscure questions about the process of the play during the last two months. The shuffles come closer, quicker than the normal soldiers, urgency in the walk of whoever is coming.

I sit up straighter. Lev squares his shoulders as he plants himself in front of the bars, folding his arms.

"I told you we would end up here," he says with his nose in the air, a confidence that someone like him shouldn't be able to hold.

"This all affects you too, you know." I pull my legs up, draping my arms across my knees.

"And yet, I am on this side of the bars and you are on that side." I haven't seen Lev look this smug before, with the smile of a madman to his next victim.

"If the royals go down, you are out of a job. Your title doesn't save you. You are just a block in an unstable build. One tremor, and it all gets knocked over, Lev. I wouldn't have that confidence if I were you." It's nice to shed a layer of my lies. To show a bit more of who I truly am without the deception I have had to sport for so long.

Camouflage is everywhere in nature, my uncle used to tell me. He would show me the toads with their textured backs to match the soil, and the lizards with scales like bark. I have always been nothing more than a butterfly with eyes on her wings. A shadow concealed in plain light.

"Hedeon will persevere. We have for ages, and that will not stop with this reign. You are just a girl with some divisive words." He speaks as if he is the one sitting on the throne.

"At least I stand for what I believe in, instead of shrinking back in silence." He doesn't know I know of his wife and how he hasn't written poetry since her death, but it still feels good to finally say these words.

"You are nothing against an empire—you don't understand that in this moment, but you will soon."

"Did you come down here just to taunt me?" I glance to the breeze that just waltzed through the window. It is strange the sun should be out when the world is turning to ash.

"The queen sent me to fetch you." The words are glass, shattering on his tongue.

He unlocks the gate and leads me up the stairs. We come out somewhere deep in the Zamak. The hallways are empty, no maids or servants wander like they did before. Before I came and erupted their world.

I knew the play was going to create some talk, conversations between Court and the Crown. I never could have pictured myself here. No part of my mind imagined this outcome. I didn't know I held such power.

Is a revolution still a revolution if it was started by accident?

We turn through the carcass of the Zamak, the breeze the only breath. We pass through the bridge that runs over Court. The trees dying of thirst already, the floor dull from lack of use. The stalls are covered in curtains. I am not sure the walls of Court have ever witnessed this much silence.

Lev doesn't seem to notice. He carries on through the halls until we arrive at the room in which I have eaten many dinners with the royal family. I'm not sure when the monster's den turned into a haven, but I'm just realizing it now, as dread returns, dread I haven't felt since the first weeks of eating in here. Lev pushes the double doors open, striding in without waiting to be accepted. I make note of it but can't ponder his new confidence because of the scene I enter into.

The queen stands in the sitting area, just past the dinner table. Many nights, we all lounged in here. I was a fish among whales, but they now see themselves as mice among a viper. Cal stands off to her right, at a distance, and Raven is immediately to her left. They all stare at me, but Milena is the only one who meets my eyes. If the royals were taught one thing, it was how to keep emotion off their faces. Lev takes his place at the back of the room, now a silent observer, all his pageantry distinguished.

"Damira," Milena strikes. I stand naked in front of her, or at least that is what she believes, all my lies stripped bare. I still wear the midnight gown I accidentally fell asleep in after the play. It is torn and tattered now from sleeping in a cell for six days.

"Do you have any idea how much you have cost my kingdom?" I can't read her voice, can't read if execution or banishment is in my future. Would Calix barter for my survival? Would Raven? I can't look at them, nor can I bear to see if they feel the betrayal as I do.

"That wasn't my intention—"

"Then what was your intention?" Milena cuts me off, the first indication that she might be mad enough to snap her fingers and have my head.

"It was to show that this war is costing more than it has to give. Your people are deteriorating before your eyes, and they deserve to be seen, to be heard. That was my intention. To give a voice to the people who are senselessly dying."

"You were given a command to write a story of hope."

"You did not specify which kind of hope, Moi Nachalnik."

The queen gapes at this. Actually gapes.

"I did not think this would be the outcome. I did not mean for anyone to die. Call your soldiers back, work this out with your people. Please," I beg, almost on my knees. "You have a chance to stop this, to fix this." My words are soft, my eyes digging into hers like the claws of someone falling down a well. "Please."

"We are far beyond talking, Damira. My kingdom is out of control, thanks to you. They need to know who is in charge, that outrage and riots are not acceptable in Hedeon. This is all because of you. Their blood is on your hands and your hands only." She takes a step forward, solidifying her words as my fate.

I will not be killed. I will be forced to live with this guilt.

The doors slam open behind me, bouncing off the wall in fury.

"There you are!" the dreadful old lady screeches. I turn around to the queen mother wobbling in on her cane.

"I was just coming to talk with you in the prison, but to my surprise, guess who wasn't there?" Her voice is nails on a chalkboard.

"Mother, we are speaking with Damira." The words are pointed, something that wasn't meant for me to understand.

"That is all I wanted to do as well." She hobbles over to stand by the queen, in the space Calix left at her right.

A small memory flashes through my mind at the queen mother's snarl. In Reine, we had monkeys with grins that never meant anything good. They were dangerous, tearing through flesh with a blink. You had to be careful with these animals. My grandfather would shoot them on sight, explaining that something wasn't right in their mind, and the best way to deal with them was to exterminate them.

The queen mother smiles like one of those monkeys.

And I am left defenseless.

"I was talking with a sweet boy just yesterday, he goes by the name of Deacon. I believe you know him, the composer of the wonderful melodies in your play," she smiles, taking no care to the plummeting of my stomach.

I nod slowly. She doesn't go on until I acknowledge her.

"He was such a sweet boy." She lets me weigh the words she places so carefully.

He *was* such a sweet boy.

I take a step back, hitting a wall. I look up to the guard hovering over me. Grey uniform, black stripe. Back to the queen mother and her wicked smile. Lev stands a few steps behind her, for the first time, his eyes don't have that confidence he usually weightlessly carries.

"They all were rather nice people. I spoke to a few of them, though, under the circumstances, they weren't too—talkative. Shame, I rather liked the last play we had on tour. Talented individuals all gone to waste." Her smile grows with every word. I can't move, can't run. I just keep pressing back into the soldier not giving an inch.

"Mother, what did you do?" the queen breathes behind the queen mother who is moving toward me now.

"I knew you were trouble the moment I laid eyes on you, but no one listened to me. Well, let's see if the people listen now. I know how to run this kingdom, and people like you are easily silenced. Their blood is pooled outside the Arman doors, their bodies left to rot as a public spectacle. Let's see who fights back now. Let's see who dares to rise up knowing exactly what their future will be."

"You monster! You— You—" I scream, not knowing what insult I could possibly hurl. The tears interrupt before I can decide. I wail and launch myself at her. The wall reaches out from behind me and pins my arms back. I kick against him, screaming inaudible insults. The queen mother laughs close to my face.

I can hardly see her, tears blurring my vision. I can't hear anything being discussed by the Crown behind the monster in front of me. I kick and twist, but the wall has a good grip on me. I shout and wail.

Gone.

How could they all be gone?

Deacon and Pasha and Myka and Calliope and Anoki.

Kolyo, Dilean, Ira.

Dead.

Because of me and my words.

All their stories coming to one pinnacle and ending there because of me.

Pasha's laugh and Calliope's tears, and Deacon's stories. Never to be heard again.

Their blood outside the theatre doors. The place they all loved more than anywhere else, tainted in the last moments of their lives.

I should be there with them.

I wish I was.

31

I HARDLY NOTICE BEING carried back to my cell, thrown down, and left until they figure out what to do with me. Let them kill me, let them drain my blood as a public spectacle too, let no one else do what I have done.

I curl on my side where I was left, not having anything in me to move. I cry more, yell more, say their names, one by one.

They will not be forgotten.

Deacon and Pasha and Myka and Calliope and Anoki.

Kolyo, Dilean, Ira.

I sleep, I think. Their eyes flash through my mind, their smiles, their talents. Their beautiful, beautiful lives. I just saw them, how could they now be gone? If I could only get out of here, I could run to the Arman, and surely, they would be waiting for me on the stage, stretching and preparing for practice. I was just hugging Pasha. We ended the night with Dilean telling jokes and all of us so alive.

I wake with a gasp, choking on the tears I must have been crying in my sleep.

Calix sits at a distance, his knees pulled up, his eyes tracing my face.

"You are from Reine." His words fly out in the dark like a bat from a cave.

"I—" My throat is raw from all the screaming.

"You lied to me," he cuts me off. "You are a spy. You are the reason we had to fall back from Cotea—the reason our soldiers at the front line didn't get their supplies, but instead, were met with Reinen guns." He shakes his head, the curls that usually fall over his forehead are pushed back, his hands having run through them enough to flatten them.

I wish I was hearing this from Tenny or from the soldiers themselves back in Reine. That's where I was supposed to hear this beautiful information. We were all supposed to be safely back home when I heard this victory. Me and Aunt Selah and Uncle Sumood and Myla.

Calix moves his head into the lone streak of sunlight as he searches for his next words on the cell's floor between us. I wonder if he will find words for me there too. My breath catches at the sight of a yellow and purple bruise across his cheek.

He notices my surprise, offering an explanation I don't deserve. "When my mother found out I knew what the play was about, she struck me."

It's clear that it was a bit more than a single strike.

"You knew?"

I feel like those broken statues, long neglected in the graveyard down the Krepost. Things that once held beauty, once held use and meaning, discarded because their worth diminished over time. Unable to move from their burial place.

"I was in practice with you a few times a week. You don't think I caught on? Though admittedly, I just assumed you were trying to weaken the war as a whole. It never occurred to me at that time that you might have been from Reine."

He doesn't add *darling* to the end of his words, we are past terms of endearment now. I can't even be mad that I miss it. I hate myself for more consequential reasons now. There is only anger in his eyes. I stay silent, but that's not what Calix is looking for.

He stands up, and I instinctively follow.

"How dare you!" His anger moves beyond a simmer. "You have been sneaking around the Zamak for months, pretending to be friends with Rave, pretending to care about Alek and Anya, pretending to—" He cuts himself off, shaking his head, throwing his hand down as he paces.

I should be worried about how the Crown is taking all of this, what this means if Tenny is still in a cell, but all I can think of are my aunt and uncle, and that Calix knows exactly where to find them—if they aren't already long gone.

"The only reason you are not on a stake on the steps of the Arman with the others is because my grandmother wants to make a larger, more public spectacle of your death." His eyes snap down to mine as he stills abruptly.

I am a statue, discarded because my worth is diminished. I can't say anything, can't ask the questions that halt on my tongue. All I can do is stand broken in front of him.

"Say something, Damira!" he shouts. I have never seen Calix this enraged. I have seen him bitter and angry and sorrowful, but I have never seen him this full of fury. He is a king to match the queen mother. It shakes me out of my stupor, enough to find a few words.

"How did you find out I am from Reine?"

The anger only grows on his face, his jaw clenched tight, his normal paleness worsened.

"That is what you care about? Out of all the things I said, you only want to focus on that part?" he scoffs.

I dig for my words in the anger that is an endless pool in my core. "I have my family to think about, Calix. If I am found out, what will happen to them? That is all I care about, keeping them safe. I am not going to sit here and beg for your forgiveness. Your family murdered mine!"

Calix takes a step back as the words hang in the air. Surely if he had enough time to think on the truth that I am from Reine, he came to this conclusion on his own, but he still seems caught off guard. He takes a shaking breath, but keeps his eyebrows set firm against the realities that now separate us.

"I was ten," I continue. "My parents, my siblings. Gone because of this stupid war your grandmother and mother, and now you, keep fanning the flame of. I couldn't have told you any of this, not when I am trying to conserve what little this war has left me with." I don't bother keeping my voice down. If I am already found out, then it doesn't matter, I can be as reckless as I please.

"You started uprisings across Hedeon!"

How fragile the mighty Hedeon must be if a single girl's silly story can take it down. How ready was the flame to catch, that barely a spark could set it ablaze? My initial response is to laugh before the harsh realities of those implications put me next to the others outside the Arman.

"I wanted to start a conversation. I didn't mean for all of this to happen. How many times do I have to say that? I never wanted to start another war, I wanted to end the one being fought now!" My vision is stained crimson, blood coating my eyes so I will forever be reminded of my mistakes.

"You could have just given my mother what she wanted. You could have written a play about dresses and dragons, and we could have all moved on with our lives."

"Of course, I wish I had done that now! I wish and pray to The Faits that I could go back and silence my ambition. If you came here to lecture me on the consequences of my actions, rest assured, I understand them full well, Prince."

I have no fight left in me, even though the anger hasn't subsided—I'm not sure it will ever subside—I have no more will to make him or anyone else see my side of this story.

Calix takes a step forward, but not to me. He moves anxiously, from the inability to sit still. "I have been trying to slowly undo the cruel things my family has done, for years I have been pulling back our war efforts in whatever way I can. You have gone and thrown that all away. My mother is more angered than ever, and who do you think she is going to take it out on? Your people!"

He paces a few steps. I can see where he finds his anger. I would be mad at myself too. I *am* mad at myself. Calix has been fighting to end the war, and thus, fighting for my own people by default for years, and all I have done is greatly messed things up, for him, for myself, for Reine. For Hedeon.

How did I once find the prince to be as uncaring as his grandmother? He could never murder a company of people when he has actively been trying to undermine such heinous acts.

"How did you find out I am from Reine?" I ask again. If there is anything I do before I am marched to my death, I will make sure, somehow, that if my aunt and uncle are still in Hedeon, they won't be associated with my stupidity. Calix takes a deep breath, clearly still more fight in him. It's easy to fight when all your friends haven't been killed.

"My grandmother. She intercepted one of your spies on his way back from the war front. She didn't know who they had gotten their information from, but it was clear it was someone from inside the Zamak. We had thought it was your friend, at first, but the information the spy was found with was not common knowledge, not papers from a general or ones that could be so easily found." His anger boils over, fleeing the heat until all that is left is desperation at the bottom of the pot. "The information came from the papers from my room. You were the only one it could have been, and after the play, there was little doubt in anyone's mind."

"I'm sorry," I rush out, surprising us both with my apology. "I felt terrible about that even as I was doing it."

"You saved thousands of people. It would have been a blood bath," he whispers, appearing unsure of whether he should share this information with me or not. He continues with clenched fists. "I hadn't agreed with my mother to march on Cotea, we didn't have the numbers or strength, both sides would have suffered greatly, and by the calculations I figured, neither side would have come out with much to gain. Though plenty of our soldiers are captured now, they are not piled high waiting for the ground to thaw." It's not gratitude that comes from Calix. Not even a truce. But it is a sort of admitting that this isn't the main reason he is past anger when he looks at me.

I don't speak in the silence. The absence of screaming has never sounded so sweet. Calix doesn't move to go—he still has a clenched jaw holding in more words to hurl at me. I meet his eyes and look at him for the first time since the world turned in on itself. Besides the bruise from his mother across his cheek, the lack of sleep has taken its toll. He's been crying, as I am sure the whole kingdom of Hedeon has. Teardrops are now as common as mirrors in the Zamak. If only it didn't take everyone seeing their reflection in the salt water to finally realize that something is wrong.

"I—" Calix opens his mouth to speak again, but he's having just as hard a time finding the words as I am. We can only stare at each other.

I am still in my tattered dress, hair pushed back from my face that I am sure is covered in dirt from sleeping against the ground for days. Despite my appearance, despite that I am imprisoned, this is the first time it feels like Calix and I are on level ground. No more lies to create boundaries between us. I am destined for death, so my allegiances hardly matter anymore. And yet, for all that Calix is against, what I was raised to believe, there is something admirable about him. When I hid my motives and lied about who I was, Calix never bothered to put on a front with me. He presented himself exactly as he was, pushing past the years of tales his mother formed around him.

Perhaps that is why this situation stings deeper than it should.

"Were you ever going to tell me?" he asks, pleads.

"I was going to go back home after the play was over," I admit, without looking into his eyes. He runs a hand over his face, shaking his head. I keep staring at the ground.

"After all of that, you were just going to leave." He doesn't have to add the word 'me' to the end of his sentence. I know it's there.

"I'm sorry." I push back tears. I have cried for the dead too many times in my life. I don't need to cry for the living too.

"Your words don't mean anything to me, Damira!" he yells. I take a step toward him, but I'm not sure why I do. Maybe I was hoping that the culmination of everything I have burdened him with would be heavy enough to keep him from moving away. I was wrong. He takes a step back, shaking his head, gearing up for another fistful of words. Instead of throwing them, though, he takes a breath, closing his mouth as he rethinks.

"I thought you cared for me," he whispers, ashamed. "I showed you who I was. Despite my mother and her stupid stories, I showed you who I was, and I thought—"

I didn't know I had anything left in me to break. I keep finding new depths within myself, and I wish I could just crawl to the bottom of the well inside of me and lie there, unable to hurt anyone ever again.

"You weren't supposed to happen. I didn't know we would get close, and I certainly didn't expect to care about you. But I do, I care about you a lot, Cal. And I can't change where I was born or what our families have been through."

I don't know where Sumood is, but I can hear him already reprimanding my words, telling me I am building my walls too high. But I started to let them fall, and I ended up crying over all of my dead friends. Maybe he isn't right about everything.

Calix takes me in, a few tears trailing down his cheek. We are perfect reflections of one another. Just when I think that maybe he is rethinking, maybe his anger will subside, he speaks.

"I can't look at you anymore."

He turns and leaves.

I crumble to a pile on the ground. I am out of tears, out of pleas, out of any energy to call after him.

I just stare, a piece of my heart I didn't even know he owned, smashed against the floor.

Hours pass, maybe days, who bothers to keep track anymore? I stay on the ground, my limbs too heavy to move from the place from where I will have to be scraped up. I'm not sure if they haven't bothered to feed me, or if I just haven't reached a mealtime yet.

How could I have overlooked the queen mother in all of my scheming? I was sure Milena wouldn't touch the Arman, and now, there is little victory in being right about that aspect. I never even thought twice about the queen mother coming down on them. How could I have saved Hedeon soldiers from massacre but not my own friends?

Footsteps come from down the hall, pulling me from my thoughts before they turn any darker.

"Damira," a whisper so faint, I almost think it's Deacon, Pasha, or Calliope whispering to me from the other side.

"Damira," my damned name comes again, a little louder this time. I look between the bars, squinting against the dark. I guess the sun set somewhere in the past hours, or maybe the smoke of the burning Krepost is that thick.

I hope the fires swallow me whole.

"Faits, Damira." Tenny comes through the shadows. I don't bother rushing to her, I have all the time I could ever want.

"You look terrible," she mutters, starting to work at the locks in the gate. I just stand back, letting her do whatever she's come for. Maybe I know too much about the Network, maybe she's come to kill me before I can cause any more problems. If I am going to be killed one way or another, I would rather it be by someone from Reine.

The gate swings open on rusted hinges. She curses under her breath. Footsteps echo off the hallways. "Come on. Now!" She has to grab my hand and drag me.

We wind through the dark halls, through rows and rows of cells that only remind me of Calliope's dad. If there are people in these cells, they keep to the shadows and don't call out to us.

"Through here," Tenny whispers as she points to an open cell at the end of the chamber. Footsteps somewhere behind us are quickening. Moonlight filters through a small window, but it is still hard to see. We enter a cell, a dead end. Tenny doesn't fret though, bending down to the broken wooden floor and pulling up a slat. It pulls open a trapdoor with it, a hole looking into darkness that stares up at us.

"You're going to need this." She pulls a rag from her pocket and hands it to me, the putrid smell already wafting up from the abyss. I tie the rag around my nose, she does the same with one similar. It smells of sandalwood oil. Of home. I almost lose it.

"After you."

I take a final breath in the moonlight and descend. Rung by rung, I lower myself until I hit the mud. The landing jolts my ankle, but I don't have time to think about the nuisance. By the time Tenny has climbed down, pulling the door back over us, my eyes have adjusted. The footsteps from the distance don't echo through the wood over our heads.

"We need to put as much space between us and this castle as quickly as possible," Tenny moves quickly as she explains. "Not many people know about that hatch, it is a plumbing escape from when the prison used to be some other nightmare of a building. I'm sure enough people know about it, though, that they will check here eventually."

I listen to Tenny's words, but the smell of sandalwood at my nose takes me back home to the woods outside my house, laughter mixing with the summer breeze. I run toward a creek, barefoot and careful not to step on any of the flowers that bloom. A woman waits at the bank, her trousers rolled up so she can put her feet in the water. Her face isn't clear, but she tilts her head back, absorbing the sun like the wildflowers I try not to step on.

"Sweetheart," the woman calls, when she glances back and sees me. Her arms are opened, and I fling myself to her. She pulls me around, so I sit in her lap.

"What are you doing?" I giggle, putting a flower I had picked into the braid of her hair.

"Talking with the water," the woman pokes my nose.

"What is it saying to you?" I look over my shoulder to the water that streams along.

"That you should be in lessons, wildflower."

I roll my eyes. "Mom." I drag out the word. Mom. She is my mom.

"Why don't you listen too, and tell me what you hear?" She sits me down beside her, but suddenly, I would much rather be inside in lessons, but I don't know why.

The memory dissipates before I can latch onto the ending of it.

I step in a puddle, the sound making me jump. I shake off the water from my boot. At least, I hope it's just water. I can't tell what color it runs in this horrible light.

"Better not to know," Tenny glances back at me, reading my mind. I nod my head.

We turn corners, feeling our way down a few flights of falling-apart stairs. The footsteps that were following us on ground level have reappeared behind us. They're light steps, a single pair. Tenny doesn't look too concerned, so I try not to be either. Light grows in front of us, creating a halo around Tenny as she leads me. I can feel the cool air on my skin. Freedom. I might actually get out of this alive. The revelation doesn't excite me as it should.

A loud splash comes from behind us. The pair of footsteps is suddenly closer than they were mere moments ago. I almost take off running, but Tenny grabs my hand, stilling me and putting a finger to her mouth. She takes a few quiet steps forward, not wanting our own echoes to be heard.

"Damira." My name cuts the silence from the other end of the tunnel.

Calix.

"Damira," he calls again, quietly. I meet Tenny's eyes through the moonlight that barely hits us. She shakes her head.

I know I should cut my losses, follow Tenny into the night air. But it's him.

It's Calix.

"Calix," I call back, loud enough for him to hear me, but still as quiet as I can be. Tenny sighs from behind me. I will make it up to her. I just have to see him, speak to him, once more.

He comes from the shadows, around a corner in the tunnels. He doesn't wield a sword or gun or anything that says he is about to turn both of us in.

"What are you doing?" I ask, but by the shock on his face, it seems I am the one who should be answering the question.

And so I do. "It was either this or death. Tell me you would have chosen differently," I sigh.

He shakes his head slightly.

"I wouldn't have. I just—" he runs a hand through his hair. I'm not sure where he put the anger that he was wearing last time we were standing like this, but his back slumps with desperation now.

He moves slowly, one hand up in surrender and one hand to a strap on his shoulder. Tenny takes a step closer to me from behind. I hold my hand out to her, pausing her. Cal extends a burlap bag between us. I take it tentatively. It's full of supplies. Rope, food, a blanket.

"I was going to get you out after the play if it came down to it. Then everything happened, and after I learned what my grandmother had planned for you, I was glad to not let the supplies I had gathered go to waste," he admits. I never want to know what she was planning.

"Thank you."

"Just because you betrayed me doesn't mean I wish to see you dead. Duplicity does not annul love."

Perhaps these words are worse than torture.

I hand the bag of supplies to Tenny as he continues talking. "If you are heading south, stay out of Anelly. Rebellion just broke out there. The Krepost has been something of an epicenter, uprisings have been rippling for days. Stories have always kept our citizens fed, it is no wonder your words have spread so fast when we don't have coin enough to feed them." He looks between Tenny and me.

I don't know how to say goodbye to him. I didn't want an opportunity to say goodbye. I wanted to leave his life abruptly, just as I entered it. The more I talk to him, the more damage I risk causing, and I have already uprooted his life enough. He deserves better than this.

"How did you get out of our cells?" he asks Tenny with a look of realization. She gives him a grin, not giving anything away. I hadn't even thought to ask. I have been too preoccupied with the prince in front of me and the blood on my hands.

A rock skips in the passageway behind Calix, kicked up by someone quiet enough to sneak up on us all. Her voice echoes before I have a chance to squint down the tunnel.

"And where exactly do you think you are going?"

32

R AVEN STANDS WITH TWO soldiers at her back, perfectly concealed by the darkness. I don't know how they managed to go undetected, but Tenny, now at my side, looks just as surprised as I am.

"Raven?" I take a step forward, instinctively trying to stand in front of Tenny, to guard her.

"Two traitors for the effort of one." Her eyes jump between me and Calix, not bothering with Tenny behind us.

I glance between the twins, not sure what to say. Raven, Calix and me. It couldn't have ended any other way. I just never thought we would all be on opposing sides. The realization seems to flood Raven as well, but she doesn't look as caught off guard as I feel.

"I was tipped off that Tenny here found a way to get you out, Damira, and that you—" She turns to her brother, forgetting about me for the time being as much more important matters are unfolding. She doesn't exactly smile, but the resolve of why she came down here is clear on her face. "You were here with them. Mother will be forced to name me heir, she won't be able to ignore this kind of betrayal," she laughs, the gift of a lifetime delivered straight into her lap.

"You're going to turn me in as a traitor because you want to rule Hedeon? Listen to your words, Rave—you're being insane." Calix holds his hand out like he's calming a foal, putting himself between Raven and me.

"Why would me taking the throne be that insane, Cal? Because I could never be as smart as you? Because I wouldn't know how to read the ledgers like you? Because you think I don't have what it takes? I have been in your shadow with every breath in my life. I am tired of being overlooked because you were born a few moments before me. I would be the better leader, and we both know that, so I am doing what it takes to get there." Her face twists with each word. The shedding of a mask. She takes a few steps forward, causing us to push further back toward the light at the tunnel's end.

"Raven, let's just talk about this," Calix pleads.

"I am tired of talking, no one ever listens to me. All you think I am fit for is planning parties and spending coin. You and mother never gave me a chance. This will be the last time that mistake is made."

"And so, you think this is the best option? What are you going to do from here?"

"Throw you in the dungeons or give you the chance to abdicate the throne to me." The speed at which she answers tells me what I don't want to admit—this has been planned for longer than the chaos I let loose, probably longer than I have been in the Krepost.

"You know I can't abdicate the throne. So that would leave you to make me and Damira rot in a cell for the rest of our lives? You can't want that."

I take my eyes off the twins and glance at the guards with her. Grey uniform with a black stripe down the side. I still on the face of the soldier to Raven's left.

Kover.

"Raven—" I manage out. She follows my glare and sees it land on her guard.

"Come with me." Raven changes her focus on her brother and turns it to me, taking a few steps. Her words soften around the edges, the animosity only overflowing when it comes to her twin.

"Kover has been spying on us?" I ask.

"He did say he would keep an eye on you."

"From the very beginning?"

She nods, allowing me the patience she won't allow Calix. How did she not have me killed earlier? How had I been so trusting? My stomach turns from all the ways Raven could have betrayed me in the past weeks.

"I thought we could keep you out of this, Damira. I didn't want you caught in the crossfire of a feud between Calix and me, because you truly are my friend. If you come back with me, I can find a way to pardon you, to send you back to Reine without being wanted by the Crown any longer."

For her, it was never about the war between our kingdoms, it has really only ever been the war between her and Calix that she cares about. Which means she will put herself at the queens' wills trying to prove her worthiness, leaving our two kingdoms to continue warring as long as her puppet masters will it to be so.

"You would pardon me, but not your own brother?" I still ask, even though I know her words are only empty promises. Everyone in this tunnel knows that if I returned to the Zamak, there would be no way I'd be allowed to leave with my head still on my shoulders.

"Grandmother would be so proud," Cal interrupts before she can answer.

I check on Tenny behind me who takes a few steps back, silently instructing me to do the same with a hand on my wrist. I creep back with her as her eyes scan the walls of the tunnel.

"At least grandmother didn't disgrace the Hendrick's name," Raven throws the accusation at Calix.

And that's enough to solidify my allegiances. If Raven admits to aligning herself with her grandmother, even in this small way, I cannot find it in me to even try and hear her out.

"I have little care to a last name. I care about our people, and the life we can't give them as long as this war continues."

"And that lack of care is why the throne can't be allowed to go to you. You would ruin the legacy our family worked so hard to build."

"A legacy built on the graves of your own people, is no legacy at all, Raven." I step in front of Cal now, abandoning Tenny behind me. She lets out a sigh of exasperation that only I am close enough to hear. "You can still let us go."

Raven sighs, shaking her head. "You know I can't do that, Damira." She straightens her shoulders, finally understanding where I have drawn my line.

We have overstayed the luck The Faits have given us.

I had always thought Calix was the twin who follows every rule, but I have gotten it backward. Raven does not have the courage to go against her mother and grandmother. She has shown me that from the beginning, always doing whatever she can to please them despite her own thoughts.

"Take me and let them go," Cal takes a few steps toward her, trying to place himself between us again.

"Calix, I have no choice about this." And I am sure, in her mind, she doesn't. Raven and Cal were taught that the world is black and white. Calix has decided to start seeing the greys, but Raven still doesn't have that kind of scope.

"Please," Calix's voice breaks in the simple word.

I glance at Tenny, who is way too calm, she almost even has a smile. She pulls me back again, still at a slower pace so not to draw attention.

Raven ignores Calix, having already given him his sentence.

"Damira, I wish I could be sorry." Her eyes burrow into mine, clawing out all the solace we found in each other over the last two months and leaving nothing but gaping holes of more loss.

I open my mouth again to speak, but a buzz of electricity screeches above our heads. All of us glance up in unison. Right above my head, a small, red light flashes. Cal's eyes snap down to me. In a breath, he looks back to Raven and then throws himself on me, launching us backward as an explosion rumbles off the walls of the tunnel. Raven screams. I can't see anything around Calix's body pushing me into the ground. That and my eyes squeezing shut.

Silence falls like the rubble. I peek over Calix's shoulder, the haze so thick I can hardly see the light that should stream in through the tunnel's opening. I cough on the dirt that flies in the air, even through the rag at my nose. Calix is heavy on me, peering down to see if I am alright.

"We need to go," Calix pulls himself up, but I can hardly hear him over the ringing in my ears. My head screams, but Cal takes my hand and leads us toward the dim light at the end of the tunnel. My already throbbing ankle protests to more movement. I keep the tears at bay, but between the pounding in my head, the burning in my ankle and the conversation with Raven, I don't know how I will manage many more steps.

I glance back, the debris settling, revealing the cave-in. The tunnel is completely obstructed. Raven and her guards on one side. Tenny, Calix and I on the other. Even if he could have found a way to talk Raven down, to live the life he was born to, Calix now has no choice.

"Damira," Calix calls, pulling me forward with him.

"Are you both okay?" Tenny yells. "I didn't want to have to do that, but I wasn't sure there would be another way for us to get out. We had that installed so that no one could follow Damira and I out of the tunnel. We were supposed to be far from it before I set it off, but I guess it worked this way too." She's on her feet, a device in hand that I'm assuming set off whatever caused the tunnel to collapse.

"I'm okay." I finally shake off the surprise and get my wits about me with help from the cool breeze beckoning us into the night. At the same time, Calix takes on the dazed look I managed to slip off.

"Cal," I tug at his hand, still wrapped around mine. He stares at the cave, at the past that is no longer his future. We climb down the small drop-off into the night, every movement making me just aware of how bad my ankle is.

"We have to move," Tenny jogs off into the forest ahead of us. Cal moves with me, shaking off whichever thought trapped him.

I glance back, shocked at the sight. We are at the base of the Krepost, the Zamak watching over us from the distance. Smoke rises in various places from the front of the mountain. Yells and gunshots still pollute the air, even after what I guess is at least two weeks since the play.

"We need to move." It's Calix's turn again to pull me by our intertwined hands, but I'm stalled. Evidence of the damage I've caused rises from the ash of the Krepost.

"Go back," I turn to him quickly. "You can still make this right with Raven, and keep your own position."

His face is tense and unreadable. Even though he is by my side, running in the same direction, the openness that was once so easy between us has become stiff. He isn't mad, though, not as he was. Quarrels between two people who love each other always dissipate with more pressing matters. That isn't to say I am in love with Calix or that he could ever be in love with me, but sometimes, with certain people, you can never be indifferent. You can never go back to nothingness.

"No. They won't let me back, not after all that." He shakes his head, and suddenly, I am in an endless loop of Calix looking between me and Raven, and then throwing himself on me so I don't get buried by rubble. Over and over, he is throwing himself on me. Choosing me.

We might not ever find our way back to each other in the way we once were, but he will always mean something to me. And how fitting that is. A grand ending, Calix said. We deserve a grand ending. Well, nothing ever ends beautifully. In books and in plays, we end everything with a bow, wrapping up loose ends and pretending that life cascades into a well-constructed stop. Closure is a fable we make up to comfort us from the stage.

"You'll be branded a traitor if you come with us," I remind him, as if he could ever forget.

"It appears I've already made my decision." Calix stands by my side as we stare up to the Zamak. He glances at me, tracing my face with his eyes in that same way he did all those weeks ago, when neither of us knew who the other was. Calix will always be loyal to Hedeon, even if he just chose to save my life over staying with his sister. But I still can't help longing for the look he gives me now, when he says, "I made my decision some time ago."

Tenny yells from the woods behind us. "We need to go. Now!"

We share one last look. His eyes are rimmed red—as red as the blood that now paints his kingdom.

And then we run.

ACKNOWLEDGEMENTS

Firstly, thanks God for giving me this gift I love so dearly, and for giving me the dream that would later be turned into WELL-LIT SHADOWS after I told you I wanted to write a book about the importance of the arts.

I have enough words to write many books, but I will never have enough words to fully express the gratitude I have for my parents. Thank you both for giving me every opportunity to follow my dreams. Thank you Father, my human dictionary, for letting me call you at all hours asking for a word. Thank you Momma, for pretending to listen when I start rambling on about my fictional worlds. Thank you Emmy (and Suki Azula), for being my number one fan(s). Thank you Josh, for reading draft after draft and getting in deep debates with me about my world building (and I guess, for naming this book). Thank you to all my family, it would take another novel to name you all, but your support and prayers have gotten me here.

I've said it once and I'll say it again—Madison has listened to me ramble on about imaginary people and imaginary worlds since we were 10. She hears about my ideas before most anyone else. Thank you Madison, for it all.

To those I dedicated the book to, and all my Chicago family I left unnamed—this book was written in my favorite city and you all watched me labor over it for months. Thank you for letting me bring my laptop to movie nights and hangouts and listening to me verbally work through plot holes for days on end. There is truly no one like you all.

My lovely editor Tahnya Abraham, thank you for loving this book enough to take a chance on me. The fact that you believed in this book as much as you did strengthened my confidence in myself. I have to also thank Isabell for connecting me with Tahnya and being the head of my Colorado fan club. Isabell, you're truly a one-of-a-kind friend, and I don't know what I would do without you.

Evelyn Andersen, thank you for my gorgeous cover. Time and time again you read my mind for exactly what I wanted this cover to be and I couldn't be more thankful.

Thank you to everyone I talked to about this publishing process and all those that were eager to give me advice! I couldn't have made it to the finish line without your guiding lights.

There are many more people I could thank, but I will run out of page space, so I will leave it at this—everyone who has been in my life in the past two years has helped me make this book. From encouragement, to connecting me to people, to checking in on my sanity, I am truly blessed to be surrounded by people who support me.